ROBYN CARR

JEAN BRASHEAR
VICTORIA DAHL

Midnight Kiss

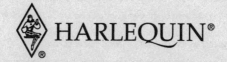

TORONTO • NEW YORK • LONDON
AMSTERDAM • PARIS • SYDNEY • HAMBURG
STOCKHOLM • ATHENS • TOKYO • MILAN • MADRID
PRAGUE • WARSAW • BUDAPEST • AUCKLAND

ISBN-13: 978-0-373-83743-4

MIDNIGHT KISS

Copyright © 2010 by Harlequin Books S.A.

The publisher acknowledges the copyright holders of the individual works as follows:

MIDNIGHT CONFESSIONS
Copyright © 2010 by Robyn Carr

MIDNIGHT SURRENDER
Copyright © 2010 by Jean Brashear

MIDNIGHT ASSIGNMENT
Copyright © 2010 by Victoria Dahl

Recycling programs
for this product may
not exist in your area.

Printed in U.S.A.

CONTENTS

MIDNIGHT CONFESSIONS

Robyn Carr

CHAPTER ONE

SUNNY ARCHER WAS SERIOUSLY considering a legal name change.

"Come on, Sunny," her uncle Nathaniel said. "Let's go out on the town and see if we can't put a little of that legendary sunshine back into your disposition!"

Out on the town? she thought. In *Virgin River?* A town of about six hundred? "Ah, I think I'll pass…"

"C'mon, sunshine, you gotta be more flexible! Optimistic! You can't lick this wound forever."

Maybe it was cute when she was four or even fourteen to say things like "Sunny isn't too sunny today!"

But this was December 31 and she had come to Virgin River to spend a few quiet days with her uncle Nate and his fiancée Annie, to try to escape the reality of a heart that wouldn't heal. And if the hurt wasn't bad enough, her heart had gone cold and hard, too. She looked at her watch—4:00 p.m. Exactly one year ago at this time she was having her hair and makeup done right before slipping into a Vera Wang wedding gown, excited, blushing and oblivious to the fact that her fiancé Glen was getting blitzed and ready to run for his life.

"I'm not really in the mood for a New Year's Eve bash, Uncle Nate," she said.

"Aw, sweetheart, I can't bear to think of you home alone, brooding, feeling sad," Nathaniel said.

And feeling like a big loser who was left at the altar on her wedding day? she wondered. But that's what had happened. How was she supposed to feel?

"Nate," Annie said under her breath, "this might be a bad night to push the party idea.…"

"Ya think?" Sunny said sarcastically, noting to herself that she hadn't been so irritable and sarcastic before becoming an abandoned bride. "Listen, you guys, please go. Party like rock stars. I actually have plans."

"You do?" they both asked hopefully.

"I do. I'm planning a ceremonial burning of last year's calendar. I should probably burn three years' worth of them—that's how much time and energy I invested in the scumbucket."

Nate and Annie were speechless for a moment; they exchanged dubious looks. When Nate recovered he said, "Well all-righty then! We'll stay home and help with the ceremonial burning. Then we'll make some popcorn, play some monopoly, make some positive resolutions or something and ring in a much better new year than the last."

And that was how Sunny, who wasn't feeling at all accommodating, ended up going to the big Virgin River blast at Jack's Bar on New Year's Eve—because she just couldn't let her uncle Nate and sweet, funny Annie stay home to watch her sulk and whimper.

THERE HAD BEEN A LONG HISTORY in Sunny's family of returning to the Jensen stables for a little rest and rejuvenation. Sunny and her cousins had spent countless vacations around the barn and pastures and trails, riding, playing, inhaling the fresh clean air and getting a regular new lease on life. It had been Sunny's mother's idea that she come to Virgin River for a post-Christmas revival. Sunny's mom was one of Nate's three older sisters, and Sunny's grandpa had been the original owner and veterinarian of Jensen's Clinic and Stable. Now Uncle Nate was the vet and Grandpa was retired and living in Arizona.

Sunny was her mama's only child, age twenty-five; she had one female cousin, Mary—who it just so happened had managed to get *her* groom to the church. Since Uncle Nate was only ten years older than Sunny at thirty-five, she and her cousin had had tragic crushes on him. Nate, on the other hand, who had grown up with three older sisters, thought he was cursed with females.

Until he was thirty, anyway. Then he became a little more avuncular, patient and even protective. Nathaniel had been sitting in the church on New Year's Eve a year ago. Waiting, like everyone else, for the groom to show, for the wedding to begin.

The past year had passed in an angry, unhappy blur for Sunny. Her rather new and growing photography business had taken off—a combination of her kick-ass website and word of mouth—and rather than take a break after her personal disaster, she went right back to work. She had scheduled shoots, after all. The catastrophic twist was that she specialized in engagement, wedding, anniversary, belly and baby shots—five phases of a couple's life worth capturing for posterity. Her work, as well as her emotional well-being, was suffering. Although she couldn't focus, and she was either unable to sleep or hardly able to pull herself out of bed, she pressed on the best she could. The only major change she'd made in her life was to move out of the town house she had shared with Glen and back into her mom and dad's house until she could afford something of her own. She had her workroom in the basement of her parents' place anyway, so it was just a minor shift in geography.

During the past year at her parents', Sunny had a revelation. The driving reason behind most young women her age wanting their own space, their independence and privacy, was their being involved in a serious relationship. Since she was determined not to repeat past mistakes by allowing another man into her life, there was no need to leave the comfort, security and economy of her parents' house.

She was trying her hand at photographing sunrises, sunsets, landscapes, seascapes and pets. It wasn't working—her images were flat and uninteresting. If it wasn't bad enough that her heart was broken, so was her spirit. It was as if her gift was lost. She'd been brilliant with couples, inspired by weddings—stills, slideshows, videos. She saw the promise in their eyes, the potential for their lives. She'd brought romance to the fat bellies of pregnant women and was a veritable Anne Geddes with babies! But now that she was a mere observer who would never experience any of those things firsthand, everything had changed. Not only had it changed, it pierced her heart each time she did a shoot.

When she confessed this to Annie, Annie had said, "Oh, darling, but you're so young! Only twenty-five! The possibilities ahead are endless if you're open to them!"

And Sunny had said, "I'm not upset because I didn't make the cheerleading squad, Annie. My fiancé dumped me on our wedding day—and my age doesn't matter a damn."

THE TOWN WAS CARPETED in a fresh blanket of pretty white snow, the thirty-foot tree was lit and sparkling as gentle flakes continued to fall, and the porch at Jack's Bar, strung with lights and garlands, was welcoming. There was a friendly curl of smoke rising from the chimney and light shone from the windows.

Nate, Annie and Sunny walked into the bar at 8:00 p.m. and found the place packed with locals. Jack, the owner, and Preacher, the cook, were behind the bar. There was a festive table set up along one whole wall of the room, covered with food, to which Annie added a big plate of her special deviled eggs and a dill-speckled salmon loaf surrounded by crackers.

"Hey, looks like the whole town is here," Nate said.

"A good plenty," Jack said. "But I hope you don't see anyone here you want to kiss at midnight. Most of these folks won't make it that long. We have a strong skeleton crew that will stay late, however. They're busy getting all the kids settled back at Preacher's house with a sitter—it's going to be a dormitory. Vanessa and Paul's two are bunking in with Preacher's little Dana, my kids are sleeping in Preacher's room, Cameron's twins are in the guest room, Brie and Mike's little one is borrowing Christopher's room because he's planning on sitting up until midnight with the sitter. Oh, and to be very clear, the sitter is there for all the *little* kids—not for Chris," Jack added with a smile. "He's eight now. All man."

"Jack, Preach, meet my niece Sunny. Sunny, this is Jack and Preacher, the guys who run this place."

She gave them a weak smile, a nod and a mumbled nice to meet you.

"Hop up here, you three. As soon as you contribute your New Year's resolution, you get service," Jack said. "The price of admission is a food item and a resolution."

Sunny jumped up on a bar stool, hanging the strap of her large bag on the backrest. Jack leaned over the bar and eyed the big, leather shoulder bag. He peered at her with one brow lifted. "Going on a long trip right after the party?"

She laughed a little. "Camera equipment. I never leave it behind. Never know when I might need it."

"Well, by all means, the first annual New Year's Eve party is your canvas," Jack said. He slid a piece of paper and pen toward her.

Sunny hovered over it as if giving it careful thought. She knew if she said her resolution was to get this over with as soon as possible, it would open up the conversation as to why she now and would forever more find New Year's Eve the most reprehensible of holidays.

"Make it a good one, Sunny," Jack said. "Keep it generic and don't sign it—it's anonymous. There's a surprise coming right after midnight."

Sunny glanced at her watch. God, she thought. At least four hours of this? I'll never make it! She wrote on her slip of paper. "Give up men."

DREW FOLEY WAS A SECOND-YEAR orthopedic resident at UCLA Medical and had somehow scored ten days off over Christmas, which he'd spent in Chico with his two sisters, Marcie and Erin, their guys Ian and Aiden and his new nephew. The three previous Christmases he'd spent with his family, and also his former fiancée, Penny. That somehow seemed so long ago.

When surgical residents get days off, they aren't *real* days off. They're merely days on which you're not required in surgery, clinic, class, writing reports or being verbally beaten to death by senior residents and attending physicians. But there was still plenty of studying to do. He'd been hitting the books straight through Christmas even with the distraction of family all around, including Marcie's new baby who was really starting to assert himself. With only a few days left before he had to head back to Southern California, he borrowed the family's isolated cabin on the ridge near Virgin River so he could study without distraction. He'd managed to focus completely for a couple of days and had impressed himself with the amount of academic ground he'd covered. As he saw it, that bought him a New Year's Eve beer or two and a few hours of satellite football on New Year's Day. On January 2 he'd head back to Erin's house in Chico, spend one more evening with the family, then throw himself back into the lion's den at UCLA Medical.

He grabbed his jacket. It was New Year's Eve and he'd spent enough time alone. He'd swing through town on his way to Fortuna to collect his beer, just to see what was going on. He'd be surprised if the only bar and grill in town was open, since Jack's Bar wasn't usually open late on holidays. In fact, the routine in Virgin River on regular days was that Jack's shut down before nine, open till ten at the latest, and that was only if there were hunters or fishermen in the area. This was a town of mostly farmers, ranchers, laborers and small-business owners; they didn't stay out late because farm chores and animals didn't sleep in.

But to his surprise, once in town he found that the little bar was hopping. It made him smile—this was going to save him some serious mountain driving and he'd get to have a beer among people. When he walked into the packed bar he heard his name shouted. "Ho! Doc Foley! When did you hit town?"

This was the best part about this place. He'd only been up here maybe a half dozen times in the past couple of years, but Jack never forgot anyone. For that matter, most of Jack's friends and family never did either.

He reached a hand across the bar in greeting to Jack. "How's it going, Jack?"

"I had no idea you were up here!" Jack said. "You bring the family along?"

"Nah, I was with the family over Christmas and came up to get a little studying done before I have to get back to residency. I thought I'd better escape the girls and especially the baby if I intend to concentrate at all."

"How is that baby?" Jack asked.

Drew grinned. "Red-headed and loud. I'm afraid he could be a little rip-off of Marcie. Ian should be afraid. Very, very afraid."

Jack chuckled. "You remember my wife, Mel."

"Sure," he said, turning toward the town's renowned midwife and accepting a kiss on the cheek. "How are you?"

"Never better. I wish we'd known you were up here,

Drew—I'd have made it a point to call you, invite you."

Drew looked around. "Who knew you folks ripped up the town on New Year's Eve. Is everyone here?"

"Pretty good number," Jack said. "But expect this to change fairly quick—most of these folks will leave by nine. They start early. But I'm hanging in there till midnight," he assured Drew. "I bet I can count on one hand the number of Virgin River residents willing to stay up for a kiss at midnight."

And that's when he spotted her. Right when Jack said *kiss at midnight* he saw a young woman he'd be more than willing to accommodate when the clock struck twelve. She was tucked back in a corner by the hearth, swirling a glass of white wine, her golden hair falling onto her shoulders. She seemed just slightly apart from the table of three women who sat chatting near her. He watched as one of those women leaned toward her to speak, to try to include her, but she merely nodded, sipped, smiled politely and remained aloof. Someone's wife? Someone's girl? Whoever she was, she looked a little unhappy. He'd love to make her happier.

"Drew," Jack said. "Meet Nate Jensen, local vet."

Drew put out his hand, but didn't want to take his eyes off the girl. He said, "Nice to meet you," but what he was thinking was how long it had been since just looking at a beautiful woman had zinged him in the chest and head with almost instant attraction. Too long! Whoa, she was a stunner. He'd barely let go of Nate's hand, didn't even catch the guy's response because his ears were ringing, when he asked Jack, "Who is that blonde?"

"That's my niece," his new acquaintance said. "Sunny."

"Married? Engaged? Accompanied? Nun? Anything?"

Nate chuckled. "She's totally single. But—"

"Be right back," Drew said. "Guard my beer with your life!" And he took off for the corner by the hearth.

"But…" Nate attempted.

Drew kept moving. He was on automatic. Once he was standing right in front of her and she lifted her eyes to his, he was not surprised to find that she had the most beautiful blue eyes he could have ever imagined. He put out his hand. "Hi. I'm Drew. I just met your uncle." She said nothing, didn't even shake his hand. "And you're Sunny. Sunny Jensen?" he asked.

Her mouth fixed and her eyes narrowed. "Archer," she corrected.

Drew gave up on the shake and withdrew his hand. "Well, Sunny Archer, can I join you?"

"Are you trying to pick me up?" she asked directly.

He grinned. "I'm a very optimistic guy," he said pleasantly.

"Then let me save you some time. I'm not available."

He was struck silent for a moment. It wasn't that Drew enjoyed such great success with women—he was admittedly out of practice. But this one had drawn on him like a magnet and he was unaccountably surprised to be shot down before he'd even had a chance to screw up his approach. "Sorry," he said lamely. "Your uncle said you were single."

"Single and unavailable." She lifted her glass and gave him a weak smile. "Happy New Year."

He just looked at her for a moment, then beat a retreat back to the bar.

Jack and Nate were watching, waiting for him. Jack pushed the beer toward him. "How'd that work out for you?"

Drew took a pull on his beer. "I must be way out of practice," he said. "I probably should'a thought that through a little better...."

"What? Residency doesn't leave time for girls?" Jack asked with a twist of the lip.

"A breakup," Drew explained. "Which led to a break from women for a while."

Nate leaned an elbow on the bar. "That a fact? Bad breakup?"

"You ever been around a good one?" Drew asked. Then he chuckled, lifted an eyebrow and said, "Nah, it wasn't that it was so bad. In fact, she probably saved my life. We were engaged, but shouldn't have been. She finally told me what I should've known all along—*if we got married, it would be a disaster.*"

"Bad fit?"

"Yeah, bad fit. I should have seen it coming, but I was too busy putting titanium rods in femurs to pay attention to details like that, so my bad. But what's up with Sunny Archer?"

"Well," Nate said. "I guess you probably have a lot in common."

"Uh-oh. Bad breakup?"

"Let's just say, you ever been around a good one?"

"I should've known. She didn't give me a chance. And here I thought I'd bungled it."

"Gonna go for round two?" Jack asked him.

Drew thought about that a minute. "I don't know," he said with a shrug. "Maybe I should wait until she gets a little more wine in her."

Nate slapped a heavy hand on Drew's shoulder. "That's my niece, bud. I'll be watching."

"Sorry, bad joke. I'd never take advantage of her, don't worry about that," Drew protested. "But if she shoots me down twice, I could get a serious complex!"

CHAPTER TWO

DREW NURSED HIS BEER slowly and joked around with Jack and Nate over a plate of wings, but the subject of breakups had him thinking a bit about Penny. There were times he missed her, or at least he missed the idea of what he thought they would be.

He had met her while he was in med school. She was a fellow med student's cousin and it had been a fix up. The first date had gone smoothly; the next seven dates in as many weeks went even better and before he knew it, he was dating Penny exclusively. They had so much in common, they grew on each other. She was an RN and he was studying medicine. She was pretty, had a good sense of humor, understood his work as he understood hers and in no time at all they had settled into a comfort zone that accommodated them both. And it didn't hurt that the sex was satisfying. Everything seemed compatible.

Penny had been in charge of the relationship from the start and Drew didn't have to think about it much, which suited him perfectly. He was a busy guy; he didn't have a lot of time for flirtation or pursuit. Penny was very well-equipped to fill him in on their agenda and he was perfectly happy to go along. "Valentine's Day is coming up," she would say. "I guess we'll be doing something special?"

Ding, ding, ding—he could figure that out easy. "Absolutely," he would say. Then he'd get a reservation, buy a gift. Penny thought he was brilliant and sensitive and all was right with his world.

It had been working out effortlessly until he asked her to go to Southern California with him, to live with him. His residency in orthopedic surgery was beginning, he'd dated Penny exclusively for a couple of years and it seemed like the natural progression of things. "Not without an engagement ring," she'd said. So he provided one. It had seemed reasonable enough.

But the move from Chico changed everything. It hadn't gone well for Penny. She'd been out of her element, away from her job, friends and family, and Drew had been far too stressed and overworked to help her make the transition. She was lonely, needed attention, time, reassurance. And he had wanted to give it to her, but it was like squeezing water out of a rock. It wasn't long before their only communication was in the form of arguing—make that fighting. Fights followed by days of not speaking or nights in which she cried into her pillow and wouldn't take comfort from him, if he could stay awake long enough to give it.

Drew shook off the memory and finally said to Nate, "So, tell me about Sunny, who, if you don't mind me saying, might be better named Stormy.…"

"Well, for starters, jokes about her name don't seem to be working just now," Nate replied.

"Ahh," he said. Drew was distracted by a sudden flash and saw that it was none other than Stormy Sunny herself with the camera, getting a shot of a couple in a toast. "What's with the camera?"

"She's a photographer, as a matter of fact. A good

one," Nate said. "She started out studying business in college but dropped out before she was twenty-one to start her own business. My sister Susan, her mother, almost had a heart attack over that. But it turned out she knew exactly what she was doing. There's a waiting list for her work."

"Is that a fact?" he said, intrigued. "She seems kind of young…"

"Very young, but she's been taking great pictures since she was in high school. Maybe earlier."

"Where?"

"She lives in L.A. Long Beach, actually."

Long Beach, Drew thought. Like next door! Of course, that didn't matter if she wouldn't even talk to him. But he wasn't giving anything away. "Is she a little artsy-fartsy?" Drew asked.

Nate laughed. "Not at all—she's very practical. But lately she's been trying some new stuff, shooting the horses, mountains, valleys, roads and buildings. Sunrises, sunsets, clouds, et cetera." Nate looked over at Sunny as she busily snapped pictures of a happy couple. "It's kind of nice to see her taking pictures of people again."

Drew watched Sunny focus, direct the pair with one hand while holding her camera with the other. Her face seriously lit up; her smile was alive and whatever it was she was saying caused her subjects to laugh, which was followed by several flashes. She was so animated as she took five or six more shots, then pulled a business card out of the pocket of her jeans and handed it to the couple. She was positively gorgeous when she wasn't giving him the brush. Then she retreated to her spot by the hearth and put her camera down. He noticed that the second she gave up the camera, her face returned to its seriousness. The sight of her was immediately obscured by partiers.

He wanted one of those business cards.

"Hey, buddy, you didn't make out your resolution," Jack said, passing him a slip of paper and pen. "That's the price of admission."

"I don't usually do resolutions," Drew said. "Well, except every morning when I resolve to fly under the radar of the senior residents."

"Because?" Jack asked.

Sometimes Drew forgot that few people knew what the life of a junior resident was like. "Because they're sociopaths with a mean streak."

"Ah," Jack said as if he bought that. "Maybe that's your resolution—to avoid sociopaths? When you've written one, it goes in the pot here."

"And then?" Drew asked.

"When you're getting ready to leave, you can draw one—maybe you'll get a better one than you wrote. Give you something new to strive for."

Drew laughed. "I dunno. This is such a crazy idea," he said. "What if the one I draw is to bike across the U.S.?"

Jack looked around. "Nah," he said. "No danger of that around here. You could draw one that says to remember your annual mammogram, however. Now get on it," he said, tapping the paper on the bar.

Chuckling, Drew wrote. Then he scratched it out. Thinking about the grumpy but beautiful woman in the corner he wrote "Start the new year by giving a new guy a chance." Then he folded it in half and shoved it in his pocket; he asked for a new piece of paper. On his second try he wrote "Don't let past hurts ruin future possibilities."

Then he took a bolstering swallow of his beer and said, "Excuse me a second." And off he went to the other side of the room.

He stood in front of Sunny, smiled his handsomest smile and said, "So. You're a photographer."

She looked up at him, her expression deadpan. "Yes," she said.

"You like being a photographer?" he asked.

Again there was that pregnant pause before she said, "Yes."

"What do you like best about it?"

She thought for a moment. Then she said, "The quiet."

He had to ask himself why in the world he was interested. She was beautiful, but Drew had never been drawn by beauty alone. He'd known lots of gorgeous women who fell short in other areas, thus killing his interest instantly. For a woman to really intrigue him she had to be fun, smart, good natured, energetic, driven by something besides her looks and above all, *positive*. So far this one, this Sunny, had only looks going for her and it was not enough. Still, for unknown reasons, he lingered. "The quiet," he repeated. "Anything else?"

"Yes. It doesn't require any other people. I can do it alone."

"Just out of curiosity, are you always this unapproachable, or is it just at New Year's Eve parties?"

She shrugged. "Pretty much always."

"Gotcha. One last question. Will you take my picture?"

"For what occasion?" she asked.

Nothing came to mind. "Passport photo?" he attempted.

"Sorry. I don't do passport photos."

He smiled at her. "Well, Sunny—you're in luck. Because that's all I got. You are, as you obviously wish to be, on your own."

OH, I'M SUCH A BITCH, she thought as she watched Drew's back weave through the people to return to the bar. When he sat up on the stool beside her uncle, she cringed in embarrassment. She adored her uncle Nate and knew how much he cared about her, how it had hurt him to see her in pain on what was supposed to have been her wedding day, how it killed him to see her struggle with it for so long afterward. But while she knew Nate had nothing but sympathy for her, she realized he was running short on patience with her bitterness and what could only be described as attitude a full year later.

He wasn't the only one. Friends had tried to encourage her to let go of the heartache and move on. If she didn't want to date again, fine, but being pissed off all the time was not only wearing on friendships, it was hurting business. And she was hearing a lot about the fact that she was only twenty-five! She wasn't sure if twenty-five was so young it excused her for making such a mistake on Glen or if that meant she had decades left to find the right guy!

Then, right after she arrived in Virgin River, Annie had taken her aside, sat her down and said, "This rage isn't going to help you get on with your life in a positive way, Sunny. You're not the only one who's been dumped. I found out the man I was supposed to marry had three full-time girlfriends he lived with—each of us part time, of course."

"How'd he manage that?" Sunny had asked, intrigued and astonished.

"He obviously kept a very careful calendar. He was in sales and traveled. When I thought he was selling farm equipment, he was actually with one of the other girlfriends."

"Oh, my God! You must have wanted to *kill* him!"

"Sure. I was kind of hoping my dad or one of my brothers would do it for me, but when they didn't I got past it. I realize I wasn't left at the altar with a very expensive, non-refundable wedding to pay for, like you were. I can't imagine the pain and humiliation of that, but even so, I was very angry. And now I'm so grateful that I found a way to get beyond that because if I hadn't, I would never have given Nate a chance. And your uncle Nate is the best thing that ever happened to me."

What Sunny wanted to tell Annie was that the pain and humiliation wasn't the worst part—it was that her friends and family *pitied* her for being left. What was wrong with her, that he would do that?

She knew what was wrong, when she thought about it. Her nose was too long, her forehead too high, her chest small and feet big, her hips too wide, she hadn't finished college and she took pictures for a living. That they were good pictures didn't seem to matter—it wasn't all that impressive. She sometimes veered into that territory of "if I had been a super model with a great body, he'd never have left me." Intellectually she knew that was nonsense, but emotionally she felt lacking in too many ways.

Instead she said to Annie, "Did you know? Did you ever have a hint that something was wrong?"

She shook her head. "Only when it was over, when I looked back and realized he never spent a weekend with me, and I was too trusting to wonder why he hadn't ever asked me to join him on a business trip to one of the other towns where he stayed overnight on business. Oh, after it was all over, I had lots of questions. But at the time?" She shook her head. "I didn't know anything was wrong."

"Me either," Sunny said.

"I probably didn't want to know anything was wrong," Annie added. "I don't like conflict."

Sunny didn't say anything. She was pretty well acquainted with her own denial and that hurt just about as much as the hard truth.

"Well, there was one thing," Annie corrected. "After it was all over I wondered if I shouldn't have been more desperate to spend every moment with *him,* if I loved him so much. You know—Nate gets called out in the middle of the night pretty often, and I never make a fuss about it. But we both complain if we haven't had enough time together. We need each other a lot. That never happened with Ed. I was perfectly fine when he wasn't around. Should have tipped me off, I guess."

No help there, Sunny thought. Glen had complained constantly of her Fridays through Sundays always being booked with shoots. There were times she worked a sixteen-hour day on the weekends, covering three weddings and receptions and a baptism. Slip in some engagement slide shows, photos of babies, whatever had to be done for people who worked Monday through Friday and who only had weekends available. Then from Monday through Thursday she'd work like a dog editing and setting up proofs.

Glen was a California Highway Patrolman who worked swing shifts to have weekends off and she was always unavailable then.

She revisited that old argument—wait a minute! Here was a clue she hadn't figured out at the time. Glen had a few years seniority with CHP, so why would he work swings just to have those weekends off when he knew she would be tied up with her clients the entire time? She'd been rather proud of the fact that it hadn't taken her long to develop a strong clientele, to make incredibly good money for a woman her age—weddings were especially profitable. But she'd had to sacrifice her weekends to get and keep that success.

So why? It would have been easy for him to get a schedule with a Tuesday through Thursday, her lightest days, off. In fact, if he had been willing to take those days off, and work the day shift regularly, they could have gone to bed together every night. He said at the time that it suited his body clock, that he wasn't a morning person. And he *liked* to go out on the weekends. He went out with "the boys." The *boys?* Not bloody likely....

After being left at the church a couple of his groomsmen had admitted he'd been having his doubts about the big, legal, forever commitment. Apparently he'd worried aloud to them, but all he ever did was argue with her about it. *We don't need all that! We could fly to Aruba, get married there, take a week of sailing, scuba diving...* He hadn't said the commitment was an issue, just the wedding—something Sunny and her mom were having a real party putting together. So she had said, "Try not to worry so much, Glen—you'll get your week in Aruba on the honeymoon. Just be at the church on time, say your lines and we'll be diving and sunning and sailing before you know it."

Sunny shook her head in frustration. What was the point in figuring it out now? She grabbed her coat, her camera and headed out the door. The snow was still gently falling and she backed away from the town Christmas tree, snapping photos as she went. She zoomed in on some of the military unit patches used as decorations, caught snowflakes glistening against gold balls and white lights, captured angles of the tree until, finally, far enough away, she got the whole tree. If these came out the way she hoped, she might use them for something next Christmas—ads or cards or something.

Then she turned and caught a couple of good shots of the bar porch, the snow drifting on the rails and steps and roof. Then of the street with all the houses lit for holiday cheer. Then the bar porch with a man leaning against the rail, arms crossed over his chest—a very handsome man.

She lowered the camera and walked toward Drew. There was no getting around the fact that he was handsome—tall and built, light brown hair, twinkling brown eyes, and if she remembered right, a very sexy smile. He stood on the porch and she looked up at him.

"Okay, look, I apologize," she said. "It's not like me to be so rude, so 'unapproachable' as you call it. I got dumped, okay? I'm still licking my wounds, as my uncle Nathaniel puts it. Not a good time for me to respond to a come-on from a guy. I'm scared to death to meet a guy and end up actually liking him, so I avoid all males. That's it in a nutshell," she added with a shrug. "I used to be very friendly and outgoing—now I'm on guard a lot."

"Apology accepted. And I had a bad breakup, too, but it was a while ago. Water under the bridge, as they say."

"You got dumped?"

He gave a nod. "And I understand how you feel. So let's start over. What do you say? I'm Drew Foley," he said.

She took another step toward the porch, looking up at him. "Sunny Archer. But when? I mean, how long ago did you get dumped?"

"About nine months, I guess."

"About?" she asked. It must not have impacted him in quite the same way if he couldn't remember the date. "I mean—was it traumatic?"

"Sort of," he said. "We were engaged, lived together, but we were arguing all the time. She finally told me she wasn't willing to have a life like that and we had to go our separate ways. It wasn't my idea to break up." He shrugged. "I thought we could fix it and wanted to try, but she didn't."

"Did you know?" she asked. "Were you expecting it?"

He shook his head. "I should have expected it, but it broadsided me."

"How can that be? If you should have expected it, how could it possibly have taken you by surprise?"

He took a deep breath, looked skyward into the softly falling flakes, then back at her. "We were pretty miserable, but before we lived together we did great. I'm a medical resident and my hours were…still are hideous. Sometimes I'm on for thirty-six hours and just get enough time off to sleep. She needed more from me than that. She…" He looked down. "I don't like calling her *she* or *her*. *Penny* had a hard time changing her life in order to move in with me. She had to get a new job, make new friends, and I was never there for her. I should have seen it coming but I didn't. It was all my fault but I couldn't have done anything to change it."

"Where are you from?" she asked him.

"Chico. About four hours south of here."

"Wow," she said. "We actually do have some things in common."

"Do we?" he asked.

"But you're over it. How'd you get over it?"

He put his hands in his front pants pockets. "She invited me to her engagement party three months ago. To another surgical resident. Last time I looked, he was on the same treadmill I was on. Guess he manages better with no sleep."

"No way," she said, backing away from the bar's porch a little bit.

"Way."

"You don't suppose…?"

"That she was doing him when she was supposed to be doing me?" he asked for her. "It crossed my mind. But I'm not going there. I don't even want to know. All that aside, she obviously wasn't the one. I know that now. Which means it really *was* my fault. I was hooking up with someone out of inertia, not because I was insanely in love with her. Bottom line, Sunny, me and

Penny? We both dodged a bullet. We were not meant to be."

She was speechless. Her mouth formed a perfect O. Her eyes were round. She wished she'd been able to take her own situation in such stride. "Holy crap," she finally said. Then she shook her head. "I guess you have to be confident to be in medicine and all."

"Aw, come on, don't give the study all the credit. I might actually have some common sense." He took a step down from the bar porch to approach her, his heel slid on the step and he went airborne. While he was in the air, there were rapid flashes from her camera. Then he landed, flat on his back, and there were more flashes.

Sunny stood over him, camera in hand. She looked down at him. "Are you all right?"

He narrowed his eyes at her. It took him a moment to catch his breath. "I could be paralyzed, you know. I hope I was hallucinating, but were you actually taking my picture as I fell?"

"Well, I couldn't catch you," she said. Then she smiled.

"You are sick and twisted."

"Maybe you should lie still. I could go in the bar and get the pediatrician and the midwife to have a look at you. I met them earlier, before you got here."

He looked up at her; she was still smiling. Apparently it didn't take much to cheer her up—the near death of a man seemed to put her in a better mood. "Maybe you could just show them the pictures...."

She fell onto her knees beside him and laughed, her camera still in hand. It was a bright and happy sound and those beautiful blue eyes glittered. "Seriously, you're the doctor—do you think you're all right?"

"I don't know," he said. "I haven't moved yet. One wrong move and I could be paralyzed from the neck down."

"Are you playing me?"

"Might be," he admitted with a shrug of his shoulders.

"Hah! You moved! You're fine. Get up."

"Are you going to have a drink with me?" he asked.

"Why should I? Seriously, we're a couple of wounded birds—we probably shouldn't drink, and we certainly shouldn't drink together!"

"Get over it," he said, rising a bit, holding himself up on his elbows. "We have nothing to lose. It's a New Year's Eve party. We'll have a couple of drinks, toast the New Year, move on. But give it a try not so pissed off. See if you can have some fun." He smiled. "Just for the heck of it?"

She sat back on her heels and eyed him warily. "Is this just more inertia?"

His grin widened. "No, Sunny. This is part chivalry and part animal attraction."

"Oh, God.… I just got dumped by an animal. So not looking for another one."

He gave her a gentle punch in the arm. "Buck up. Be a big girl. I bet you haven't let an interested guy buy you a drink in a long time. Take a chance. Practice on me. I'm harmless."

She lifted one light brown brow. "How do I know you're harmless?"

"I'm going back to sacrifice myself to the gods of

residency in two days. They'll chew me up and spit me out. Those chief residents are ruthless and they want revenge for what was done to them when they were the little guys. There won't even be a body left. No one will ever know you succumbed to having a beer with me." And then he smiled with all his teeth.

She tsked and rolled her eyes at him.

He sat up. "See how much you like me? You're putty in my hands."

"You're a dork!"

He got to his feet and held out a hand to her, helping her up. "I've heard that, but I'm not buying it yet. I think if you dig deep enough, I might be cool."

She brushed off the knees of her jeans. "I'm not sure I have that kind of time."

CHAPTER THREE

ONCE DREW GOT UP AND MOVED, he limped. He claimed a wounded hip and leaned on Sunny. Since she couldn't be sure if he was faking, she allowed this. But just as they neared the steps, the doors to the bar flew open and people began to spill out, laughing, shouting, waving goodbye.

"Careful there," he yelled, straightening up. "I just slipped on the steps. They're iced over. I'll get Jack to throw some salt on them, but take it slow and easy."

"Sure," someone said. "Thanks, Drew."

"Be careful driving back to Chico," someone else said.

"Say hello to your sisters," a woman said. "Tell them to come up before too long, we miss them."

"Pinch that cute baby!"

"Will do," Drew said in response, and he pulled Sunny to the side to make way for the grand exodus. The laughing, joking, talking people, some carrying their plates and pots from the buffet table, headed for their cars.

"What the heck," Sunny said. "It's not even nine o'clock!"

Drew laughed and put his arm back over her shoulder to lean on her. "This is a little town, Sunny. These folks have farms, ranches, orchards, vineyards, small businesses and stuff like that. The ones who don't have to get up early for work—even on holidays—might stay later. And some of the folks who are staying are on call—the midwife, the cop, the doctor." He grinned. "Probably the bartender. If anyone has a flat on the way home, five gets you ten either Jack or Preacher will help out."

"Do you know all these people?"

"A lot of them, yeah. I'll give you the short version of the story—my sister Marcie was married to a marine who was disabled in action and then later died. She came up here to find his best friend and sergeant—Ian Buchanan. She found him in a run-down old cabin up on the ridge, just over the county line, but the nearest town was Virgin River. So—she married him and they have a baby now. My oldest sister, Erin, wanted a retreat up here, but she couldn't handle a cabin with no indoor bathroom or where you'd have to boil your bath water and chop your wood for heat, so she got a local builder to renovate one into something up to her standards with electricity, indoor plumbing and a whirlpool tub." He laughed. "Really, Marcie's pretty tough, but if Erin risked breaking a nail, that would make her very cranky." He looked at Sunny and smiled. "It used to be a lean-to, now it should be in *Architectural Digest*. Anyway, I've been up here several times in the past couple of years, and Jack's is the only game in town. You don't have to drop into Jack's very many times before you know half the town. I'm hiding out in the cabin for a few days to get some studying done, away from my sisters and the baby. I have to go back on the second. I just swung through town for a beer—I had no idea there was a party."

They just stood there, in front of the porch, his arm draped across her shoulder. It was kind of silly—she was only five foot four and he was easily six feet, plus muscular. He didn't lean on her too heavily.

"Is it very hard, what you do? Residency?"

"It doesn't have to be. It could be a learning experience, but the senior residents pile as much on you as they can. It's like a dare—who can take it all and keep standing. That's the part that makes it hard." Then he sobered for a second. "And kids. I love working with the kids, making them laugh, helping them get better, but it's so tough to see them broken. Being the surgeon who puts a kid back together again—it's like the best and worst part of what I do. Know what I mean?"

She couldn't help but imagine him taking a little soccer player into surgery, or wrapping casting material around the arm of a young violinist. "Your sister was married to a soldier who was killed…?"

"She was married to a marine. Bobby was permanently disabled by a bomb in Iraq. He was in a nursing home for a few years before he died, but he never really came back, you know? No conscious recognition—the light was on but no one was home. They were very young."

"Were you close to him?"

"Yeah, sure. He was two years older and we all went to high school together. Bobby went in right after graduation. Ian was a little older, so I didn't know him until Marcie brought him home." He laughed sentimentally. "She's something, Marcie. She came up here to find Ian, make sure he was all right after the war and to give him Bobby's baseball card collection. She brought him home on Christmas eve and said, 'This is

Ian and I'm going to marry him as soon as he can get used to the idea.'"

"This is why," she said softly. "This is why you can move on after getting dumped by your fiancée. You've seen some rough stuff and you know how to count your blessings. I bet that's it."

He turned Sunny so she faced him. Of course he couldn't lean on her then, but he got close. "Sunny, my family's been through some stuff… Mostly my sisters, really—they had it toughest. But the thing that keeps me looking up instead of down—it's what I see at work everyday. I'm called on to treat people with problems lots bigger than mine—people who will never walk again, never use their arms or hands, and sometimes worse. Orthopedic pain can be terrible, rehab can be extended and dreary.… Tell you what, Sunshine—I'm upright, walking around, healthy, have a brain to think with and the option to enjoy my life. Well, I'm not going to take that for granted." He lifted a brow, tilted his head, smiled. "Maybe you should spend a little time in my trauma center, see if it fixes up all those things you think you should worry about?"

"What about your chief residents?" she asked, showing him her smile.

"Oh, them. Well, I pretty much wish them dead. No remorse, either. God, they're mean. Mean and spiteful and impossible to please."

"Will you be a chief resident someday?"

His smile took on an evil slant. "Yes. But not soon enough. Watch yourself on these stairs, honey." Before opening the door for Sunny, he stopped her. "So—want to find a cozy spot by the fire and tell me about the breakup that left you so sad and unapproachable?"

She didn't even have to think about it. "No," she said, shaking her head. "I'd rather not talk about it."

"Fair enough. Want to tell me how you got into photography?"

She smiled at him. "I could do that."

"Good. I'll have Jack pour you a glass of wine and while he's doing that I'll scatter some salt on those icy steps." He touched her pink nose. "Your mission is to find us a spot in that bar where we can talk. If I'm not mistaken, we're the only two singles at this party."

SUNNY WENT BACK TO THE PLACE near the fire where she had left her camera bag and put her camera away. She glanced over at Drew. He stood at the bar talking with Jack; Jack handed him a large canister of salt.

And suddenly it was someone else standing at the bar, and it wasn't this bar. Her mind drifted and took her back in time. It was Glen and it was the bar at their rehearsal dinner. Glen was leaning on the bar, staring morosely into his drink, one foot lifted up on the rail. His best man, Russ, had a hand on his back, leaning close and talking in Glen's ear. Glen wasn't responding.

Why hadn't she been more worried? she asked herself in retrospect. Maybe because everyone around her had been so reassuring? Or was it because she *refused* to be concerned?

Sunny wasn't very old-fashioned, but there were a few traditional wedding customs she had wanted to uphold—one was not seeing her groom the day of her wedding. So she and her cousin Mary, who was also her matron of honor, would spend the night at Sunny's parents' house after the rehearsal dinner. Even still, she remembered thinking it was a little early when Glen kissed her goodnight that evening.

"I'm going out with the boys for a nightcap, then home," he said.

"Is everything all right?" she asked.

"Sure. Fine." His smile was flat, she knew things were not fine.

"You're not driving, are you?"

"Russ has the keys. It's fine."

"I guess I'll see you tomorrow." She remembered so vividly that she laid her palm against his handsome cheek. "I can't wait for tomorrow."

He didn't move his head, but his eyes had darted briefly away. "Me, too."

When Russ came over to her to say good-night, she had asked, "What's bothering Glen?"

"Oh, he'll be fine."

"But what is it?"

Russ had laughed a bit uncomfortably. "Y'know, even though you two have been together a long time, lived together and everything, it's still a pretty big step for a guy. For both of you, I realize. But guys... I don't know what it is about us—I was a little jittery the day before my wedding. And it was absolutely what I wanted, no doubt, but I was still nervous. I don't know if it's the responsibility, the lifestyle change..."

"What changes?" she asked. "Besides that we're going to take a nice trip and write a lot of thank-you notes?"

"I'm just saying... I've been in a bunch of weddings, including my own, and every groom I've ever known gets a little jumpy right before. Don't worry about it. I'll buy him a drink on the way home, make sure he gets all tucked in. You'll be on your way to Aruba before you know it." Then he had smiled reassuringly.

"Will you ask him to call me to say good-night?" she asked.

"Sure. But if he's slurring by then, don't hold it against me!"

She'd been up late talking to Mary; they'd opened another bottle of wine. By the time they fell asleep it was the wee hours and they'd slept soundly. In the morning when she checked her cell phone, she found a text from Glen that had come in at three in the morning. *Going to bed. Talk to you tomorrow.*

She wanted to talk to him, but she thought it would probably be better if he slept till noon, especially if there was anything to sleep off, so he'd be in good shape for the ceremony. All she wanted was for the wedding to be perfect! She had many bridely things to do and was kept busy from brunch getting a manicure and pedicure, surrounded by the women in her family and her girlfriends.

The New Year's Eve wedding had been Sunny's idea. It had been born of a conversation with the girls about how they'd never had a memorable New Year's Eve— even when they had steady guys, were engaged or even married. Oh, there'd been a few parties, but they hadn't been special in any way. Sunny thought it would be fantastic—a classy party to accompany her wedding, something for everyone to remember. An unforgettable event.

Little did she know.

She'd been so busy all day, she hadn't worried that she never heard from Glen. She assumed he was as oc-cupied with his guys as she was with her girls. In fact, it hadn't really bothered her until about five, still a couple of hours till the wedding. She called him and when he didn't pick up, she left him a voice mail that she loved him, that she was so happy, that soon they would be married and off on a wonderful honeymoon.

It's very hard for a photographer to choose a photographer; almost no one was going to measure up to Sunny's expectations. But the very well known Lin Hui was trying her best, and started snapping shots as soon as the girls showed up at the church with hairdressers and professional makeup artists in tow. Her camera flashed at almost every phase of preparation and in addition captured special memories—shiny, strappy heels against flowers, female hands clutching white satin, mothers of the bride and groom embracing and dabbing each other's eyes. But the poor thing seemed very nervous. Sunny assumed it was because of the challenge of shooting another professional. She had no idea it was because Lin couldn't find the groom for a photo shoot of the men in the wedding party.

It happened at six forty-five, fifteen minutes before the ceremony was to start. Sunny's father came into the wedding prep room with Russ. Both of them looked as if someone had died and she immediately gasped and ran to her father. "Is Glen all right?"

"He's fine, honey." Then he sent everyone out of the room including Sunny's mom and the mother of the groom. He turned to Russ and said, "Tell her."

Russ hung his head. He shook it. "Don't ask me what's got into him, I really can't explain. There's no good reason for this. He said he's sorry, he just isn't ready for this. He froze up, can't go through with it."

She had never before realized how fast denial can

set in or how long it can last. "Impossible. The wedding is in fifteen minutes," she said.

"I know. I'm sorry—I spent all day trying to get through this with him. I even suggested he just show up, do it, and if he still feels the same way in a few months, he can get a divorce. Honest to God, it made more sense to me than this."

She shook her head and then, inexplicably, laughed. "Aw, you guys. This is not funny. You got me, okay? But this isn't funny!"

"It's not a joke, baby," her father said. "I've tried calling him—he won't pick up."

"He'll pick up for me," she said. "He always picks up for me!"

But he didn't. Her call was sent to voice mail. Her message was, "Please call me and tell me I'm just dreaming this! Please! You can't really be ditching me at the church fifteen minutes before the wedding! Not you! You're better than this!"

Russ grabbed her wrist. "Sunny—he left his tux in my car to return. He's not coming."

Sunny looked at her father. "What am I supposed to do?" she asked in a whisper.

Her father's face was dark with anger, stony with fury. "We'll give him till seven-fifteen to call or do something honorable, then we make an announcement to the guests, invite them to go to the party and eat the food that will otherwise be given away or thrown out, and we'll return the gifts with apologies. And then I'm going to kill him."

"He said he'll pay back the cost of the reception if it takes his whole life. But there's no way he can pay me back for what he asked me to do today," Russ said. "Sunny, I'm so sorry."

"But *why?*"

"Like I said, he doesn't have a logical reason. He can't, he said." Russ shook his head. "I don't understand, so I know you can't possibly."

Sunny grabbed Russ's arm. "Go tell his mother to call him! Give her your cell phone so he'll think it's you and pick up!"

But Glen didn't pick up and his mother was left to growl angrily into the phone's voice mail right before she fell apart and cried.

Before they got even close to seven-fifteen everyone nearby was firing questions at Sunny like it was her fault. Why? Did he talk to you about this? Was he upset, troubled? Did you suspect this was coming? You must have noticed something! How can you not have known? Suspected? Were you having problems? Arguing about something? Fighting? Was his behavior off? Strange? Was there another woman? It didn't take long for her to erupt. "You'll have to ask *him!* And he's not even here to ask! Not only did he not show up, he left me to try to answer for him!"

At seven-ten, right before her father made an announcement to the wedding guests, Sunny quietly got into the bridal limo. She took her bouquet—her beautiful bouquet filled with roses and orchids and calla lilies—made a stop at her parents' house for her purse and honeymoon luggage and had the driver take her home.

Home. The town house she shared with Glen. Her parents were frantic, her girlfriends were worried, her wedding guests wondered what went wrong. She wasn't sure why she went home, maybe to see if he'd moved out while she was having a manicure and pedicure. But no—everything was just as she'd left it. And typical of Glen, the bed wasn't made and there were dirty dishes in the sink.

She sat on the edge of their king-size bed in her wedding gown, her bouquet in her lap and her cell phone in her hand in case he should call and say it was all a bad joke and rather than pulling out of the wedding he was in the hospital or in jail. The only calls she got were from friends and family, all worried about her. She fended off most of them without saying where she was, others were forced to leave messages. For some reason she couldn't explain to this day, she didn't cry. She let herself fall back on the bed, stared at the ceiling and asked herself over and over what she didn't know about this man she had been willing to commit a lifetime to. She was vaguely aware of that special midnight hour passing. The new year didn't come in with a kiss, but with a scandalous breakup.

Sunny hadn't had a plan when she went home, but when she heard a key in the lock she realized that because she'd taken the bridal limo and left her car at her parents', Glen didn't know she was there. She sat up.

He walked through the bedroom door, grabbing his wallet, keys and change out of his pockets to drop onto the dresser when he saw her. Everything scattered as he made a sound of surprise and he automatically reached for his ankle where he always kept a small, back-up gun. Breathing hard, he left it there and straightened. Cops, she thought. They like always having *some-*

thing, in case they happen to run into someone they put away…or a pissed-off bride.

"Go ahead," she said. "Shoot me. It might be easier."

"Sunny," he said, breathless. "What are you *doing* here?"

"I *live* here," she said. She looked down at the bouquet she still held. Why had she clung to that? Because it was sentimental or because it cost 175 dollars and she couldn't return it? "You can't have done this to me," she said almost weakly. "You can't have. You must have a brain tumor or something."

He walked into the room. "I'm sorry," he said, shaking his head. "I kept thinking that by the time we got to the actual date, the wedding date, I'd be ready. I really thought that."

"Ready for what?" she asked, nonplussed.

"Ready for that life, that commitment forever, that next stage, the house, the children, the fidelity, the—"

She shook her head, frowning in confusion. "Wait a minute, we haven't found a house we like and can afford, we agreed we're not ready for children yet and I thought we already had commitment…" His chin dropped. "Fidelity?" she asked in a whisper.

He lifted his eyes and locked with hers. "See, I haven't really done anything wrong, not really. I kept thinking, I'm not married yet! And I thought by the time—"

"Did you sleep with other women?" she asked, rising to her feet.

"No! No! I swear!"

She didn't believe him for a second! "Then what *did* you do?"

"Nothing much. I partied a little. Had drinks, you know. Danced. Just went out and sometimes I met girls, but it didn't get serious or anything."

"But it did get to meeting, dancing, buying drinks. Talking on the phone? Texting little messages? Maybe having dinner?"

"Maybe some of that. A couple of times."

"Maybe kissing?"

"Only, maybe, twice. At the most, twice."

"My God, have I been brain damaged? To not know?"

"When were we together?" he asked. "We had different nights off, we were like roommates!"

"You could have fixed that easy! You could have changed your nights off! I couldn't! People don't get married or have fiftieth anniversary parties on Tuesday nights!"

"And they also don't go out for fun on Tuesday nights! I guess I'm just a bad boy, but I enjoy a ball game or a run on a bar or club on a weekend when people are out! And you were never available on a weekend! We talked about it, we *fought* about it! You said it would never change, not while you took pictures."

"This isn't happening," she said. "You stood up two hundred wedding guests and a trip to Aruba because I work weekends?"

"Not exactly, but... Well... Look," he said, shaking his head. "I'm twenty-six. I thought you were probably the best thing for me, the best woman I could ever hook up with for the long haul except for one thing—I'm not ready to stop having fun! And you are—you're all business. Even that wedding—Jesus, it was like a run-away train! Planning that astronomical wedding was like a second job for you and I never wanted anything that big, that out of control! Sunny, you're way too young to be so old."

That was one way to deliver what she could only describe as a punch to the gut. Of all the things she thought she knew about him, she hadn't given enough credence to the fact that even at twenty-six, he was younger than she. More immature. He wanted to have *fun.* "And you couldn't tell me this last month? Or last week? Or *yesterday?*" She stared at him, waiting.

"Like I said, I thought I'd work it out in my head, be ready in time."

Talk about shock and awe. "You're an infant. How did I not realize what a liability that could be?"

"Excuse me, but I lay my life on the line every day! I go to work in a bulletproof vest! And you're calling me an *infant?*"

"Oh, I'm so sorry, Glen. You're an infant with a dick. With a little, tiny brain in it." She took a breath. "Pack a bag. Take some things and see if you can find a friend who will take you in for a few days. I'll move home to my mom and dad's as soon as I can. I hope you can make the rent alone. If I recall, I was making more money with my boring old weekend job than you were with your bulletproof vest."

Sunny sat back on the bed, then she lay down. Still gowned in a very big wedding dress, holding her valuable bouquet at her waist, Sunny closed her eyes. She heard Glen rustling around, finding clothes, his shaving kit, the essentials. Her mind was completely occupied with thoughts like, will the airline refund the money for the first-class tickets because the groom didn't show? How much non-refundable money had her parents wasted on a wedding that never happened? Would the homeless of L.A. be eating thousands of dollars worth of exquisite food discarded by the caterer? And since her name was also on the lease to this townhouse, would fun-man Glen stiff her there, too? Hurt her credit rating *and* her business?

"Sunny?" Glen said to her. He was standing over her. "Wake up. You look so… I don't know… *Funereal* or something. Like a dead body, all laid out." He winced. "In a wedding dress…"

She opened her eyes, then narrowed them at him. "Go. Away."

SUNNY GAVE HER HEAD a little shake to clear her mind and looked up to see Drew standing in front of her. He held a glass of wine toward her. "I salted the steps, got you a wine and me a beer. Now," he said, sitting down opposite her. "About this photography of yours…"

"It happened a year ago," she said.

"Huh? The picture taking happened a year ago?" he asked.

"The wedding that never was. Big wedding—big party. We'd been together three years, engaged and living together for one, and all of a sudden he didn't show. I was all dressed up in a Vera Wang, two hundred guests were waiting, little sausages simmering and stuffed mushrooms warming, champagne corks popping…and no groom."

Total shock was etched into his features. "Get out!" he said in a shocked breath.

"God's truth. His best man told me he couldn't do it. He wasn't ready."

Suddenly Drew laughed, but not unkindly, not of humor but disbelief. He ran his hand through his hair. "Did he ever say *why?*"

She had never told anyone what he'd said, it was too embarrassing. But for some reason she couldn't explain, she spit it right out to Drew. "Yeah. He wasn't done having fun."

Silence reigned for a moment. "You're not serious," Drew finally said.

"Deadly. It was all so stunning, there was even a small newspaper article about it."

"And this happened when?" he asked.

"One year ago. Today."

Drew sat back in his chair. "Whoa," was all he could say. "Well, no wonder you're in a mood. Fun?" he asked. "He wasn't done having *fun?*"

"Fun," she affirmed. "That's the best explanation he could come up with. He liked to party, go to clubs, flirt, dance, whatever… He's a Saturday-night kind of guy and just wasn't ready to stop doing that and guess what? Photographers work weekends—weddings, baptisms, et cetera. Apparently I'm a real drag."

Drew rubbed the back of his neck. "I must be really backward then. I always thought having the right person there for you, listening to your voice mails and texting you to pick up her dry cleaning or saying she'd pick up yours, someone who argued with you over what sushi to bring home or what went on the pizza, someone who would come to bed naked on a regular basis—I always thought *those things* were fun. Sexy and fun."

She grinned at him. "You find dry cleaning sexy?"

"I do," he said. "I really do." And then they both laughed.

CHAPTER FOUR

SUNNY SAT FORWARD, elbows on her knees, a smile on her face and said, "I can't wait to hear more about this—the things you find sexy. I mean pizza toppings and dry cleaning? Do go on."

He took a sip of his beer. "There is a long list, Miss Sunshine, but let's be clear—I am a boy. Naked tops the list."

"Yes, there are some things all you *boys* seem to have in common. But if I've learned anything it's that showing up naked regularly apparently isn't quite enough."

"Pah—for men with no imagination maybe. Or men who don't have to push a month's worth of work into a day."

"Well, then…?" she asked. "What?"

"I like working out a budget you'll never stick to. There's something about planning that together, it's cool. Not the checkbook, that's not a two-person job— it's dicey. No two people add and subtract the same, did you know that? And the chore list, that turns me on like you wouldn't believe. Picking movies—there's a real skill to that. If you can find a girl who likes action then you can negotiate three action movies to every chick flick, and you can eventually work up to trading chick flicks for back rubs." He leaned close to whisper. "I don't want this to get out, but I actually like some of the chick flicks. I'm picky, but I do like some."

"Shopping?" she asked.

"I have to draw the line there," he said firmly. "That just doesn't do it for me. If I need clothes or shoes I take care of it as fast as I can. I don't like to screw around with that. It's boring and I have no skills. But I get that you have to look at least half decent to get a girl to like you." He smiled. "A pretty girl like you," he added.

"Then how do you manage that? Because tonight, you weren't even aware there was a party and you don't look that terrible."

"Why, thank you," he said, straightening proudly. "I either ask my oldest sister, Erin, to dress me—the one who made the lean-to into a showplace—or failing that I just look for a gay guy working in clothing."

She burst out laughing, not realizing that Nate, Annie, Jack and a few others turned to look. "That's awful, shame on you!"

"Gimme a break—I have gay friends. You can say anything you want about them but the common denominator is—they have fashion sense. At least the guys I know do."

"Then why not ask a gay friend to go shopping with you?"

"I don't want to mislead anyone," he said with a shrug.

"Sure you're not just a little self-conscious about your…um…somewhat *flexible* status?"

He leaned so close she could inhale the Michelob on his breath. His eyes locked on hers. "Not flexible about that. Ab. So. Lutely. Not." Then he smiled. "I only swing one way."

She couldn't help it, she laughed loudly. Happily.

"You gotta stop that, my sunshine. You're supposed to be miserable. You were left at the altar by a juvenile idiot a year ago tonight. We're grieving here."

"I know, I know," she said, fanning her face. "I'm going to get back into depression mode in a sec. Right now, tell me another thing you find impossibly sexy, and keep in mind we've already covered that naked thing."

"Okay," he said. He rolled his eyes skyward, looking for the answer. "Ah!" he said. "Her lingerie in the bathroom! It's impossible. Hanging everywhere. A guy can't even pee much less brush his teeth or get a shower. I hate that!" And there was that wicked grin again. "Very sexy."

"Okay, I'm a little confused here. You hate it? And it's very sexy?"

"Well, you have to be a guy to get this. A guy goes into the bathroom—which is small like the rest of your house or apartment until you're at least an evil senior resident—and you put your face into all the satin and lace hanging all over the place. You rub it between your palms, wear a thong on your head for a minute, have a couple of reality-based fantasies, and then you yell, 'Penny! Get your underwear out of here so I can get a shower! I'm late.'"

She put her hands over her face and laughed into them.

His eyes glowed as he looked at her. "Be careful, Sunny. You're enjoying yourself."

She reached across the short space that separated them and gave him a playful slug. "So are you! And your breakup was more recent."

"Yeah, but—"

He was about to say *but not more traumatic*. At least he wasn't left in a Vera Wang gown hiding from two hundred wedding guests. But the door to the bar opened and in came the local Riordans—Luke, Shelby and little Brett, their new baby. Luke was holding Brett against his chest, tucked under his jacket. Drew jumped to his feet. "Hey! Son of a gun!" Then he grabbed Sunny's hand and pulled her along. He turned to her and said, "Kind of family. I'll explain."

Leaving Sunny behind him a bit, he grabbed Shelby in a big hug and kissed her cheek. He grabbed Luke, careful of the baby and Luke scowled at him and said, "Do *not* kiss me!"

"All right, but gee, I'll have to really hold myself back," Drew said with a laugh. He winked at Sunny before he pulled her forward. "Meet Sunny, here visiting her uncle. Sunny, remember I told you about the sister who turned the shack into a showplace? That's Erin—and while she was up here finding herself, she also found Luke's brother Aiden. They're engaged. That makes me almost related to these guys and little Brett."

Shelby reached out to shake Sunny's hand. "I heard you'd be visiting, Sunny. We know Nate and Annie. I sometimes ride with Annie."

"Hey, I thought you said you weren't coming out tonight," Jack said from behind the bar. "Baby sleeping and all that."

"We should'a thought that through a little better," Luke said. "Brett prefers to sleep during the day and is a regular party animal at night."

Mel moved closer and said, "Aww, let me have him

a minute." She pulled the little guy from Luke and indeed, his eyes were as big as saucers—he was wide awake at nine-thirty. Mel laughed at him. "Well, aren't you something!"

Shelby said to Sunny, "Mel delivered him. She gets really invested in her babies."

"Let's have your resolutions," Jack said. "Then I'll set you up a drink and you can graze the buffet table."

"What resolutions?" Luke wanted to know.

Jack patted the fishbowl full of slips of paper on the bar. "Everyone has contributed their number one, generic resolution. You know the kind—quit smoking, lose ten pounds, work out everyday. We're going to do something fun with them at midnight. A kind of game."

"I don't do games," Luke said.

"Lighten up, it's not like charades or anything. It's more like cracking open a fortune cookie."

"I don't do resolutions," Luke said.

"I'll do his," Shelby said, sitting up at the bar. "I have some ideas."

"Easy, baby," Luke said. "You know you don't like me too perfect. Rough around the edges caught you in the first place."

Shelby glanced over her shoulder and smiled at him. Nate, who was sitting beside her, leaned in and pretended to read her resolution. "No more boys' nights out or dancing girls?" he said. "Shelby, isn't that a little strict for our boy Luke?"

Luke just laughed. So did Shelby.

Sunny took it all in. She had always liked to be around couples who were making that whole couple thing work—understanding each other, give and take, good humor, physical attraction. She'd done a lot of weddings. They weren't all easy and pleasant. A lot of the couples she photographed she wouldn't give a year.

Drew whispered in her ear. "Shelby is a full-time nursing student. She and Luke run a bunch of riverside cabin rentals and while Shelby goes to school and studies, Luke not only takes care of the cabins and house, but Brett, too. I think dancing girls are way in the past for Luke."

"Hmm," she said. She went for her camera and started taking pictures again, and while she did so she listened. Sunny could see things through the lens that were harder to see with the naked eye. For her, anyway.

She learned that Vanessa and Paul Haggerty were more conventional. She was home with the children while he was a general contractor who did most of the building and renovating around Virgin River, including the reconstruction of that old cabin for Drew's sister, the cabin Drew was staying in. Abby Michaels, the local doctor's wife, had a set of toddler twins and was overseeing the building of a house while her husband, Cam, was at the clinic or on call 24/7. The situation was a bit different for Mel and Jack Sheridan. The local midwife was always on call and Jack had a business that was open about sixteen hours a day—they had to shore each other up. They did a lot of juggling of kids and chores—Jack did all the cooking and Mel all the cleaning. If all the jokes could be believed, apparently Mel could burn water. Preacher and Paige worked together to raise their kids, run the kitchen and keep the accounting books at the bar. Brie and Mike Valenzuela had a child and two full-time jobs—she was an attorney, he was the town cop. And Sunny already knew that Uncle Nate and Annie were partners in running the Jensen Clinic and Stable. Their wedding was scheduled for May.

Lots of interesting and individual methods of managing the realities of work, family, relationships. She wondered about a couple who would split up because one of them wasn't available to party on Saturday nights. She already knew that wasn't an issue among these folks.

While she observed and listened, she snapped pictures. She instructed Mel to hold the Riordan baby over her head and lower him slowly to kiss his nose. She got a great shot of Jack leaning on the bar, braced on strong arms spread wide, wearing a half smile as he watched his wife with a baby she had delivered, a proud glow in his eyes. Preacher was caught with his huge arms wrapped around his little wife, his lips against her head. Paul Haggerty put a quarter in the jukebox and danced his wife around the bar. Cameron Michaels was clinking glasses with Abby Michaels and couldn't resist nuzzling her neck—Sunny caught that. In fact, she caught many interesting postures, loving poses. Not only was there a lot of affection in the room, but plenty of humor and happiness. God, she never used to be the type that got dragged down.

When Sunny was focusing the camera, she didn't miss much. Maybe she should have been looking at Glen through the lens because clearly she missed a lot about him. Or had she just ignored it all?

She wondered if this was all about it being New

Year's Eve, being among friends and the promise of a brand-new start, a first day of a new year. That's what she'd had in mind for her wedding—a new beginning.

Then she spotted Drew, apart from the crowd, leaning against the wall beside the hearth, watching her with a lazy smile on his lips. He had one leg crossed over the other, one hand was in his front jeans pocket and he lifted his bottle of Mich, which had to be warm by now since he'd been nursing it for so long. She snapped, flashed the camera, making him laugh. He posed for her, pulling that hand out of his pocket and flexing his muscles. Of course it was impossible to see his real physique given the roomy plaid flannel shirt. He put his leg up on the seat of a nearby chair, gave her a profile and lifted the beer bottle—she liked it. He grinned, scowled, stuck his tongue out, blew raspberries at the camera—she snapped and laughed. Then he crooked his finger at her for her to come closer and she took pictures as she went. When she got real close he pulled the camera away.

"Let's get out of here," he whispered. "Somewhere we can talk."

"Can't we talk here?" she asked.

He shook his head. "Listen," he said.

She listened—the jukebox. Only the jukebox. He turned her around. Every single eye was on them. Watching. Waiting. She turned back to Drew. "Everyone knows," she said. "We are the only single people, we're both single and miserable—"

"Single," he said. "I'm not miserable and I know you intended to be miserable, but that's not really working out for you. So?" he asked with a shrug. "Wanna just throw caution to the wind and see if you can enjoy the rest of the evening?"

"I can't enjoy it here?"

"With all of them watching you? Listening?" he asked with a lift of the chin to indicate the bar at large.

When she turned around to look, she caught everyone quickly averting their eyes and it made her laugh. She laughed harder, putting her hand over her mouth.

"Don't do that," he said, pulling her hand away. "You have an amazing smile and I love listening to you laugh."

"Where would we go?"

"Well, it's only ten. I could take you to Eureka or Fortuna—there's bound to be stuff going on, but I'd prefer to find somewhere there's not a party. I could show you the cabin Erin turned into a showplace, but I don't have any 'before' pictures. Or we could take a drive, park in the woods and make out like teenagers." He grinned at her playfully. Hopefully.

"You're overconfident," she accused.

"I've been told that. It's better than being underconfident, in these circumstances at least."

"I have to speak to Uncle Nathaniel," she said.

He touched her cheek with the knuckle of one finger. "Permission?"

She shook her head a little. "Courtesy. I'm his guest. Grab our coats."

The walk across the bar to her uncle was very short and in that time she realized that Drew wasn't overconfident—*Glen* was overconfident. He preened, and had always managed to strike a pose that accentuated his height, firm jaw, strong shoulders. Drew clowned around. Laughed. Drew seemed to be pretty easygoing and took things as they came. But she'd known him for two whole hours. Who knew what secrets he harbored?

But what the hell, Sunny thought. I can experiment with actually letting a male person get close without much risk—I'm never going to see him again. Who knows? Maybe I'll recover after all.

"Uncle Nate," she said. "I'm going to go with Drew to see if anything fun is happening in Fortuna or Eureka. If you're okay with that."

"Well," he said. "I don't actually know—*ow!*"

Annie slugged him in the arm. "That's great, Sunny," she said. "Will you come back here or have Drew take you home?"

She shrugged and shook her head. "I don't know. Depends on where we are, what's going on, you know. Listen, if the cells worked up here, I'd call, but…"

"Your cell from Fortuna or Eureka to my home phone works. Or to Jack's land line. We'll be here till midnight," Nate said. Then he glared briefly at Annie. "Jack, can you give her your number?"

"You bet," Jack said, jotting it on a napkin. "I've known Drew and his family a couple of years. You're in good hands, Sunny."

"Does he have four-wheel drive?" Nate asked.

Sunny grinned. "Oh, you're going to be a fun daddy, yessir." Then she walked back to Drew and let him help her slip on her jacket.

"Where did you say we were going?" Drew asked.

"I said Fortuna or Eureka, but I want to see it—the cabin."

He grabbed his own jacket. "Hope I didn't leave it nasty."

"And is that likely?" she wanted to know.

"Depends where my head was at the time," he said. He rested her elbow in the palm of his hand and began to direct her out of the bar. As they were leaving he put two fingers to his brow and gave the gawkers a salute.

Sunny was trying to remember, what was the first thing Drew had said to her? She thought it was something simple, like "Hi, my name is Drew." And what had been Glen's opening line? With a finger in her sternum he had said, "Yo. You and me."

CHAPTER FIVE

"I'M NOT SURE THAT was the best thing to do," Nate Jensen said right after Sunny and Drew left. "I'm supposed to be looking after her, and I let her go off with some guy I don't even know."

"She was *laughing!*" Annie stressed. "Having fun for the first time in so long! She didn't need your permission, Nate. She was being polite, telling you where she was going so you wouldn't worry."

"You did fine," Jack said. "Drew's a good guy. A doctor, actually—in his residency now."

"But is he the kind of guy who will take advantage of a girl with a broken heart?" Nate asked. "Because my sister…"

"I don't know a thing about his love life," Jack said. "He said he'd had a breakup, so that might make them sympathetic to each other. I'll tell you what I know. Every time I've talked to him he's seemed like a stand-up guy. His brother-in-law was a disabled marine in a nursing home for a few years before he died, and Erin said that Drew, along with the rest of the family, helped take care of him. Erin thinks that had an impact on him, drew him to medicine. And…he has four-wheel drive. That should put your mind at ease."

"She *was* smiling," Nate admitted. "You should'a been there last year. Sitting in that church, waiting for the wedding to start. Just like in all things, the rumors that the groom didn't show started floating around the guests, maybe before Sunny had even heard it. It was awful. How do you not know something like that is coming? How could she not know?"

Jack gave the bar a wipe. "You can bet she's been asking herself that question for about a year."

"TELL ME ABOUT THE photography business," Drew said as they drove.

"You don't have to ask that," she said. "I can tell you're a gentleman and that's very polite, but you don't have to pretend to be interested in photography. It bores the heck out of most people."

He laughed at her. "When I was a kid, I took pictures sometimes," he said. "Awful pictures that were developed at the drugstore, but it was enough to get me on the yearbook staff, which I only wanted to be on because Bitsy Massey was on it. Bitsy was a cute little thing, a cheerleader of course, and she was on the yearbook committee—most likely to been sure the lion's share of the pictures were of her. I was in love with her for about six months, and she never knew I was alive. The only upside to the whole thing? I actually like taking pictures. I admit, I take a lot with my cell phone now and I don't have any aspirations to go professional, but I wasn't just being polite. In fact," he said, reaching into his pocket for his cell, "I happen to have some compound fractures, crushed ankles, ripped out shoulders and really horrible jaw fractures if you'd like to—"

"Ack!" she yelled, fanning him away with her hand. "Why in the world would you have those?"

"Snap 'em in E.R., take 'em to report and explain how we treated 'em and have the senior residents shoot us down and call us fools and idiots. So, Sunny—how'd it happen for you—picture taking? A big thug named Rock who liked to pose for you?"

"Nothing of the sort," she said indignantly. "I got a camera for Christmas when I was ten and started taking pictures. It only takes a few good ones before you realize you *can*. Take good pictures, that is. I figured out early what they would teach us about photography in college later—to get four or forty good pictures, just take four hundred. Of course, some subjects are close to impossible. Their color, angles, tones and shadows just don't work, while others just eat the camera, they're so photogenic. But…" She looked over at him. "Bored?"

"Not yet," he answered with a grin.

"It was my favorite thing," she said. "My folks kept saying there was no real future in it and I'd better have a backup plan, so I majored in business. But friends kept asking me to take pictures because I could. Pretty soon I had the moxie to ask them to at least pay the expenses—travel costs like gas for the car, film, developing, mounting, that sort of thing. Me and my dad put a darkroom in the basement when I was a junior in high school, but right after that we went digital and got a really good computer, upscale program and big screen. I built a website, using some of my stock for online advertising, and launched a price list that was real practical for people on a budget—but the product was *good*. My darkroom became a work room. I could deliver finished portraits in glossy, matte, texture, whatever they wanted, and I could do it quickly. Friends told friends who told friends and by my sophomore year I was booked every weekend for family reunions, birthday parties, christenings, weddings, engagement parties, you name it. The only thing I didn't have when I dropped out of school to do this full-time was a studio. Since I did all my shooting on location at the site, all I needed in a studio was a desk, computer, big-screen monitor, DVD player and some civilized furnishings, plus a whole lot of albums and DVDs and brochures of photo packages. The money was good. I was set up before I was set up. I was lucky."

"I bet you were also smart," Drew said.

She laughed a bit. "Sort of, with my dad running herd on my little business all the time. He wasn't trying to make me successful, he was looking out for me, showing me the pitfalls, helping me not fail. When it became my means of income, I think he was a little ambivalent about me quitting college. And my mom? Scared her to death! She's old-fashioned—go get a practical job! Don't bet on your ingenuity or worse, your talent!"

"Your guy," Drew asked. "What did he do?"

"Highway Patrol. He liked life on the edge."

"Did he like your photographs?"

Without even thinking she answered, "Of him. He liked being in front of the camera. I like being behind it."

"Oh, he was one of the photogenic ones?"

"He was," she admitted. "He could be a model. Maybe he is by now."

"You don't keep in touch?"

"Oh, no," she said with a mean laugh.

"Not even through friends?"

"Definitely not through friends." She turned to look at him. "You? Do you keep in touch?"

He shrugged but his eyes were focused on the road. "Well, she's going to marry one of the residents at the hospital. We're not in the same service—he's general surgery. But she turns up sometimes. She's polite. I'm polite." He took a breath. "I hate that. I don't know how she feels, but I don't feel polite."

"So you are angry," she said, a note of surprise in her voice.

"Oh, hell yes," he replied. "It's just that sometimes the line is blurred, and I get confused about who I'm angriest with—her or me. She knew what she was signing up for, that residents don't have a lot of time or money or energy after work. Why couldn't we figure that out without all the drama? But then, I'm guilty of the same thing—I was asking way too much of her. See? Plenty of blame to go around."

There was quiet for a while. The road was curvy, banked by very tall trees heavy with snow. The snow was falling lightly, softly. The higher they went, the more snow there was on the ground. There were some sharp turns along the road, and a few drop-offs that, in the dark of night, looked like they were bottomless. He drove slowly, carefully, attentively. If he looked at her at all, which was rare, it was the briefest glance.

"Very pretty out here," she said quietly.

He responded with, "Can I ask you a personal question?"

She sucked in her breath. "I don't know...."

"Tell you what—don't answer if it makes you the least bit uncomfortable," he suggested.

"But wouldn't my not answering tell you that—"

"Did you fall in love with him the second you met him? Like right off the bat? Boom—you saw him, you were knocked off your feet, dead in love?"

No! she thought. "Yes," she said. She looked across the front seat at him. "You?"

He shook his head first. "No. I liked her right away, though. There were things about her that really worked for me, that work for a guy. Like, for example, no guessing games. She was very up-front, but never in a bitchy way. Not a lot of games with Penny, at least up until we got to the breaking-up part of our relationship. For example, if we went out to dinner, she ordered exactly what she liked. If I asked her what she'd like to do, she came up with an answer—never any of that 'I don't care' when she really did care. I liked that. We got along, seemed like we were paddling in the same direction. I wanted to be a surgeon, and she was a nurse who liked the idea of being with a doctor, even though she knew it was never easy on the spouse. When I asked her if she wanted to move in with me before the residency started she said, 'Not without a ring.'" He shrugged. "Seemed reasonable to me that we'd just get married. I'm still real surprised it didn't work out that way. I really couldn't tell you exactly when it stopped working. That's the only thing that scares me."

She stared at his profile. At that moment she decided that if she ever broke a bone, she'd want him to set it. "But by then you were madly in love with her, right? By the time you got to the ring?"

"Probably. Yeah, I think so. The thing is, Penny seemed exactly right for me, exactly. Logical. Problems that friends of mine had with wives or girlfriends, I didn't have with Penny. Guys envied me. I thought she was the perfect one for me."

She heard Glen's voice in her head. *I thought you were the best thing for me, the best woman I could ever hook up with for the long haul....*

"Until all this fighting started," he went on. "Things had been so easy with us, I didn't get it. I thought it was all about her missing her friends, me working such long hours, that kind of thing. I'm still not sure—maybe it was about another guy and being all torn up trying to decide. But really, I thought everything was fine."

"What is it with you guys?" she said hotly. "You just pick out a girl who looks like wife material and hope by the time you get to the altar you'll be ready?"

Drew gave her a quick glance, a frown, then looked back at the road. And that's when it happened—as if it fell from the sky, he hit a buck. He knew it was a buck when he saw the antlers. He also saw its big, brown eyes. It was suddenly in front of the SUV—his oldest sister's SUV that he had borrowed to go up to the cabin. Though they weren't traveling fast, the strike was close, sudden, the buck hit the front hard, was briefly airborne, came down on the hood, and rolled up against the windshield with enough force for the antlers to crack it, splinter it.

Drew fought the car, though he could only see clearly out of the driver's side window. He knew that to let the SUV go off the road could be disastrous—there were so many drop-offs on the way to the cabin. He finally brought the car to rest on the shoulder, the passenger side safely resting against a big tree.

Sunny screamed in surprise and was left staring into the eyes of a large buck through the webbed and cracked windshield. The deer was lying motionless across the hood.

Drew turned to Sunny first. "Sunny…"

"We hit a deer!" she screamed.

"Are you okay? Neck? Head? Back? Anything?" he asked her.

She was unhooking her belt and wiggling out of it. "Oh, my God, oh, my God, oh, my God! He's dead! Look at him! He's dead, isn't he?"

"Sunny," he said, stopping her, holding her still. "Wait a second. Sit still for just a second and tell me—does anything hurt?"

Wide-eyed, she shook her head.

He ran a hand down each of her legs, over her knees. "Did you hit the dash?" he asked. "Any part of you?"

She shook her head. "You have to help the deer!" she said in a panic.

"I don't know if there's much help for him. I wonder why the airbags didn't deploy—the SUV must've swept the buck's legs out from under him, causing him to directly hit the grille, and since the car kept moving forward, no airbags. Whew, he isn't real small, either."

"Check him, Drew. Okay?"

"I'll look at him, but you stay right here for now, all right?"

"You bet I will. I should tell you—me and blood? Not a good combination."

"You faint?"

She nodded, panic etched on her face. "Right after I get sick."

He rolled his eyes. That was all he needed. "Do not get out of the car!"

"Don't worry," she said as he was exiting.

Drew assessed the deer before he took a closer look at the car. The deer was dead, bleeding from legs and head, eyes wide and fixed, blood running onto the white snow. There was some hood and grille damage, but the car might be driveable if he didn't have a smashed windshield. It was laminated glass, so it had gone all veiny like a spiderweb. He'd have to find a way to get that big buck off and then, if he drove it, he'd have a hard time seeing through the cracked glass.

He pulled out his cell phone and began snapping pictures, but in the dark it was questionable what kind of shots he'd get.

He leaned back in the car. "Can I borrow your camera? It has a nice, big flash, right?"

"Borrow it for what?"

"To get some pictures of the accident. For insurance."

"Should I take them?" she asked.

"I don't know if you'll have time before you get sick and faint."

Blood. That meant there was blood. "Okay—but let me show you how." She pulled the camera bag from the backseat, took the camera out and gave him a quick lesson, then sat quietly, trying not to look at the dead deer staring at her as light flashed in her peripheral vision.

But then, curious about where Drew was, she looked out the cracked windshield and what she saw almost brought tears to her eyes. With the camera hanging at his side from his left hand, he looked down at the poor animal and, with his right hand, gave him a gentle stroke.

Then he was back, handing her the camera. "Did you pet that dead deer?" she asked softly.

He gave his head a little nod. "I feel bad. I wish I'd seen him in time. Poor guy. I hope he doesn't have a family somewhere."

"Aw, Drew, you're just a tender heart."

"Here's what we have to do," he said, moving on. "We're going to have to walk the rest of the way. Fortunately it's only a couple of miles."

"Shouldn't we stay with the car? I've always heard you should stay with the car. What if someone comes looking for us?"

"It will be too cold. I can't keep it running all night. And if anyone gets worried by how long we're gone, they're going to look in Fortuna or Eureka. Or at least the route to those towns, which is where you told them we were going." He lifted a brow. "Why do you suppose you did that?"

She shook her head. "I didn't want my uncle Nate to think we were going somewhere to be alone. Dumb. Very dumb."

"I need a phone, a tow truck and a warm place to wait, so here's what's going to happen. Hand me the camera case." She zipped it closed and he hung it over his shoulder. "There's a big flashlight in the glove box. Grab it—I'll have to light our way when we clear the headlights. Now slide over here and when you get out, either shield or close your eyes until I lead you past the deer, because the way my night's going if you get sick, it'll be on me."

She wrinkled her nose. "I smell it," she said. "Ick, I can *smell* it!"

"Close your eyes *and* your nose," he said. "Let's get past this, all right?"

She slid over, put her feet on the ground and stood. And her spike heels on her boots sank into the frozen, snowy ground. "Uh-oh," she said.

"Oh, brother. So, what if I broke the heels off those boots? Would you be able to walk in them?"

She gasped! "They're six-hundred-dollar Stuart Weitzman boots!"

He looked at her levelly for a long moment. "I guess the photography business is going very, very well."

"I had to console myself a little after being left at the church. Giving them up now would be like another... Oh, never mind..."

"You're right," he said. "I must have lost my mind." He eased her backward, lifted her onto the seat with her legs dangling out. Then he positioned the heavy camera bag around his neck so it hung toward the front. Next he turned his back to her, braced his hands on his knees and bent a little. "Piggyback," he said. "Let's move it."

"I'm too heavy."

"No, Sunny, you're not."

"I am. You have no idea how much I weigh."

"It's all right," he said. "It's not too much."

"I'll go in my socks. It's just a couple of miles..."

"And get frostbite and from then on you'll be putting your prosthetic feet into your Stuart Weitzmans." He looked over his shoulder at her. "The sooner we do this, the sooner we're warm and with help on the way."

Sunny only thought about it for a second—she was getting cold and she liked her feet, didn't want to give them up to frostbite. She grumbled as she climbed on.

"I was just willing to leave Jack's so we could talk without everyone watching. I haven't really talked to a single guy in a year."

"Close your eyes," he said. "What does that mean, 'really talked to a single guy'?"

"Obviously I ran into them from time to time. Bag boys, mechanics, cable repairmen, cousins to the bride or groom… But after Glen, I had sworn off dating or even getting to know single men. Just not interested in ever putting myself in that position again. You know?"

"I know," he said a bit breathlessly. He stopped trudging up the hill to catch his breath. Then he said, "You lucked out with me—there's no better way to see a person's true colors than when everything goes to hell. Wrecked car, dead dear, spiked heels—it qualifies." He hoisted her up a bit and walked on.

"I'd like to ask you something personal, if you're up for it," she said.

He stopped walking and slid her off his back. He turned toward her and he was smiling. "Sunny, I can't talk and carry you—this top-of-the-line camera is heavy. Here's what you can do—tell me stories. Any stories you want—chick stories about shopping and buying six-hundred-dollar boots, or photographer stories, or scary stories. And when we get to the cabin, you can ask me anything you want."

"I'm too heavy," she said for the umpteenth time.

"I'm doing fine, but I can't carry on much of a conversation. Why don't you entertain us by talking, I'll walk and listen." And he presented his back again so she could climb on.

She decided to tell him all about her family; how

her mother, two aunts and Uncle Nate had grown up in these mountains; and how later, when Grandpa had retired and left the veterinary practice to Uncle Nate, they all went back for visits. Grandma and Grandpa lived in Arizona as did Patricia and her two sons. Auntie Chris lived in Nevada with their two sons and one daughter and Sunny, an only child, lived in Southern California.

"Am I heavier when I talk?" she asked him.

"No," he said, stopping for a moment. "You make the walk shorter."

So she kept going. She talked about the family gatherings at the Jensen stables, about how she grew up on a horse like her mom and aunts had. But while her only female cousin and best friend since birth, Mary, had ridden competitively, Sunny was taking pictures. She spoke about fun times and pranks with her cousins.

She told him how Nate and Annie had met over an abandoned litter of puppies and would be married in the spring. "I'll be a bridesmaid. It will be my third time as a bridesmaid and a lot of my girlfriends are getting married. I've never before in my life known a single woman who was left at the altar. I keep wondering what I did wrong. I mean, Glen worked out like a madman and he wanted me to work out too, but you can't imagine the exercise involved in carrying a twenty pound camera bag, running, stooping, crouching, lifting that heavy camera for literally hours. I just couldn't get excited about lifting weights on top of that. He said I should think about implants. I hate surgical procedures of any kind. Oh, sure, I've always wanted boobs, but not that bad. And yes, I'm short and my butt's too big and my nose is pointy.... He used to say wide hips are good for sex and nothing else. That felt nice, hearing that," she said facetiously. "I tried to take comfort in the sex part—maybe that meant I was all right in the sack, huh? And I'm bossy, I know I'm bossy sometimes. I liked to think I'm efficient and capable, but Glen thought it was controlling and he said it pissed him off to be controlled by a woman. There you have it—the recipe for getting left at the altar."

Then she stopped talking for a while. When she spoke again, her voice was quiet and his tread actually slowed. "I'd like you to know something. When we first met and I was so snotty and rude, I never used to be like that. Really. I always concentrated on being nice. That's how I built my business—I was nice, on time, and worked hard—that's what I attribute most of my success to. Seriously. That whole thing with Glen.... Well, it changed me. I apologize."

"No apology necessary," he said breathlessly. "I understand."

Then she was embarrassed by all her talking, talking about boobs and hips and sex to a total stranger. Blessedly, he didn't make any further comment. It wasn't long before she could see a structure and some lights up ahead. He trudged on, breathing hard, and finally put her down on the porch that spanned the front of a small cabin.

She looked up at him. "It's amazing that you would do that. I would have left me in the car."

He gave her a little smile. "Well, you wanted to see the cabin. And now you will. We'll call Jack's, let everyone know what happened, that we're all right, and I'll light the fire, so we can warm up. Then I have a few things to tell you."

CHAPTER SIX

DREW IMMEDIATELY STARTED stacking wood in the fireplace on top of some very big pinecones he used as starters.

Sunny looked around—showplace, all right. She appreciated the plush leather furniture, beautiful patterned area rug, spacious stone hearth, stained shutters, large kitchen. There were two doors off the great room— bedrooms, she assumed. It wasn't messy, though books and papers were stacked on the ottoman and beside the long, leather sofa, and a laptop sat open on the same ottoman. There was a throw that looked like it might be cashmere that was tossed in a heap at the foot of the sofa.

"Should I go ahead and call Jack's?" she asked him.

He looked over his shoulder at her and smiled. "No hurry. No way I'm getting a tow truck tonight, on New Year's Eve. In fact, I wouldn't count on New Year's Day either—I'm probably going to have to get my brother-in-law to drive up here in his truck to get me and tow Erin's car home. We're not late yet, so no one's worried." He lit a match to the starter cones and stood up as the fire took light. He brushed the dirt off his hands. "I hate to think about you being rescued too soon. I think we still have some things to talk about."

"Like?"

He stepped toward her. There was a softness in his eyes, a sweet smile on his lips. "You wanted to ask me something personal. And I have to tell you something." His hands were on her upper arms and he leaned down to put a light kiss on her forehead. "You're not too short. You're a good height." He touched her nose with a finger, then he had to brush a little soot off of it. "Your nose looks perfect to me—it's a very nice nose. And your chest is beautiful. Inviting, if you can handle hearing that from a man who is not your fiancé. I was never attracted to big boobs. I like to look at well-proportioned women. More than that, women in their real, natural bodies—implants might stay standing, but they're not pretty to me." His hands went to her hips. "And these?" he asked, squeezing. "Delicious. And your butt? One of the best on record. On top of all that I think you have the greatest laugh I've heard in a long time and your smile is infectious—I bet you can coax excellent smiles out of photo subjects with it. When you smile at me? I feel like I'm somebody, that's what. And the fact that you were a little ornery? I'm okay with that—you know why? Because when someone does something that bad to you, they shouldn't just get away with it. It hurts and turns you a little mean because it's just plain unfathomable that a guy, even a stupid guy, can be that cruel. I'm really sorry that happened, Sunny. And I hope you manage to get past it."

She was a little stunned for a moment. No one had ever talked to her like that, not that she'd given anyone a chance with the way she pushed people away. But he was so sexy and sweet it was *killing* her. "Just out of curiosity, what would you have done?"

"If I was left in my Vera Wang?" he asked, wide-eyed.

She laughed in spite of herself. "No, if you realized you didn't want to get married to the woman you were getting married to!"

"First of all, it would never have gotten that far if I wasn't sure. Invitations would never be mailed. Getting married isn't just some romantic thing—it's a lot of things, and one is a serious partnership. You have to be in the same canoe on at least most issues, but it's okay to be different, I think. Like my sisters and their guys? I would never have coupled them up, they're so different from their guys. But they're perfect for each other because they have mutual respect and a willingness to negotiate. They keep each other in balance. Plus, they love each other. Jesus, you wouldn't believe it, how much they're in love. It's almost embarrassing. But when they talk about being married, it's more about how they want their lives to go, how they want their partnership to feel."

"And you were that way with... Penny?" she asked.

"I thought I was," he said. "Thought she was, too."

"What if you're wrong next time, too?" Sunny asked.

"Is that what you're afraid of, honey?" he asked her gently.

"Of course! Aren't you?"

He stared at her for a second, then walked into the kitchen without answering. "Let's hope good old Erin stocked something decent for a cold winter night, huh?"

He began opening cupboards. He finally came out with a dark bottle of liquid. "Aha! Brandy! Bet you anything this isn't Erin's, but Aiden's. But it's not terrible brandy—at least it's Christian Brothers." He lifted the bottle toward her.

"Sure, what the hell," she said, going over to the sofa to sit. She raised the legs of her jeans, unzipped her boots and pulled them off. She lifted one and looked at it. Now why would she bring these to Uncle Nate's stable? These were L.A. boots—black suede with pointy toes and spike heels. The boots she normally brought to the stable were low-heeled or cowboy, hard leather, well worn. The kind that would've made it up that hill so she wouldn't have to be carried.

She threw the boot on the floor. Okay, she had wanted to be seen, if possible, and judge the look on the face of the seer. Her confidence was pretty rocky; she needed to feel attractive. She wanted to see a light in a male eye like the one she had originally seen in Glen's—a light she would run like hell from, but still....

Drew brought her a brandy in a cocktail glass, not a snifter. He sat down beside her. "Here's to surviving a deer strike!" he said, raising his glass to her.

She clinked. "Hear, hear."

They each had a little sip and he said, "Now— that personal question? Since I can breathe and talk again."

"It's probably a dumb question. You'd never be able to answer it honestly and preserve your manhood."

"Try me. Maybe you're right about me, maybe you're not."

"Okay. Did you cry? When she left you?"

He rolled his eyes upward to find an answer. He shook his head just a bit, frowning. "I don't think so. Didn't cry, didn't beg." He leveled his gaze at her. "Didn't sleep either, and since I couldn't sleep I worked even more hours. I kept trying to figure out where I'd gone wrong. For two years we seemed to be fine and then once the ring was on the finger, everything went to hell."

"So what *did* you do?" she wanted to know.

"I did my chores," he said. "All the things she wanted me to do that when I didn't, drove her crazy. There were little rules. If you're the last one out of the bed, make it. If you eat off a plate, rinse it and put it in the dishwasher. If something you take off is dirty it doesn't go on the floor, but in the hamper. I thought if she came back, she'd see I was capable of doing the things that were important to her."

That almost broke her heart. "Drew…"

"In medicine we have a saying, if you hear hoofbeats, don't expect to see a zebra. I was thinking horses—it's pretty common for surgeons to have relationship problems because of the pressure, the stress, the time they have to spend away from home. Horses. I brought her with me to my residency program, took her away from her mom, away from her job and girlfriends, and then I had even less time for her than I'd had as a med student. And we fought about it—about my hours, her loneliness. But when she left me, she didn't go back home. It took me so long to figure that out. I thought it meant she was still considering us. She moved a few miles away. Not because I was still a consideration, but because there was a guy. I never suspected a guy.

I didn't even know about him for six months after we broke up. It was a zebra all along."

"Ow. That must have hurt you bad."

He leaned toward her. "My pride, Sunny. At the end of the day, I missed her, hated giving up my idea of how we'd spend the rest of our lives, but it was mostly my pride that was hurt. I'm real grateful to Penny—she walked away while all we had at stake was some cheap, hand-me-down furniture to divide between us. If we weren't going to make it together, if she wasn't happy with me, I'm glad she left me before we invested a lot more in each other. See," he said, taking Sunny's hand in his, "I think I put Penny in charge and I went along, and that wasn't fair. When a man cares about a woman, he owes it to her to romance her, pursue her, *convince* her. I learned something there—you don't just move along toward something as serious as marriage unless just about every emotion you have has been engaged. Like I said, we grew on each other. Lots of times I asked myself why I thought that was enough."

"But what I want to know is, will you ever be willing to risk it again?" she asked.

"Yes, and I look forward to it," he answered.

"You're just plain crazy! A glutton for punishment!"

"No, I'm reformed. I always heard it was a good idea to fall in love with your best friend and I bought that. I thought if you could meet someone you really liked and she also turned you on, all the mysteries of life were solved. I still think you'd better be good, trusted friends with the person you marry, but by God, there had better be some mind-blowing passion. Not like when you're sixteen and carry your brain in your… Well, you know.

But next time, and there will be a next time, I want it all—someone I like a lot, trust, someone I respect and love and someone I want so bad I'm almost out of my mind."

"Do you think you'll ever find that?" Sunny asked.

"The important thing is that I won't settle for less. Now, you've had a year to think about it—what's your conclusion about what happened?"

She pursed her lips and frowned, looked down for a second, then up. "I was about to marry the wrong guy and he bolted before he could make the biggest mistake of his life. But don't look at me to thank him for it—the mess he left was unbelievable. Over a hundred gifts had to be returned, my parents had paid for invitations, a designer gown, flowers and several big dinners—including the reception dinner. Flowers were distributed to the wedding party so they wouldn't just be wasted… It was horrendous."

"Have you ever wondered," he asked her, "what one thing would make that whole nightmare a blessing in disguise?"

"I can't imagine!" she said.

Funniest thing, he thought. *Before tonight, neither could I.*

He moved very slowly, scooting closer to her. He lifted the glass of brandy out of her hand and placed both hers and his on the coffee table. He put his hands on her waist and pulled her closer, leaning his lips toward hers. He hovered just over hers, waiting for a sign that she felt something, too; at least a stirring, a curiosity, that would be enough for now. Then slowly, perhaps reluctantly, her hands slid up his arms to his shoulders and that was just what he needed. He covered her mouth with his in a hot, searing kiss. He wanted to see her face when he kissed her, but he let his eyelids close and allowed his hands to wander around to her back, pulling her chest harder against his, just imagining what more could happen between them.

The kiss was warm and wet and caused his heart to thump. He'd had quite a few brief fantasies linked to desires. Earlier, out by the Christmas tree in town, he'd had a vision of kissing her and then licking his way down her belly to secret parts that would respond to him with powerful satisfaction. He wanted nothing as much as to lie in her arms, skin on skin, and explore every small corner of her beautiful body.

But that wasn't going to happen now. Not tonight. Not tomorrow.

He pulled away reluctantly.

"I haven't been kissed in a year," she whispered. "I had decided I wasn't ever going to be kissed again. It was too dangerous."

"No danger here, Sunny. And you'll be happy to know you haven't lost your touch. You're very good at it." He looked into those hypnotic blue eyes as he pushed a lock of her hair over her ear. "If I had married Penny, if Glen had shown up when he was supposed to, I wouldn't be kissing you now. And I have to tell you, Sunny, I can't remember ever feeling so good about a kiss…"

She could only sigh and let her eyes drift closed. "We are a bad combination," she whispered.

"I can't believe that…"

"Oh, believe it." She opened her eyes. "You were a guy who just went along with what a woman wanted and I was a woman who, without even thinking about it too much, pushed a man into a great big wedding he didn't want." She swallowed and her eyes glistened. "I hate to admit this to anyone, but Glen kept telling me things—like he just wasn't comfortable with the size of that wedding, and he wasn't sure our work schedules would be good for us, or this or that. I told him not to worry, but I never changed anything. I kept saying I couldn't—that photographers work weekends. But that's not really true, they don't have to work *every* weekend. Portraits for events like anniversaries and engagements can be done before the parties are held, belly shots and babies can be done on weekdays. But the important thing is that until five minutes ago, I wasn't willing to admit our breakup had anything to do with me. And I might be admitting it to you because I'll probably never see you again."

"Listen—I might have been a go-along kind of guy, but I was never that spineless. Glen let it go too far. He doesn't get off that easy."

She gave him a weak smile. "I'm glad I met you. I didn't want to meet a guy, get to know a guy, and I sure didn't want to like a guy, but… Well, I'm not sorry."

"You know what that means, don't you?"

She shook her head.

"After you go through something like a bad breakup and you meet someone new, you check it out and you either find someone better for you, or you recognize right off that you haven't found the right one yet. But at least you keep moving forward until the guy and the life that's right for you comes into focus. And until that happens, we get to kiss."

"You're an opportunist. I could smell it on you the second I met you."

"Now you call your uncle and tell him about the deer accident, tell him we're safe and warm and I'll be looking for a tow truck in the morning. If you want him to, you can ask him if he'll come and rescue you. He can come now or later. A little later or much, much later. You could even stay the night, if you felt like it."

"No I couldn't," she said with a laugh.

"Then will you ask him to wait till after midnight? It's not that far off."

"I think I'll just wait a while to call," she said. "If I know my uncle, he'll be on the road as soon as he gets my call."

That made Drew smile. "I know I'm probably a poor substitute for the guy you wanted to be kissing at midnight, but—"

"Actually, Dr. Foley, I think maybe you're a big improvement. And I might've gone a long time without knowing that."

SUNNY WAITED A LITTLE BIT and then called her uncle, letting him know where she was, what had happened and that she was fine. While she was on the phone, Drew quickly downloaded the pictures of the bloody deer onto his laptop and deleted them from her camera. Then, while the fire roared, they sat on the leather sofa, very close together, with their feet propped up on the ottoman. At times their legs were on top of each other's. They kissed now and then. Other times they talked. Sunny didn't say too much more about Glen, and she didn't want to hear any more about Penny.

She didn't tell him that Glen wasn't always nice to

her. Oh, it went a bit further than the comment about the wide hips. Glen was the kind of guy who stayed out too late "unwinding" after work, criticized her appearance as being not sexy enough for his tastes and when they did have time together, he was never happy with how they were going to spend it—almost as if he'd rather she be working. She had thought about snatching his phone and looking at old text messages, listening to voice mails, but she was a little afraid of what she might find so she convinced herself she was being paranoid. By the time she realized it wasn't such a positive match, she was wearing a ring and had made deposits on wedding stuff.

It was too late.

But what she did want to ask Drew was, "What makes you think you'll do any better the next time you have a relationship?"

He turned to her with a smile and said, "Good! I really wanted you to ask me that." He ran the knuckle of his index finger along her cheek. "Do you have any idea what attracts men and women to each other?"

She just shook her head. "I thought it was a learned behavior...."

"Maybe, but I bet it's more. I bet it's a real primal mating thing that has no logical explanation. Like you see someone and right away, *bam,* you gotta be with that person. And I bet sometimes all the other elements fall into place, and sometimes they don't. That kind of unexplainable thing—you see a woman on the other side of the room and your heart just about leaps out of your chest. You go brain-dead and you're on automatic. All of a sudden you're walking over to her and you don't know why, you just know you have to get closer.

Everything about her pulls you like a magnet. You feel kind of stupid but you just walk up to her and say, 'Hi, my name is Drew' and hope for the best, even though she's looking at you like you're an idiot."

"Slick," she said. "Have you actually been able to use that technique very often?"

"I've never even tried it before, I swear. Listen, it's kind of embarrassing to admit this, but that never happened with Penny. It was comfortable, nice, that's all. No fireworks, no mind-blowing passion…"

"But you said it was good with her! You said sex was good."

"I might be kind of easy to please in that department. The worst sex I ever had was actually pretty good. I want what *else* there is! How did what's his name reel you in?" he asked.

Yo. Me and you!

"He wasn't too slick, as a matter of fact. He thought he was. I never told him his great pick-up line didn't impress me. Thing was, he was cute. And I worked all the time. I hadn't been out on a date in a long time and he was…" She shrugged. "Handsome and interested." She tilted her head and smiled at him. "I think I'm telling you all these things because you're safe."

His large hand closed over her shoulder. "I don't want to be safe," he said. "And I want to see you again."

"Want to go off, live our solitary lives and meet back here for New Year's Eve every year…kind of like a take-off on *Same Time Next Year?*"

"Did you know what Jack had planned for midnight?" Drew asked. "Did you write your resolution?"

She shook her head, then nodded. "I wrote that I had to stay away from men. He put it in the fishbowl."

"At midnight everyone was going to pull out a resolution, ending up with someone else's. Really corny, don't you think?" he asked her, reaching into the pocket of his jeans. "It's going to be for laughs, not for real. Some skinny girl could get a resolution to lose twenty pounds. But I wrote this one before I knew much about you." He presented a slip of paper. "Look, Sunny—it's midnight."

"No, it's not," she said. "It's like three minutes till."

"We can stretch it out," he said, handing her the paper. "I have no idea why I stuck this in my pocket. I put a different one in the fishbowl."

She took it, opened it and read, "Start the new year by giving a new guy a chance."

Her cheeks got a little pink. She was flattered, she was feeling lusty and attracted, but… "But Drew, I'm not going to see you again."

"If you want to, you will…"

"You're just looking for a replacement fiancée," she said. "And long-distance relationships are even harder to keep going than the close kind."

"We can start with football tomorrow. I have beer and wings. Unfortunately I have no car, but I bet you can wrangle one from the uncle."

"That's cute, but—"

"It's midnight," he said, closing in on her. His lips hovered right over hers. "Sunny, you just do something to me."

"Thanks," she said weakly. "Really, thanks. I needed to think I was actually attractive to someone."

"You're way more than that," he said, covering her mouth in a deep and powerful kiss. He put his arms around her waist and pulled her onto his lap, holding her against him. His head tilted to get a deeper fit over her mouth, their tongues played, her fingers threaded into his hair. At long last their lips parted. "Let's just give it a try, see where it goes."

"Can't work. I live in the south. L.A. area...."

"Me, too."

She jumped, startled. She slid off his lap. "You said Chico..."

"No, I didn't. My family is in Chico. I lived there while I went to med school, while I dated Penny, but I don't live there anymore. I'm in residency at UCLA Medical."

She slid away from him. "Uh-oh..."

He shook his head. "I'm just saying we keep getting to know each other, that's all. Neither one of us is likely to keep moving forward in a relationship that doesn't feel good. We're wiser—we know too much now. But for God's sake, Sunny, what if it's good? You gonna walk away from that?"

"I don't want to take any chances!"

"I don't blame you," he said. "It's midnight. Kiss in a new year. And just think about it."

She looked into his eyes for a long moment, then she groaned and put the palms of her hands on his bristly cheeks and planted a good, wide, hot one on his mouth.

Against her open mouth he said, *"Yeah!"* Then he moved against her mouth, holding her tight, breathing her in, memorizing the taste of her.

A car horn penetrated the night. "Awww," he groaned. "Your uncle broke every speed limit in Humboldt and Trinity Counties."

"I told him to stay at Jack's till midnight, but I knew he wouldn't listen," she said. She pulled away from him, slid down the couch and reached to the floor for her boots. Without looking at him she said, "Listen, thanks. Really, thanks. I needed to drop the rage for a while, have a real conversation with a guy, test the waters a little bit. Kiss—I needed to kiss." She zipped the first boot. Then she looked at him. "I'm just not ready for more."

"But you will be," he said. "I can hang loose until you're more comfortable."

"I'll think about that," she said, reaching for the other boot.

The horn sounded again.

"He's going to be pounding on the door real soon," she said, zipping the boot.

"Will you come back tomorrow?" he asked.

She shook her head. "I need to think. Please understand."

"But how will I find you? How will you find me?"

"Doesn't Jack know your family? Don't they know where you are?"

He grabbed her just as the horn blasted another time. He held her upper arms firmly but not painfully, and looked deeply into her eyes. "The second I saw you I lost my mind and wanted to sit right down by you and talk to you. I wanted a lot more than that, but I'm no caveman. Sunny, all I want is to know more about you, to know if there's an upside to our mistakes—like maybe the right ones were meant to come along just a little later. I'd hate to stomp on a perfectly good spark if it's meant to be a big, strong, healthy flame. I—"

There was a pounding at the door.

Sunny sighed and pulled herself from his grip. "Well, here's a bright side for you," she said. "I'm going to kill my uncle."

CHAPTER SEVEN

SUNNY THREW OPEN THE DOOR and glared at her uncle Nathaniel. "Not real patient, are you?"

Nate had his hands plunged into his jacket pockets to keep warm. He glared back. "A—you didn't go where you said you were going to go. And B—you didn't come out when I honked. Something could have been *wrong!*"

"A—I'm twenty-five and can change my plans when it suits me. And B—something could have been *right!*" She turned toward Drew. "Thank you for everything. I'll get this lunatic out of here."

"Sunny," Drew said. "UCLA Medical. Orthopedics Residency. I stand out like a sore thumb. I'm the one the senior residents are whipping and screaming at."

She smiled at him. "I'll remember. I promise."

Sunny grabbed her jacket, her camera bag and pulled the door closed behind her as she left. Nathaniel let her pass him on the porch. She stomped a little toward the truck until her skinny heels stuck into the snow covered drive and she had to stop to pull them out.

"Must've been tough, walking from that wrecked car to the cabin in those boots," Nate observed.

She glared over her shoulder at him. "He carried me."

"Are you kidding me?" Nate said. "It was two miles!"

"Piggyback," she said, trying to balance her weight on the balls of her feet until she got to the truck. She pulled herself up into the backseat of the extended cab with a grunt.

Annie, who sat in the front of the truck, had her arms crossed over her chest. When she looked into the backseat, there was a frown on her face. "Are you all right?" she asked grimly.

"Of course, I'm all right," Sunny said. "Are you angry with me, too?"

"Of course not! I'm angry with Nathaniel!"

"Because…?"

"Because you were laughing with Drew Foley and I didn't want to crash your party!"

Sunny laughed lightly. "Oh, you two," she said. "It wasn't a party," she said just as her uncle was getting behind the wheel. "It was supposed to be a tour of the cabin, but it turned into a deer accident and a two-mile trek. Poor Drew. He had to carry me because of my stupid boots."

"But were you ready to leave?" Annie asked, just as Nate put the truck in gear.

No, Sunny thought. Not nearly ready. She loved everything about Drew—his voice, his gentle touch, his empathy for kids and animals, his scent.… Oh, his scent, his lips, his *taste*. But she said, "Yeah, sure. Thanks for coming for me. Sorry if I was a bother."

"Sorry if I was a lunatic," Nate said, turning the truck around. "I have a feeling if I have daughters, Annie will have to be in charge."

"First smart thing you've said in an hour," Annie informed him.

"Well, I have a responsibility!" he argued.

Sunny leaned her head forward into the front of the cab, coming between them. "You two didn't have your New Year's kiss, did you? Because whew, are you ever pissy!"

"Some people," Annie said, her eyes narrowed at Nate, "just don't listen."

WINTER IN THE MOUNTAINS is so dark; the sun wasn't usually up before seven in the morning. But Sunny was. In fact, she'd barely slept. She just couldn't get Drew out of her mind. She got up a couple of times to get something from the kitchen, but she only dozed. At five-thirty she gave up and put the coffee on.

By the time it was brewing, Annie was up. Before coming into the kitchen she started the fire in the great room fireplace. She shivered a bit even though she wore her big, furry slippers and quilted robe.

"Why are you up so early?" Sunny asked, passing a mug of coffee across the breakfast bar.

"Me? I'm always up early—we have a rigid feeding schedule for the horses."

"This early?"

"Well, I thought I heard a mouse in the kitchen," Annie said with a smile. "Let's go by the fire and you can tell me why *you're* up."

"Oh, Annie," she said a bit sadly, as she headed into the great room. "What's wrong with me?"

"Wrong?" Annie asked. She sat on the big leather sofa in front of the fire and patted the seat beside her. "I think you're close to perfect!"

Sunny shook her head. She sat on the sofa, turned toward Annie and pulled her feet under her. "I made up my mind I wasn't getting mixed up with another guy after what Glen did to me, then I go and meet this sweetheart. He's pretty unforgettable."

"Oh? The guy from the bar?"

Sunny sipped her coffee. "Sounds funny when you put it that way. Drew—a doctor of all things. Not a guy from a bar. He was up at his sister's cabin to study and only came into town to get a New Year's Eve beer. I never should have run into him. And even though he's totally nice and very sweet, I promised him I'd never get involved again, with him or anyone else. I told him I just wasn't ready."

"Smart if you ask me," Annie said, sipping from her own steaming cup.

"Really?" Sunny asked, surprised. Wasn't this the same woman who lectured her about letting go of the anger and getting on with her life?

Annie gave a short laugh. "After what happened to you? Why would you take that kind of chance again? Too risky. Besides, you have a good life! You have work you love and your parents are completely devoted to you."

"Annie, they're my parents," she said. "They're wonderful and I adore them, but they're my parents! They don't exactly meet all my needs, if you get my drift."

Annie patted Sunny's knee. "When more time has passed, when you feel stronger and more confident, you might run into a guy who can fill some of the blank spots—and do that without getting involved. Know what I mean?"

"I know what you mean," Sunny said, looking down.

"Problem is, those kind of relationships never appealed to me much."

"Well, as time goes on…" Annie said. "I imagine you'll get the hang of it. You're young and you've been kicked in the teeth pretty good. I understand—you're not feeling that strong."

Sunny actually laughed. "I had no idea how strong I was," she said. "I got through the worst day of my life. I helped my mom return over a hundred wedding gifts…" She swallowed. "With notes of apology."

"You're right—that takes strength of a very unique variety. But you told me you don't feel too confident about your ability to know whether a guy is a good guy, a guy you can really trust," Annie said.

Sunny sighed. "Yeah, it's scary." Then she lifted her gaze and a small smile flitted across her mouth. "Some things are just obvious, though. You know what Drew said is the best and worst part of his job as an orthopedic surgery resident? Kids. He loves being able to help them, loves making them laugh, but it's really hard for him to see them broken. What a term, huh? Broken? But that's what he does—fixes broken parts."

"That doesn't mean you'd be able to count on him to come through for the wedding dance…" Annie pointed out.

But Sunny wasn't really listening. "When that deer was lying on the hood of the SUV I tried not to look, but he was taking pictures for the insurance and I had to take a peek out the windshield. He gave the deer a pet on the neck. He looked so sad. He said it made him feel bad and he hoped the deer didn't have a family somewhere. Annie, you grew up around here, grew up on a farm—do deer have families?"

"Sort of," she said softly. "Well, they breed. The bucks tend to breed with several doe and they run herd on their families, keep 'em together. They—"

"He's got a soft spot," Sunny said. "If I ever gave a new guy a chance, it would be someone with a soft spot for kids, for animals...."

"But you won't," Annie said, shaking her head. "You made the right decision—no guys, no wedding, no marriage, no kids." Sunny looked at her in sudden shock. "Maybe later, when much more time has passed," Annie went on. "You know, like ten years. And no worries— you could meet a guy you could actually trust in ten years, date a year, be engaged a year, get married and think about a family... I mean, women are now having babies into their forties! You have lots of time!"

Sunny leaned toward her. "Did you hear me? He loves helping kids. He carried me to the cabin—two miles. He petted the dead dear! And he should have broken the heels off my Stuart Weitzmans so I could walk in the snow, but he carried me instead because I just couldn't part with—" Sunny looked at Annie with suddenly wide eyes. "What if he's a wonderful, perfect, loving man and I refuse to get to know him because I'm mad at Glen?"

Annie gave Sunny's hand a pat. "Nah, you wouldn't do that. You're just taking care of yourself, that's all. You don't have a lot of confidence right now. You're a little afraid you wouldn't know the right guy if he snuck up on you and kissed you senseless."

Sunny touched her lips with her fingertips. "He kisses *great*."

"Oh, Sunny! You let him *kiss* you?"

Sunny jumped up so fast she sloshed a little coffee

on her pajamas. "I have plenty of confidence, I always have," she said. "I started my own business when I was twenty and it's going great. I know I get help from my dad, but I was never unsure. And I can't even think about being alone another ten years! Or sleeping with guys I don't care about just to scratch an itch—bleck!"

Annie shrugged and smiled, looking up at her. "All part of protecting yourself from possible hurt. I mean, what if you're wrong? Scary, huh?"

"Oh, crap, one hour with Drew and I knew what was wrong with Glen! I just couldn't..." She stopped herself. She couldn't stop that wedding!

"You said it yourself—you shouldn't get mixed up with another guy," Annie reminded her softly. "You wouldn't want to risk getting hurt." Annie stood and looked Sunny in the eyes. "Give it eight or ten years. I'm sure the right guy will be hanging around just when you're ready."

Sunny stiffened so suddenly she almost grew an inch. She grabbed Annie's upper arm. "Can I borrow your truck? I have something important to do."

"In your pajamas?" Annie asked.

"I'll throw on some jeans and boots while you find your keys," she said.

Sunny dashed to the kitchen, put her coffee mug on the breakfast bar and as she was sailing through the great room Annie said, "Sunny?" Sunny stopped and turned. Annie took a set of keys out of the pocket of her quilted robe and tossed them.

Sunny caught them in surprise, then a smile slowly spread across her face. Who carries their car keys in their robe? "You sly dog," she said to Annie.

Annie just shrugged. "There are only two things you have to remember. Trust your gut and take it one day at a time." Annie raised a finger. "One day at a time, sweetheart. Nice and easy."

"Will you tell Uncle Nate I had an errand to run?"

"You leave Uncle Nate to me," Annie said.

BY THE TIME SUNNY WAS standing in front of the cabin door, it still was not light out. It was only six-thirty, but there were lights on inside and the faintest glow from the east that suggested sunrise. Drew opened the door.

"We never open the door that fast in L.A.," she said.

"There weren't very many possibilities for this part of town," he said. And he smiled at her. "I'm pretty surprised to see you. Coming in?"

"In a minute, if you still want me. I have to tell you a couple of things."

He lifted a light brown brow. "About my nose? My hips?"

"About me. First of all, I never lie. To anyone else or to myself. But my whole relationship with Glen? I wouldn't admit it to anyone, but it was one lie after another. I knew it wasn't going well, I knew we should have put on the brakes and taken a good, honest, deep look at our relationship. But I couldn't." She glanced down, then up into his warm brown eyes. "I couldn't stop the wedding. It had taken on a life of its own."

"I understand," he said.

"No, you don't. It was the wedding that had become a monster—a year in the making. Oh, Glen should take some responsibility for going along with it in the beginning, but it was entirely my fault for turning off my eyes, ears and *brain* when it got closer! I'd invested in it—passion and energy and money! My parents had made deposits on everything from invitations and gowns to parties! And there was an emotional investment, too. My friends and family were involved, praising me for the great job I was doing, getting all excited about the big event! Not only did I feel like I was letting everyone down, I couldn't give it up."

"I understand," he said again.

"No, you don't! The wedding had become more important than the marriage! I knew I should snoop into his text messages and voice mails because lots of things were fishy, but I didn't because it would ruin the wedding! I should have confronted our issues in counseling, but I couldn't because I knew the only logical thing to do was to postpone the wedding! The wedding of the century!" A tear ran down her cheek and he caught it with a finger. "I knew it was all a mistake, but I really didn't see him not showing up at the last minute as a threat, so that made it easy for me to lie when everyone asked me if there were any clues that it would happen." She shook her head. "That he would leave me at the altar? I didn't see that coming. That we weren't right for each other? I managed to close my eyes to that because I was very busy, and very committed. That's the truth about me. There. I traded my integrity for the best wedding anyone had ever attended in their life! And I've never admitted that to anyone, ever!"

"I see," he said. "Now do you want to come in?"

"Why are you awake so early?" she asked with a sniff.

"I don't seem to need that much sleep. I'd guess

that was a real problem when I was a kid. Sunny, I'm sorry everything went to hell with your perfect wedding, but I'm not threatened by that. I'm not Glen and I have my own mistakes to learn from—that wouldn't happen with me. And guess what? You're not going to let something like that happen again. So the way I see it, we have only one thing to worry about."

"What's that?" she asked.

"Breakfast. I was going to have to eat canned beans till you showed up. I don't have a car. Now you can take me to breakfast." He grinned. "I'm starving."

"I brought breakfast. I grazed through Uncle Nate's kitchen for groceries," she explained. "I wasn't going to find anything open on the way over here."

"You are brilliant as well as beautiful. Now we only have one other thing to worry about."

"What?"

"Whether we're going to make out like teenagers on the couch, the floor or the bed after we have breakfast."

She threw her arms around him. "You should send me away! I'm full of contradictions and flaws! I'm as much to blame for that nightmare of a wedding day as Glen is!"

He grinned only briefly before covering her mouth in a fabulous, hot, wet, long kiss. And after that he said, "Look. The sun's coming up on a new day. A new year. A new life. Let's eat something and get started on the making out."

"You're not afraid to take a chance on me?" Sunny asked him.

"You know what I'm looking forward to the most?

I can't wait to see if we fall in love. And I like our chances. Scared?"

She shook her head. "Not at all."

"Then come in here and let's see if we can't turn the worst day of your life into the best one."

* * * * *

For Ercel, whose midnight kisses still thrill me

MIDNIGHT SURRENDER

Jean Brashear

CHAPTER ONE

Austin, Texas

"SPILL, GIRL. Who was last night's victim?" Fiona Sinclair asked.

"What makes you think there was one?" Jordan Parrish responded to her best friend.

Fiona rolled her eyes. "Because you date like a guy, trolling the waters, snagging the juicy ones and playing with them till you're bored, then throwing them back in. And when's the last time you didn't go out on a Friday night?"

"Fee…" Marly Preston, the third member of Girls' Night, eased between them, a fresh wine bottle in hand. "Don't badger Jordan. You'll hurt her feelings. More wine?"

"Shark lawyers don't have feelings, sweetie." Fiona grinned at Jordan. Jordan stuck out her tongue in response. She and Fiona always played rough, and kind-hearted Marly always worried.

"Anyway, how are we old married ladies supposed to live vicariously through her if she plays her cards close to the vest?" Fiona asked. "We depend on you, Jordan."

"It's her business," Marly protested, "and she doesn't have to share the details of her sex life…unless she wants to?" Her eyebrows rose at the end of the sentence, along with her voice.

Jordan couldn't help laughing. Even after five kids, Earth Mother Marly still possessed an innocent air that life couldn't seem to erase. The room around them reflected her nurturing tendencies: bright splashes of color, soft cushions she'd upholstered, candles made by hand, needlework and thriving plants everywhere.

"Nobody worth mentioning," Jordan sighed. "I'm thinking of taking a break."

Fiona snorted.

"You don't think I will?"

"Seriously?" Fiona finished the last of her wine and held out the glass for Marly to refill. "No."

"I know someone you need to meet," Marly piped up. "There's this amazing carpenter who works for David, Will Masterson. He's—"

Jordan flashed her palm. "Stop right there. No matchmaking. You promised." She rested her head on one fist. "If only real men were like the ones you write in your romance novels, Fee."

"You'd never let them be the alpha male, shark girl."

"Stop teasing her, Fee." Marly turned to Jordan. "There are plenty of good men."

"Yeah, right. When's the last time *you* dated, Mrs. I-Married-My-High-School-Sweetheart?"

Marly refused to rise to the bait. "Yes, well, this guy Will's special. You'll meet him at Thanksgiving."

"Oh, brother…" Jordan groaned. "If he's so great, what's he doing at your annual gathering of lost souls?"

"You'll be there," Fiona pointed out.

Jordan made a face at her, then returned her attention to Marly. "Look, I know you mean well. You and David are still so gooey in love, even after five kids, it's sickening. You think everyone should be like you, but not everyone can pull off your miracle. You're the one who's special."

"I'm only a housewife."

"Are you kidding me? You run rings around both of us. I mean, look at you—you cook like a dream, raise five amazing children, you tend a huge garden, you sew, upholster furniture—look around you. This place is gorgeous, and you did all of it."

"But my kids are growing up and won't need me as much soon. You're a successful lawyer who meets all kinds of fascinating people and parties every night. Fee has a family *and* a career."

Fiona sat up straight, worry on her features. "Want to talk about it?"

Marly shook her head. "No, I'm fine. I'm just saying—"

The back door to the kitchen opened, spilling noise inside. Jordan glanced at her watch. David had taken the kids out for the evening, but it was now Sam's bedtime. Time for them to go.

Sam streaked into the room and threw himself into his mother's arms. Marly hugged him tightly, while over her little boy's shoulder she glanced at her husband. David's smile seemed a little forced.

Jordan traded glances with Fiona. Usually you could feel the energy and love in the air between those two, but tonight Marly had sounded almost…dissatisfied.

A shiver ran through Jordan. Her faith in the institution of marriage was minimal at best. Her parents had delighted in making her the rope in their constant tug of war, and the best day of her life had been when they'd parted just before she turned eight. Not that they didn't still use her as a weapon, but they'd moved to opposite coasts and now that she was grown, she could dodge them fairly easily most of the time.

If Marly and David were having trouble…what hope was there for anyone else? Which was why Jordan would never, ever try married life herself. She was a realist.

Some people were meant for the vine-covered cottage, the puppies and kittens and babies.

She was not one of them.

Other people got married because they couldn't stand being alone.

She was fine on her own. She liked living on the edge, keeping her options open. Staying light on her feet.

No shackles for her.

And definitely no illusions.

WILL MASTERSON AROSE with the chickens, as usual.

Literally. His rooster was a walking alarm clock.

The far east Austin neighborhood where he lived was an old one with large lots and a country feel to it. Plenty of room for his big garden, his chicken coop and the woodworking shop he'd made from a detached garage that had—like the house—been close to falling down when he'd bought the place for a song.

And one day, it would be perfect for a whole pack of children.

His family still hoped he'd return to Ireland, settle down with a nice country girl and raise a large family, as most of his siblings were doing. He'd had the same intention once, that after a few months of traveling across the United States, a place with which he'd been fascinated while growing up, he'd return home.

That had been seven years ago. He'd recently applied for citizenship in this big, rowdy country that suited him like a second skin. He missed his family, yes, but he'd found home. Not *the* woman yet, no, but that would come in time. Will continued to work on the house in which he and she would raise babies—and he could picture her, perfectly. She'd have curves, real ones, that gave a man a handful of woman to love. She'd bake bread, sew, garden with him, appreciate the simple life and be a good partner to him. No, he wasn't a throwback as some of his friends accused—he would appreciate and support her career if she had one, could teach her to bake bread if she didn't know how or make it himself as he currently did. They would share values, however, and that would make all the difference—any rough edges could be smoothed out.

He was looking for a Marly, really. David Preston, the builder for whom he subcontracted trim carpentry, was married to the woman of Will's dreams, the perfect mother and wife who had created a refuge where David could retreat at the end of a long day.

Too bad she was taken, he thought, smiling. Marly swore she was going to find the right woman for him, and he'd gladly accepted her help. Will believed in his heart the woman of his dreams was out there somewhere.

He simply had to be patient.

And he was nothing if not a patient man.

CHAPTER TWO

JORDAN ARRIVED AT THE Preston home on Thanksgiving Day with wine and chocolates in hand. She left the cooking to Marly. "So where's the paragon?"

"Out there," responded the Preston's eldest daughter, Christy. She pointed Jordan to a window in the kitchen overlooking the front porch.

So this was Will Masterson, huh? However much Jordan disliked Marly organizing her love life, she had to admit that the man had a beautiful baritone voice.

He wasn't half-bad-looking, either, at least from his strong profile. Though seated, he was clearly an imposing man, built like a lumberjack. Jordan leaned against the sill and watched his big hands finger the guitar strings with surprising agility. Notes of astonishing richness and depth emerged from the guitar, intertwining with his voice and that of the second Preston daughter Sarah's in a melody so haunting that all activity around the house had stopped.

Jordan listened, instantly caught up in the spell, and was astounded to feel her eyes fill. She couldn't remember the last time she'd cried, but not to respond to the pain and longing in this music would require a heart made of stone.

He looked up suddenly and caught her gaze.

She quickly looked away.

When the last notes died off, there was a long hush of respect for something extraordinary. Then from all quarters burst enthusiastic applause.

Will nodded and smiled, then his gaze returned the window.

Jordan retreated from view.

Just then, Sam skidded out on the porch. "Wow! Can you teach me to do that? Only not something so girly?"

Everyone broke up with laughter, including Will.

"Like this, you mean?" Will launched into a rousing tune filled with war and bloodshed and enough battles to thrill a little boy's urge for mayhem and set everyone's toes tapping.

Jordan smiled as she turned to help Marly.

"I told you he was amazing," her friend said. "He's restoring an old house, he builds furniture like an artisan, gardens, cooks—"

"Then you take him. *So* not my type."

"Maybe your type needs changing."

"How about we talk about Girls' Night instead?" Jordan retorted. "So what was up with you?"

Marly's mouth went tight. "Nothing. Would you get me some ice from the utility porch?"

Jordan's eyes widened at her friend's icy tone. Suddenly she wished she hadn't come. She always counted on Marly's warm nature and usually felt right at home with her family, but today…everything felt wrong. And having the big Irishman lurking… Holidays gave her the willies at the best of times. This wasn't one of them.

As she yanked on the stubborn latch of the ice chest,

Jordan broke a nail down to the quick. She swore darkly and sucked on her finger.

"Is that any way for a lady to talk?"

Jordan whirled around, face-to-handsome-face with the last man on earth she wanted to be near. "I'm no lady. Anyway, you shouldn't sneak up on people."

"I had no mind to scare you. Would you be needing some help?"

"I'm doing fine, thank you." She dropped her injured finger to her side.

"So I see. Let me take a look at that." He stepped forward, extending his hand. "I'm Will Masterson."

She stuck her own hand behind her back. "I know who you are. Marly's playing matchmaker again, you do realize."

"Me? With you?" His eyes rounded.

"You don't have to sound so insulted. You're not my type, either, just so you know."

"Certain of that already?"

"You're not?"

"You're one to make snap judgments, are you?"

She shrugged. "Saves time."

He flashed a bright smile. "And clearly you'd like me to go away. Are you always so prickly or is it Marly's intentions that have put the burr up your lovely behind?"

"It's my behind, and I'll thank you not to be watching it."

A lovely low rumble shook him. "Now, I'm thinking any man with eyes could not possibly accommodate that demand, begging your pardon. It's a very fine derriere, and I suspect you know that."

His blue eyes twinkled with amusement that only

irritated her more. "Well then, why don't you open this big ole ice chest for li'l ole me?" She batted her lashes. "Marly needs more ice inside."

The corners of his eyes crinkled with his rumbling laughter, his cheeks denting with dimples. He leaned past her and picked up the chest as though it weighed nothing. "Why, of course, darlin'," he answered in falsetto. "Just tell this poor dumb mick where you'd be wanting it." The gleam in his eyes said he knew her game but he was too good-natured to mind.

Jordan narrowed her gaze, then stuck her nose in the air and sauntered inside. She'd make it through the meal, then she was history.

Marly, what the devil were you thinking?

WILL SURVEYED the group numbering nearly thirty scattered around the huge dining table and assorted card tables strung into one long banquet. He rose from his seat, wineglass in hand. "To Marly, who brings new meaning to the words *domestic goddess*."

"Hear, hear," replied David. "Best of all, *my* domestic goddess." He bent to his wife and gave her a lingering kiss. Marly blushed and looked away.

"Get a room, you two. There are innocent children present," Jordan teased from her place beside Will.

The eldest Preston boy, fifteen-year-old Davy, stared at Jordan adoringly. He and twelve-year-old Joseph seemed to think the lady lawyer was hot. Will couldn't disagree—if, that is, one had a self-destructive bent. She was a skinny, bad-tempered siren, and if for a moment as she'd watched him sing, he'd thought he'd seen something in her...

He had more regard for himself, that fine derriere notwithstanding.

"They do that stuff all the time, Jordan—you know that," Sam piped up. "We just ignore them."

The assembled group rang with laughter.

"Do you have Thanksgiving in Ireland, Will?" asked Sarah.

"No, darlin', we lack the essential ingredients—Pilgrims and the native tribes. A pity, I'm thinking. I have to admit that my first experience with Thanksgiving was a revelation, though never have I had these foods prepared more deliciously than today."

Jordan stirred. "I agree, but I have no idea why you put yourself through this, Marly. You cook for three days, and in forty-five minutes, it's demolished. What's the point?"

Marly shrugged. "A woman's lot in life."

"Not this woman," Jordan muttered.

Will glanced to see if Marly had heard. "Must you?" he asked Jordan, keeping his voice low.

"What?"

"Your cynicism is misplaced here."

She arched one eyebrow. "Marly's used to it."

"You do her no service."

"Where do you get off, telling me what I can and can't say to my friend?" she whispered furiously.

"Some friend you are, but we'll discuss this later." They were beginning to draw attention.

"We won't speak at all, if I have any say." Jordan turned to the middle Preston son, Joseph, on her other side. The boy was clearly smitten with her.

She said not another word to Will as the meal wound down. He was inclined to be grateful. Her short spiky black hair was as sharp as her attitude, and she was rude to boot.

She was surely wrong about Marly's intentions. Marly wouldn't do such a thing to him. Jordan couldn't be further from the woman of his dreams.

A FEW HOURS LATER, however, the woman was still on Will's mind as he returned home after a long day. He had worked at the jobsite before going to the Preston home because there was trim to run, and he'd wanted the space and quiet to do it properly. There was a peace to be found in measuring and cutting, fitting pieces together in a joint so smooth and sweet that no one would be able to spot it easily.

He should be tired and ready for bed, but he wasn't. His thoughts kept returning to the prickly lady lawyer, who hadn't hung around long after the meal. He didn't know why he should be sparing her one second's consideration.

Except that he couldn't seem to stop remembering his first sight of her as she watched him sing.

She'd had her heart in her eyes, he'd have sworn it. No matter what a harridan she'd been afterward— aggravating, supercilious, insulting. In those first brief seconds, he'd thought he'd spotted something quite different.

He'd almost have said the woman was lonely.

At the time, however, he hadn't been aware of how out of character such vulnerability would be, how difficult she actually was.

But then there was her behavior with the Preston children. Around them, everything about her softened. Her claws retracted and she could be almost…sweet.

The contrasts made him want to dig deeper.

And here he'd said he had no self-destructive instincts. He shook his head as he unlocked his workshop. A warm, furry shape appeared beside him, the scarred head bumping the side of his knee.

"Good evening, my friend," Will greeted Finn, the half-blind border collie he'd found on another jobsite a few months back. He dug his fingers into the now-silky hair that had once been matted and full of burrs, his fingers kneading the old dog's neck and shoulders.

Finn groaned and leaned into him.

Will sank to his haunches and sent the dog into ecstasy, his tail thumping eagerly on the wood floor. At the commotion, another figure appeared in the doorway, Moira, the mama cat who'd once owned this space until he and she had made their peace with one another. She twined her way past Finn and rubbed against his leg. "How are you, darlin'?"

He gave both animals a good stroking—and then he laughed. *My Will, the savior of strays,* his mum called him. He had a radar for a lost cause, a sad case, she claimed. Perhaps so, but if he had one grain of sense in his thick skull, he'd ignore any such notions about Jordan Parrish.

Will rose and walked to his workbench, studying the jewelry box that was his current project, wondering exactly who he was making it for. He didn't always know until he was finished, but the making of something new was a challenge, a puzzle to be solved.

He would spend an hour or so at the end of this long day focusing only on these pieces of wood that would become something beautiful, and he would cease to care if the lady lawyer was lonely.

He didn't need the headache.

You're not my type, she'd said. Nor was she remotely his own.

Resolutely Will put his hands to work, and after a bit, his mind followed, leaving all thoughts of sad-eyed women behind.

JORDAN HAD HIT A COUPLE of clubs that were open even on Thanksgiving night, had danced until her restless feet hurt. She'd flirted, been propositioned, had considered and dropped several candidates, but in the end, she'd returned to her Sixth Street loft alone.

Now she sat on her second-floor windowsill, one leg propped up, the other dangling over empty air. Looking down, she watched the entertainment district stragglers, wondering if any felt her watching their little dramas unfold. Across the street, a decrepit Ford van crawled away, carrying the house band to a wee-hours breakfast where they'd laugh and talk and divide the night's take among them.

Someone whistled back behind her, a tune so achy and sad she wanted to beg him to stop.

"Hey, gorgeous," a graveled voice called right below her.

Jordan looked down.

Guitar strapped across his back, he was young…too young, but wise in the ways of the street, she could see that. Hard times rode the planes of his face, nestled in the long hair drifting over his shoulders. "Whatcha doin' up there, pretty lady?"

Jordan smiled. "Not much. You?"

He shrugged. "Just gettin' by." He pantomimed strumming his guitar. "Playin' some tunes…takin' it as it comes." He smiled, slow and sweet. "Layin' down tracks for tomorrow."

Jordan leaned her cheek against her knee. "That ole tomorrow. She's not so easy to get to sometimes."

He chuckled. "You are so right, sweet one." He pulled his guitar around the front. "Maybe I can help you along."

Jordan nodded, feeling a pinch in her heart at the kindness of a stranger.

He began strumming, then blended his smooth voice with words she couldn't make out.

It didn't matter. The melody spoke for itself. He played about love and longing…about pain and parting and nights when you don't think you'll make it until tomorrow.

Then, just when she was about to leap inside and slam the window, he switched to a melody so light, so hopeful that Jordan's heart lifted, just a little.

Not much. But sometimes, even a little was enough.

She leaned her head back against the frame and closed her eyes, drifting inside the cradle his music had made for her. For moments that felt safely endless, she let him wrap a soft, cozy cocoon of music around her, and her heart rested.

Unlike the way Will's music had made her feel exposed.

She frowned at the thought of him.

When the last notes trailed off, Jordan bent forward. "Would you…do you want to come up?"

He smiled and let his gaze slide over the length of her. "With legs like those, I won't say it's not tempting."

Then he shook his head. "But that's not what you need, is it?"

Jordan chewed at her lower lip, then shook her head. "I think I can sleep now. Thank you."

He slanted a lazy salute. "That's thanks enough for me." Turning to go, he looked back one more time. "Sleep tight, pretty lady." Then he shambled off.

With a lump in her throat, Jordan climbed back inside her loft, closing the window behind her.

CHAPTER THREE

THE COUNTRY-WESTERN bar where Will let himself be dragged after work several days later was one frequented by an odd mix of cowboys, construction workers and white-collar types who liked to kick back a few and dance. With its live music and core crowd of regulars, it was, in some ways, as close to the little pub in his village as he'd encountered in the States.

For some of the guys from David's jobsite, this was their usual after-work stop, and Will found himself not averse to indulging in a beer on this day. Even if he'd sell his soul for a good Guinness.

Uncharacteristically, David had accompanied them. Will sat beside him at the bar, raised his glass of the brew they had on tap and studied it. "There is much I like about this country," he mused aloud. "But what passes for beer cannot be counted among that company." He shook his head. "Swill, pure swill."

"Hey, now," complained the man next to him.

"Maybe you should open your own bar," David suggested, staring down into his drink. "You like to gab enough. You'd make a good bartender."

"Possibly, but I need the fresh air and sunshine." Will glanced over. "You know, I can't recall ever seeing you accompany the men before."

David continued to stare morosely. "I usually go

home after work. I like doing that." He rested his head on one fist. "You don't join them often, either."

"I'm remodeling a house in my spare time," Will reminded him.

"You'd have an easier go of it if you leveled the place and started from scratch."

Will smiled. "But where would be the challenge in that?"

"You do seem to like a test." He paused, then spoke again. "Speaking of adversity, let me give you a friendly word of warning—stay away from Jordan. I saw you together at our place. She's bad news."

"What makes you say that?" Not that he disagreed.

"I've spent a good ten years watching her discard men like used tissues. A man-eater, that one. I have no idea why she and Marly are friends." David fastened his eyes on the bar. "But then, I'm not sure I know anything about Marly these days."

Will was honestly shocked. "Your wife is an angel."

David shrugged. "She is. But something's bothering her, and she's not sharing it with me."

"Women have their secrets."

"Not Marly. We've been together forever. I know her mind like I know my own." He shook his head. "At least, I thought I did."

"Could her friends help you?"

"I would have said no, that Marly confides everything in me, but…" He sighed. "I could ask Fiona, I guess."

"What about talking to Jordan?"

David snorted. "She's the last person I'd take advice from when it comes to human relationships."

Again, Will couldn't argue.

"I mean, she's sexy as hell, no question, and if you want a roll in the hay, I have no doubt she's very talented. She always has a string of men ready to do the honors."

Will frowned. "I thought she was a good friend. Your kids like her."

David's jaw flexed. "I used to like her fine, too, but lately I wonder about her influence. Maybe Marly's regretting what she missed because we married so young and started having children right away. Jordan's life probably looks very attractive to her, no responsibilities, nothing to tie her down."

"I wonder. I have a sense that Jordan might be lonely."

A bark of laughter. "Jordan? Get real." David glanced in the mirror behind the bar, and his brow wrinkled. "Speak of the devil...she does get around, doesn't she?"

Will followed his stare and spotted Jordan striding across to the bar on those long, long legs, her lithe figure showcased in a tight black pinstriped skirt and severely tailored red silk blouse. Work clothes, he supposed, but with the addition of red stilettos, she looked anything but buttoned-up.

She was quickly welcomed by the bartender and offered a stool by one of the regulars. She gave each man around her a smile that seemed genuine, bantering with them and making every man near her vie for her attention. *Man-eater* was not the right description for her; Jordan Parrish was a siren, yes, but with a surprising dash of friendly chum mixed in. In no time she had her audience eating from her hand.

"I'd better shove off." David signaled the bartender to bring his check. "I'll be late for Joseph's game if I don't get cracking."

Just then Jordan glanced into the mirror, and her gaze fastened on Will's. He felt a visceral and very unwelcome punch, but he carefully kept his face neutral and merely lifted his beer in salute.

She arched one eyebrow, then pointedly turned away.

Friendly perhaps, but not to him. And didn't that just stir the competitor in him?

David rose and clapped his hand on Will's shoulder. "Look, I didn't mean to talk out of school about Marly. We'll be fine."

Will jolted and blinked. "I imagine you will. You're not a stupid man, and your lady is a queen among women."

David grinned. "That she is." Then he followed Will's gaze and frowned. "I wouldn't, my friend."

"Wouldn't what?" Will dissembled.

David shook his head. "Your funeral. Just don't say I didn't warn you."

Will touched his forehead in salute. "Forewarned is forearmed."

"You'd need some serious armor with that one. Well, see you." He turned away, then back. "Oh—I'm supposed to find out if you'll be around for Christmas."

"That's family time," Will responded.

"Are you going home to Ireland?"

"No, not this year. One of my sisters is having a baby in January, so I'll see them then."

"Then come be with us. As you might have noticed, Marly has a generous definition of family. You won't be the only non-Preston in attendance, I assure you." He winked. "Jordan will probably be there, if you feel like living dangerously."

"Does she have no family?"

"In name only. Parents are divorced, live on opposite coasts. They specialize in using Jordan as ammunition against each other. She's usually with us on holidays." David waved to him. "See you in the morning."

Will nodded absently. There might be the explanation for Jordan's behavior. Not that it was any concern of his. He should head out, as well. There was Sheetrock calling his name.

But just then he noticed Jordan on the small dance floor, smiling and flirting outrageously with her current partner.

Will pondered holding Sheetrock…or holding Jordan.

No contest. At any rate, one more encounter with her would surely cure him of this curious fascination. He threw some money down on the bar, and headed her direction.

As he approached, she glanced over her shoulder, then quickly turned her back on him, redoubling her attention on her partner, putting a dangerous sway in those slim hips he wouldn't mind getting his hands on.

She's a man-eater. Discards men like tissues.

Hadn't he had his own taste of her sharp tongue? Indeed, but suddenly Will found himself smiling. She was bad tempered and difficult, but didn't that add to the challenge she presented? His perfect woman hadn't yet made her appearance, and while he was patiently waiting, maybe he would unlock the puzzle of Jordan Parrish. It wasn't as though his heart would get involved, after all. He was saving that for the woman of his dreams.

Meanwhile, two could play Ms. Parrish's game.

When Jordan glanced over and narrowed her eyes at him as if to warn him off, he stifled the grin that threatened and instead walked right past her toward a woman sitting with her friends. This woman was definitely more his type with her generous curves and sweet face. "Would you care to dance?"

"Me? I, uh…" She glanced at her friends.

"Only the one dance. I swear my mum would tell you I'm just a wee bit stubborn but on the whole, quite harmless."

"You're Irish," said one of her friends.

"You are, aren't you?" The first woman smiled. "I love your accent."

"Ah, but you're the one with the lovely dulcet tones."

Her friend grinned. "If you don't want him, Sue Anne, I do."

He smiled right back. "Perhaps you two ladies would also favor me with a dance."

"I'm taken," said one.

"I'm not," said the second.

"Get in line," said Sue Anne.

Will laughed and drew her out on the dance floor where they chatted easily and he never once spared a glance for Jordan.

At the end of that song, he escorted Sue Anne back and claimed her friend. The third woman said her boyfriend was out of town, so she wanted her turn, too.

"Oh, but I would never nip another man's woman. My mum would tan my backside."

"Drat," sighed the woman. "A gentleman."

This time Will had a more difficult time ignoring Jordan completely because she somehow wound up right next to them. When he glanced her way, she gave him her best come-hither look, then redoubled her efforts to charm her current dance partner, her movements sinuous and seductive. When the man's hands slid around to grab the derriere Will had admired, he had to contain a glower.

"Uh-oh," said his partner. "Lovers' quarrel?"

"Not a bit."

"She keeps watching you, you know, when you're not looking."

Will bit back a satisfied smile. "You don't say."

"Want me to go tell her she's stupid for doing whatever it is that has you dancing with us instead of her?"

Will laughed heartily and was pleased to see Jordan's head whip in his direction. "A friend of mine calls her a man-eater."

The woman glanced over. "She looks like one. Sue Anne's much nicer."

"I'm sure. And much more my type." Will sighed. "But there's that stubborn part of me my mum would warn you about. I'll play this hand out."

"My advice? Get Sue Anne's phone number first."

Will chuckled. "Perhaps I shall." The music stopped, and he escorted her back to their table, pausing long enough to visit for a few minutes, leaving with not one but two phone numbers even after Sue Anne's friend told Sue Anne the score.

Will left them, debating simply leaving now.

The band began again, a slow, smoky tune, and he reversed course, snagging Jordan from her current companion. "My turn, mate."

The man protested, but Will's expression stopped him. He shrugged and moved off.

Jordan jerked in his grasp. "I didn't say I wanted to dance with you."

"Hush." He drew her into him and began moving.

She remained stiff. "What, you want to give me another lecture?"

He merely held her more snugly against him. "Sh-h. I like this song."

He saw the mutiny in her eyes along with the confusion. Bit by bit, though, she relented, and he smiled to himself, tucking her head into his shoulder and swinging them around so that she had no choice but to hang on to him.

Soon she quit resisting completely, then swiveled her hips against him in a blatant invitation Will badly—*badly*—wanted to pursue.

Instead, he whirled them again.

And began to sing to her.

Jordan lifted her head, a line forming between her eyebrows, and he could see her working up an argument.

But to his amazement, she subsided and simply danced, their bodies surprisingly attuned to each other. Once in a while, she'd look at him, baffled.

But she didn't move away.

They danced that dance and two more before the band took a break, exchanging not one word the entire time.

As their bodies separated, Will could see her gearing up again to seduce him, to make him simply one of the many, so he seized the initiative to keep her off balance. "Good evening to you, Jordan. I'll see you soon." He kissed her knuckles when he wanted to kiss her beautiful mouth. "Would you be needing a ride home first?"

Her lips parted, her eyes at first confused, then anger reappeared. "Of course not. Anyway, the night's barely begun." She studied his reaction with a sideways glance.

I do believe I have your number, Ms. Parrish. "Tomorrow's a work day," he said blithely. "You'll need your sleep."

"Bed perhaps," she all but purred. "I don't need much sleep."

He clamped down as every instinct he had prodded him to drag her out of there and seize what she so blatantly offered.

But that would make him forgettable like all the others.

Oh, no, sweetheart. We'll play this my way. "I'll wish you sweet dreams, then." He turned to go.

"Good night and good riddance." Vexation filled her tone.

Will didn't let himself turn back.

But he left with a smile on his face.

CHAPTER FOUR

SHE WANTED TO SIT ON HER windowsill, damn it. Jordan stared in frustration at the cold drizzle that had set in before she arrived home from work the next night. She needed to think, needed more space to prowl. The walls of her loft were closing in. The weather was nasty, but she had to get out of here, away from the silence. CDs didn't get it; TV was worse. She'd picked up two different books and thrown both of them down in disgust.

Making up her mind quickly, she strode toward her coatrack, but the sharp crack against the window drew her up short.

What the—?

There it was again. Pea gravel. Sharp little clicks against her window.

Why didn't whoever it was just use the buzzer?

When the third shower of stones clinked, Jordan strode across the floor in a huff, jerking the window open.

She leaned out. "Why don't you use the stupid buzz—?" The words dried up in her throat at the sight of the man on the sidewalk. Will Masterson. Jerk.

Under the hood of his coat, his face creased in a smile. "If you wouldn't be answering the phone when I call, why should I expect you to answer the buzzer?"

He'd walked out on her the night before, when she wasn't through with him. And yes, thanks to caller ID, she'd ignored a phone call earlier. "So you threw rocks at my window?"

"Ah, but gently, sweetheart, with exactly the right touch. Just as I'd treat a woman, you see."

"You probably think that." She shrugged indifferently. "Men often overrate their performance." Now he'd be insulted and go away.

But of course he didn't do that. Instead, he threw back his head and laughed, that deep, rolling sound that reached right past every barrier she could put up.

"Does that work with your usual sort? If so, I'm thinking you've not met the right man yet."

"Are you applying for the position? I'll warn you I don't keep anyone around long."

His eyes widened in mock horror. "The poor lads allow you to send them away?"

"I prefer to sleep alone."

"Well, then, darlin' Jordan, you've clearly not slept with the proper man. A pity, that is."

"You think you're him?" Her tone dripped condescension.

"Now, don't be getting ahead of yourself. I haven't even decided if I like you yet." His smile was unrepentant.

She had to grin back. His unfailing good humor made him difficult to stay mad at. "You are too much, Will Masterson. I can't decide if you're dumb as a post or the most arrogant man I've ever met."

"While you're pondering, I'll be right up. Hit the lock."

"Wait—I didn't say you—"

Too late. He'd already disappeared from sight.

Jordan slammed the sticky window down, shivering from the cold air that had filled the room. She should just leave him out there in the rain. It was so bone-deep cold that he'd soon leave.

But until he did, she was trapped in here, the same cage she'd been clawing to escape.

Damn the man. Suddenly, Jordan laughed out loud. What the hell—she'd been wanting entertainment, but she'd never in a million years imagined it being Will. She crossed the floor and punched the button, wondering just when she'd lost control of the situation.

Probably about five seconds after they'd met.

But she'd get it back, and then she'd boot him out, just like the others.

He didn't knock but instead turned the knob and walked right in, standing in the doorway dripping. "That's my girl. I knew you wouldn't leave a poor man to freeze."

Jordan nodded toward the coatrack on the wall. "Hang up your coat right there."

He did so, even going so far as to pull off his boots, but his eyes were busy taking in the space around him. She had a sense of all her secrets being bared.

Will took his sweet time, not moving from where he stood, barely less imposing in his socks. He glanced up, and his face wreathed in smiles. "A pressed tin ceiling," he said in reverent tones. "An interesting jumble, this. There are secrets here to be mined, darlin' Jordan. A man could spend some time doing it."

"Don't get any ideas. I only took pity on a fool who'd stand out in the rain."

"That you did, sweetheart. And there'll be stars in

your crown for the doing." He rubbed his hands together. "You wouldn't happen to have a wee drop, now,
would you?"

Jordan snorted. "I never met a man who sounded
like a Pat O'Brien movie before. By that, I guess you
mean something alcoholic?"

Blue eyes twinkled. "To be sure, you've never met
a man like me before, Jordan Parrish. You may not yet
be up to the challenge, but I might be willing to take
on the task of grooming you for it."

"You wish." She shrugged nonchalantly. "I've probably got some tequila and limes. We could try body
shots."

He cocked his head. "Hmm, interesting game, that.
We never played it in my pub."

She had to chuckle. "You big faker. Marly told me
you've been in the country several years." She walked
toward the kitchen area, all too aware of his large frame
right behind her. As a tall woman, she wasn't used to
feeling dainty, but that's exactly how Will made her
feel.

"It's in the blood, Jordan darlin'. Peat fires and the
call of the auld sod. A man can't help what he is, and
I'll thank you not to make sport of me."

"Yeah, yeah, yeah. Here we go. You can have…"
But he'd left her, his concentration already switched
to something else.

Her kitchen faucet? She'd never had a man up to her
place who'd paid more attention to her loft than her
body. Right now, he was turning handles, then using
those capable hands to unscrew something on the tip
of the faucet.

He shook the metal piece and slapped it against his

palm until a tiny screen fell into his hand. Will held it up to the light, frowning. "This screen needs replacing. And how long has this faucet been dripping?"

"What business is it of yours?"

He glanced around. "I suppose it's too much to expect that you'd have a toolbox?"

"Of course I do. No twenty-first century woman is without one," she huffed.

"Lead the way, sweetheart."

Jordan grabbed for the part. "Give me that. I can take care of my own repairs, thank you very much."

"Can you now?" Placing the metal whatever-it-was and screen in her hand, he executed a sweeping invitation. "Please. I love to watch a woman work."

"I'll do it later." She slapped the parts on the counter and turned away.

"Oh, but there's no time like the present, didn't your mum teach you that?" Will relaxed against the counter, arms crossed, a big smile on his face. "Humor me. I'd so enjoy it. I'm in no hurry."

"I'm not in the mood." Jordan walked past him, drinks forgotten.

His arm shot out and wrapped around her waist, pulling her close. "Oh, darlin', I do enjoy the way you do that."

She leaned back, all too aware of how well they fit together. "Do what?"

His other hand slid up her back, tunneling into her hair, tilting her head slightly. "Lie with such arrogance." His head lowered to hers and he growled softly. "You sure you're not Irish?"

Then it was too late. His mouth covered hers, his big body surrounding her. She could smell wood shavings on him, pine and cedar and soap…and something else she could only describe as all man.

Faster than she would ever have believed, his kiss swept her mind clean of any thought but him. For one perilous, treacherous moment, she remembered how it felt to dance with him, to have her body tight against his muscled one. A part of her wanted nothing more than to snuggle up in those strong arms, to sink into the comfort of him.

No. Oh, no. But before she could end the kiss, he did, then set her back on her feet. She stifled a moan.

Regret shone in those blue eyes, and he trailed one finger down her cheek. "I'm thinking there'll be no more of that until we get something straight between us."

Jordan bristled and stepped away, fixing him with a baleful stare. "And just what might that be?"

"When you're ready to tell all those boys you're finished with them."

"And why on earth would I do that?"

"Because you'll be spending your time with me now, Jordan darlin'. And I don't share."

She laughed, though it wasn't as steady as she'd have liked. "You can't be serious."

He tapped his chest. "Don't be listening to your head now. It's the heart that's speaking to you."

"You're insane. I told you, you're not my type. Anyway, I'm still mad at you for dressing me down at Thanksgiving."

He shrugged. "You know I was right. A family like that needs supporting, not being sneered at."

"I wasn't sneering. I think they're great."

"But?"

She turned away. "They're an anomaly. Marriage isn't like that."

"David told me your parents are divorced." His gaze warmed with sympathy.

"My parents are none of your business."

"What if I want to make *you* my business?"

"Don't bother. I'm not interested."

"Liar." He approached her again.

She backed away. "We couldn't be more different. I'm a shark lawyer—and proud of it! I'm very good at what I do. You're a—"

"Careful now. Wouldn't want to let your high-and-mighty streak show too much. I'm a simple carpenter and not ashamed of it."

"I didn't say you should be. I'm not a snob."

Pity darkened his eyes. "Oh, but I think you are. Worse, I scare you. I see who you are, beyond the seductress, beyond the woman they call the man-eater."

Then, to her great surprise, he reversed course and headed for the door, pulling on his boots and sliding his arms into his coat. "I'm not afraid of you, Jordan Parrish. You won't discard me like the others. I'll go when I'm ready and not a minute before."

"First I'd have to get involved with you, and that's not gonna happen."

"It will. Get ready for it."

"It won't." But she wrapped her arms around her waist against a sudden shiver.

"I'm not saying it will be easy—God knows you're anything but, and I've surely lost my mind getting in-volved with you, but that's as it will be." He grasped the door handle, then turned back, giving her a long, soulful look she couldn't interpret. "I'm not what you think you want, sweetheart, but I'm exactly what you need."

Then he smiled and gave a tiny salute. "It's a good thing I'm a patient man, Jordan darlin'. I have a feeling I'm going to have use for all I can muster." He glanced toward the kitchen. "Just screw the end back on like it was. It will do overnight. I'll be back with the tools and parts tomorrow."

Without another word, he was out the door.

Jordan raced after him, grasping the handle with a thought to call him back, to demonstrate her disdain and leave him in no doubt of who had the upper hand.

Instead she let go and leaned back heavily against the wood, pressing trembling fingers to lips that somehow felt different. She swore, but her heart wasn't really in it. Drawing herself up resolutely, she headed to the kitchen to put her faucet back together and resume the life she liked just fine.

You have a high opinion of yourself, Will Masterson.

Insane. The man was certifiable.

And definitely not her type.

But even though her sample was brief, she knew one sure thing about him.

The man could kiss. Suddenly Jordan laughed out loud.

Certifiable, for sure. Not her type, definitely.

But able to make her toes curl?

Damn the man, yes.

Not that she'd ever tell him.

CHAPTER FIVE

WILL FOUND HIMSELF WHISTLING as he traveled the nearly deserted downtown streets at eight o'clock on Saturday morning. He'd seen her puzzlement last night, felt her body respond to his. She wanted to fight what she felt, but she was attracted, he was certain.

Not that she would like it one bit, of course. Ms. Jordan Parrish was far too accustomed to ordering men about, to calling the shots. One glimpse of those stunning legs, and a man could go blind. She used her sexuality as a weapon, as a barrier to protect a heart that he was more certain than ever needed care.

Not that she was the One, of course. No, his ideal woman was still out there somewhere and he would keep looking.

But in the meantime, he could help her, this hard-edged woman who had likely never cared for a house-plant, much less gardened. She probably lived on take-out. As for baking bread…the mere image of Jordan Parrish with flour dusting her apron and her hand buried in dough…

That made him laugh out loud.

He was quite clearly insane, of course, for getting involved. Between his inability to resist a challenge and his weakness for strays, he was, as him mum would say, a complete pudding.

But Jordan Parrish most definitely needed someone to be kind to her, to teach her that her cynicism was misplaced. That there were men with whom she could be real, men she could trust.

He wouldn't let himself get too deep, however. To get caught up in a woman like Jordan would be insanity, pure and simple. He might be a wee bit soft in the head, but he wasn't an idiot.

Yes, he felt more alive around her, on the edge of his seat to see what she would do next. Jordan was few things he wanted and many he did not.

But she was definitely never boring.

He chuckled again as he parked his truck in the deserted entertainment district, unloaded not only his tools but a sack of groceries. He'd been up for hours, but he'd bet his granny's soul Jordan was still sleeping, so he'd come prepared not only to fix her faucet but feed her, as well.

He pressed her buzzer once, then again with no answer. He set down his toolbox, already peering around him for pebbles to toss at her window.

"Oh, hell, it's you," came the irritated voice from the speaker. "Do you know what time it is?"

Will grinned. "Let me up, darlin'. I come bearing breakfast."

"I don't eat breakfast," Jordan muttered.

But she hit the button.

JORDAN UNLOCKED THE DOOR, then sank back into the nearest chair and curled up, already half-asleep.

Will strode through it seconds later, whistling.

Jordan muttered and refused to open her eyes. "Go away."

"Now, darlin'…" She could feel, actually *feel* the blasted man grinning at her. She picked up the pillow beside her and covered her face with it. "I can't believe you have the nerve to show up at, what, dawn?"

"It's hardly dawn. I've been up for hours."

She threw the pillow in the direction of his voice.

Something heavy rattled, then thumped on the floor. Footsteps sounded, along with something being set on her counter. She curled in more tightly on herself and wished just then that she'd thought to grab a blanket. It was freaking cold, and she only wore a camisole and boxers.

More footsteps, then a blanket settled over her. He even tucked it in around her legs, then pressed a kiss to her hair. "Sweet dreams," he murmured.

Then the blasted man started humming.

Jordan dragged the blanket over her head and tried to shut him out, but how on earth did you ignore a very large man clomping around your apartment, especially if the tune he was singing was quite lovely?

Then the coffee grinder kicked in.

"I hate you," she shouted.

"Hmm? What was that?"

I'm going to kill him. Dead. Worse than dead. As Jordan plotted the ways she could make Will die a slow, painful death, he blithely continued humming and clomping, pausing to chuckle now and again.

Then she smelled the coffee.

And whimpered.

Another chuckle.

Jordan was torn between plotting…and pleading.

Coffee won. "Please…" She stuck one arm out from beneath the blanket.

"In a bit. Anything good is worth the waiting. You mustn't rush things."

"Gimme."

She heard him approach. Then…nothing.

Her eyelids fluttered. The suspense was killing her. "Well?"

The blanket was peeled back. Will sank to his haunches, blue eyes alight with humor and a trace of pity. "Not a morning person, are you?"

"Coffee. I'm begging."

His smile widened. "And what would be the magic word?"

"I said please already."

"So you did." He swooped in for a quick kiss on her nose. Then he proffered a mug that smelled absolutely heavenly, holding it just out of reach. "Would this be what you're whimpering about?"

"I don't whimper." Much.

"Oh, darlin', I beg to differ. Now, what, a man has to wonder, would a creature in such dire straits be willing to give in exchange?"

"It's too early for sex."

A quick flash of very white teeth. "Oh, my…you certainly are out of sorts, aren't you? It's never too early for sex—but that wasn't what I meant."

"You're going to make me beg."

"Not exactly beg."

"I did say I hate you, right?"

"That you did. But I know it's simply that you're cross, in the way of a child." And all the while, the delectable scent of that coffee was wafting into her nostrils. "You don't really mean it."

"I might."

"No, you don't. And lucky for you, my price is quite simple and easily met. A simple 'Good Morning, Will,' that's it."

"Good morning, Will," she droned.

"Did I mention that a little enthusiasm would help?"

"God, you're annoyingly chipper in the mornings, aren't you?"

He grinned unrepentantly. "That I am."

"Good thing we're never having sex. I'd have to boot you out during the night or kill you at dawn."

"That, my dear, is another discussion altogether. I've made my conditions clear." His smile was cocky and completely unruffled as he cupped one hand behind his ear. "Now, I don't believe I heard you properly the first time."

"Good morning, Will," she said through gritted teeth.

Then she threw off the blanket and uncurled herself. "Good morning, Will." Her voice rose as she did, and he stood, too. She walked right up to where her feet touched his boots. "Good morning, Will," she shouted, her teeth bared in a grimace.

He smiled. "Could still use some work to convince me, darlin', but I'm a merciful man."

She snatched the mug and growled, then walked around him toward her bathroom.

Once inside, she slammed the door, took a healthy swallow and leaned back against the wood as her taste buds danced over the best cup of coffee she'd had in… ever.

Jordan slowly slid down the door, settled on the floor and indulged herself.

"You all right in there?" Will asked from the other side.

"Go away. I'm having a religious experience," she answered. She sipped again and closed her eyes in ecstasy.

On the other side of the wood, Will grinned.

And tried not to think about how enticing she looked in those skimpy pajamas.

"Take your time, darlin'."

Jordan smiled into her cup. "I intend to."

CHAPTER SIX

IN THE GYM A FEW DAYS LATER, Jordan finished her free-weight sets and headed toward the treadmill, wiping sweat from her forehead. In the mirrored wall, she caught a glimpse of a young guy new to the gym, a long-haired god oozing rude good health and a young man's raging hormones.

He was checking out her behind, and he didn't look away when their gazes met.

For just one moment, she paused, letting her gaze linger, allowing sheer lust to sweep through her as if at thirty-six she weren't a good ten years older than him. Then she smiled, the smile only an older woman has the confidence to hazard. His eyebrows rose, his grin spreading.

Jordan laughed and felt better than she had in days. She climbed on the treadmill and set it for half an hour, random inclines, and pushed the speed up a notch from usual.

Got to keep that butt firm and noteworthy.

Fiona arrived for her daily writing break. "What's got you so cheery today?"

"Check out the long hair over by the bench press."

"Oh, my," Fiona drawled. "Pitty pat, pitty pat."

Jordan laughed. "He likes my behind. I might keep him."

"Well, it's not like he'd be the first younger man for you."

"Again with the digs."

"You can't argue with the truth."

"I've apparently lost my ability to argue, period."

"What's that mean?" Fiona asked.

"What's what mean?" Marly said as she approached.

"Hey, stranger," Jordan greeted. "You haven't been in lately."

"I need a life," Marly replied, frowning.

"Are you okay?" Fiona asked.

"I'm fine." Marly's smile wasn't one hundred percent convincing, but her expression clearly said *bug off.* "What's with you?" she asked Jordan.

"I have a bone to pick with you, lady."

"With me?" Marly's eyebrows rose.

"Yes, you. That man has been to my house three times this week. He's fixed my faucet, my windows, and changed the lock on my door. He's driving me insane."

"What man?" Fiona asked.

"Will," Marly offered, grinning. "Has to be."

"Will?"

"Will Masterson, remember, Fiona? The big Irishman who works with David. Don't listen to a word Jordan says. He's fabulous. Remember the beautiful doors we saw at the gallery we visited the last time we went out art-gazing? Will made those."

Fiona nodded. "Those doors were works of art, not mere wood. So why is this artisan playing handyman at Jordan's loft?"

Jordan made a rude noise.

Marly simply smiled. "They met at Thanksgiving at my house, and Will's smitten. So's she."

"What?" Jordan all but shouted.

"Smitten? Our Jordan?"

"Marly's lost her freaking mind." Jordan glared at Marly. "I am not smitten. The man's insufferable."

"But how is he in bed?" Fiona asked. "You could certainly do worse than a strapping Irishman."

Jordan fell quiet.

Fiona stopped her treadmill and stared. "Oh, my. Can it be? Is there one man in Austin Jordan hasn't bagged?"

"There are lots of them," Jordan replied. "You make it sound like all I do is have sex."

Her friends didn't respond but only waited.

"Oh, all right," she snapped. "I don't know how he is in bed—are you satisfied now? The man kisses like a wet dream and he hasn't made a move on me since the first day. Worse than that, he's told me he won't take things any further until I agree to reserve myself for only him." She snorted. "As if. I can't stand the sight of him."

"Now, now," Marly soothed. "You know that's not true. Even at that first meeting, there were sparks flying between you. But I don't want him upsetting you."

"Upsetting me?" Jordan snorted. "He's driving me crazy, is what. He's relentless and so blasted cheerful. And he's sexy," she growled. "I could just murder him."

Her friends exchanged glances.

"Jordan, do you want me to have David talk to him?" Marly asked.

"No, I do not." Jordan regained control of herself.

"The man I can't handle hasn't been born. Will's just—different. Not good different, annoying different. I don't know why I've become his home improvement project, but he's got to run out of projects soon and then I'll ditch him."

Marly stiffened. "Don't you hurt him, Jordan. He's a wonderful man."

"How could I hurt someone who has the hide of a buffalo and the sensitivity of a rock?"

"Your eyes are sparkling, girlfriend." Fiona's own eyes were eagle-sharp on her. "This may be the first time I've ever seen you like this. For once, you're not bored, are you?" Then she glanced over at Marly. Marly grinned back, lifting one eyebrow.

"Just stop it, you two. This isn't funny."

Marly's peal of laughter was a welcome sound. It had been a long time since they'd heard her make it.

"It is, though. I've never seen a man fluster you before."

Jordan tossed her head. "I'm not flustered. I'm pissed."

Fiona didn't try to hold back her own laughter.

Jordan narrowed her eyes.

"I'm sorry," Fiona choked. "Swallowed wrong." She quickly averted her face, turning the laugh into a cough.

Marly carefully blanked her own face, but amusement lingered.

Fiona recovered but couldn't leave well enough alone. "You know they say that the things you fight hardest are the things you want the most."

"Fiona, you—"

"All right, you two." Marly assumed her peacemaker role. "Settle down, or I'll send you to your rooms."

"Yes, Mom." Jordan made a face at Fiona, then stuck her iPod earbuds in her ears and increased the incline on the treadmill, pointedly ignoring them.

Will was annoying. Bossy. Overbearing.

Unfortunately, also hot.

And determined to hold out until she made the promise she would never, ever make. Narrowing your options to one man was the first step on the road to delusion.

Some people weren't made for monogamy.

Jordan was one of them.

WILL MISSED A CUT on the trim board. "Blast it."

"What's up?" David appeared beside him.

"I wasted this piece, and we're short enough on what we stripped and restored." He knew his tone was irritable but couldn't seem to help it. "Never mind. I'll figure out something."

David didn't move on, however. "You okay?"

"Dandy." Will eyed another piece he might be able to toenail together with this one.… He shook his head brusquely. It wasn't like him to make such a mistake.

"You sure?"

"I said I'm—" Will exhaled in a gust. "It's nothing, really. At least, nothing you can fix."

David observed him, then began to smile. "Ten bucks the problem's initials are J.P."

Will raked one hand through his hair. "Go ahead. Say you warned me."

"No need to rub it in. What's she doing?"

"You haven't enough time, I promise. And it's my

own bloody fault." But he settled back against the wall. "I'm a patient man," he began.

David chuckled. "Well, God knows Jordan will try a saint."

Will's humor began to return. "This fish is going to take a very long line and a steady hand."

"You actually want to keep her? Jordan?"

"Of course not, but she's fragile."

"Jordan? The man-eater?"

"Don't call her that." Will's ire rose. "You don't understand her. There's a damaged child inside that shrewish woman."

"Shrew is a good description."

"David," Will said as cautiously as he could manage, "you haven't looked beneath the surface. A tender heart resides there. God blind me for wanting to be kind to that heart, but I do."

"Another one of your strays? I've seen your menagerie, watched how you slip food to the homeless guys and minister to my crew." David captured his gaze. "She'll chew you up and spit you out."

"She won't." Will shrugged. "And anyway, I said nothing of keeping her. But she can't continue as she is. She's not happy. If she would only—" He broke off. "Perhaps it's a fool's errand as you think, but I am as I am. I will not turn my back on suffering. This one is like a wild cat who spits and fights out of fear. Time and much wooing is required to gentle them. Jordan will need more than most."

"And in the end? Where is this headed?" David inquired. "You know Jordan is violently opposed to the very idea of marriage."

Will recoiled. "I'm not looking to marry the girl.

Good God, man, I want peace in my life, a woman with whom to live in contentment. You'd never have a day of it with Jordan. It's only that…" Will stared off into the distance. "I cannot leave her this way. She needs to know there are men who can be trusted. That she can allow herself to be soft. She'll never be happy otherwise."

"Well." David shook his head. "You sure don't lack ambition." He clapped Will on the shoulder. "I admire you. I think." He grinned. "Or perhaps I should have you committed. Not sure which."

"Nor am I. Might keep the straitjacket handy. A bit more time with Jordan, and I may be ripe for it."

On the other hand, he thought as he watched David leave, *perhaps it's time for a new tactic.*

A slow smile spread over his features as an idea struck him.

What was it the Yanks were fond of saying? *No guts, no glory?*

ON SATURDAY MORNING, Jordan woke early, anticipating Will's arrival. Though she told herself he deserved her bedhead and no shower, she found herself dressed and ready, coffee dripping into the pot by eight o'clock.

An hour later, still no Will.

"He said he wanted to take a look at that squeaky closet door," she muttered. She contemplated going back to bed, but she wasn't sleepy.

She spent another hour picking up and straightening the loft, though her cleaning service would be in on Monday.

At ten-thirty, she broke. Punched in the cell number she'd told him she didn't want.

His phone rang and rang. At last he picked up. "Will Masterson." His voice was distracted.

"Where are you?"

"Hmm—what?" Then his voice changed. "Why, darlin' Jordan, are you awake, then?"

She almost hung up on him. "You said you wanted to look at my closet door. How was I supposed to sleep, knowing you'd be barging in at the crack of dawn?"

"I was busy."

Busy with what? she wanted to ask but didn't. Her heart squeezed a little, and anger stirred when she realized she'd already become accustomed to him being around nearly every day.

"I might be able to drop by later," he offered.

"No need. The door doesn't bother me." *So there.* "Anyway, I have a full day." Though, she realized, not one item on her list had much appeal.

Which terrified her. "So, just…have a good day." She started to hang up.

"I was thinking," he said in a casual tone, "that perhaps you might like to see my place."

"Your place?" she echoed.

"Yes. I'm finishing a project. Since you have such a way with tools, perhaps you'd like to lend a hand."

She could hear the smile in his voice and, curse him, that charmed her. "It's not nice to mock other people."

At last, that warm chuckle she'd come to depend on. "Oh, I wasn't mocking, darlin' Jordan. You do have a certain…manner with a tool in your hand."

Normally, Jordan would assume a man saying that

was talking dirty, but this was Will, and she could never quite be sure of anything where he was concerned. "So I could be like, your apprentice?"

"There is much I would be delighted to teach you. I'm certain I've made that clear, have I not?"

"You *are* talking dirty to me, in that roundabout Irish way of yours, aren't you?"

"Me, darlin' Jordan?" His voice was all innocence. "My sainted mother would faint to hear such a thing." The smile in his tone grew more pronounced. "Perhaps you should come over and take my measure in person."

"You make me crazy, you know that?" She couldn't hold back her own laughter. This man—this impossibly aggravating and ornery and stubborn man—could make her, Jordan Parrish, giggle like the innocent girl she'd never been.

"Would that be a complaint, now?"

"What do you think?" She found herself grinning into the phone. "All right, all right, give me the address. Maybe I'll drop by later," she said, deliberately using his casual words.

"Come soon, Jordan." His tone was husky.

She shivered a little in anticipation as she wrote down the address and ended the call.

For a few moments, she stared out the window at a crisp, cool day that somehow seemed a little brighter.

CHAPTER SEVEN

OF COURSE THE WOMAN would show up for manual labor wearing skinny jeans and a tank top that bared teasing glimpses of her smooth, taut belly, topped by some fuzzy sweater that probably cost the earth. On her feet were high-heeled ankle boots.

Will groaned silently. She would cost him his sanity, no question.

But, oh, she did look delectable.

"You live practically in the country," she accused. She glanced around. "And your house is falling down."

Will couldn't help laughing. "Good afternoon to you, too." Then, unable to resist, he swooped in and placed a kiss on that sulky, sexy mouth of hers.

Jordan sighed one breathy little moan, and it was all he could do not to snatch her up, bear her inside and lay her down on his bed.

Praise Jesus and all the saints…help me. "I'll have you know that the exterior of my house is deceiving. The paint is only a primer until I figure out what colors I want. I'd like to eventually replace that octagonal window above the porch roof with a stained glass, but I haven't yet found the right one."

He continued, "I've focused first on securing the structure, then on making space livable inside. I will admit, though, that David believes I should have razed the entire house." He grinned. "But he'd be wrong. I found lovely loblolly pine floors beneath ancient scarred vinyl, and there are crown moldings that I believe were hand-carved."

She clung to her pose of nonchalance. "If you say so."

"Would you care to see for yourself?"

She hesitated. "You really like all this stuff, don't you? I mean—" She gestured around at his garden and the evidence of new trees he'd planted, shrubs he'd moved. "It's all kind of *Little House on the Prairie* or something."

"Come again?" His brow wrinkled.

"A series of books kids read, mostly girls. About a pioneer family." She shrugged. "I used to think they were kind of amazing. There was Pa and Ma and their kids, and they raised chickens and cows and—" She halted. "Well, anyway, you'd be right at home there."

He wove his fingers into hers and tugged her along. "This is how I lived in Ireland. We were not city folk. We grew our vegetables, my mum had hens for the eggs, Da raised dairy cows. We all pitched in. With eight children, it was necessary."

She caught up with him. "Eight kids? Wow. I was an only child."

And didn't that loneliness shadow her?

"Which were you?" she asked. "Don't tell me—the oldest, since you're so bossy."

He grinned. "You'd be wrong. I'm the black sheep and square in the middle. An elder sister and two older brothers, all raising families. I have two younger sisters, one married with a third baby on the way and one studying to be a nun. My two younger brothers are also bachelors but have at least stayed nearby, as my mum thinks I should have."

Jordan glanced at him sideways. "The black sheep? Really? But your mother should know you've actually done her proud." She hesitated. "I get, though, how it feels to disappoint people." Her jaw tightened. "Not that I worry about that."

"How could you possibly have disappointed your family with all you've achieved?" He was outraged on her behalf.

"It doesn't matter. They are who they are. I don't sweat it."

But she did, clearly, despite her bravado. Will's protective instincts surged. Did they not see how they'd hurt her? Could they not tell how she'd been harmed by their actions and attitudes?

"They're wrong," he said fiercely. When Jordan didn't look at him, he took her chin and turned her face to his. "How could they not be proud of you?"

Her eyes widened. "You're angry," she marveled. "At them."

"Of course I am. You were a child when they robbed you of a home."

"It's not a big deal. It was never much of a home." She glanced around her. "Nothing like this, that's for sure." She met his gaze and laid her palm against his jaw. "But thanks for defending me." Her eyes were as soft as he'd ever seen them.

He wanted to sweep her up in his arms and shield her.

Before he could, she turned away and studied his

house. "So…explain to this city slicker exactly what you've done."

Will considered her for another moment but knew she wouldn't appreciate his pity. He turned his own attention to his house.

But he didn't let go of her hand. "Allow me to introduce you to my lifetime home-improvement project," he gestured with his free arm. "Please place a donation in the jar by the door at the end of the tour, should you be so inclined. The homeowner is ever in jeopardy of impoverishment."

Jordan grinned up at him and managed a passable curtsy. "Do lead on, my good man."

"Certainly. But mind your step, miss." Though Will realized that the advice might more properly belong to him. Every glimpse of the heart behind her tough-as-nails facade made keeping his distance a little more difficult.

"So WHAT ABOUT THE project you mentioned?" Jordan asked at the end of the tour as she stared at a piece of equipment Will called a router. She could barely imagine how the crown molding above their heads had come from this tool. Or what creating it had required. "Don't you need to get back to it? Should I go?" In truth, however, she was more intrigued than she'd expected. She'd never given a second thought to how a structure was built, much less that all the pieces hadn't come from some factory.

"There's time," he replied. "Would you care to see what I'm doing?"

"Why not?"

He led her outside to a frame building, a sort of

garage that was also only painted with primer. "So will the primer be enough to protect the house and this? Isn't the weather hard on them?"

"It is, but the primer will serve for now. I have to choose my priorities. There's only me, and I must also earn what is required to fund everything. I'll need a batch of days together to paint the place all at once, and I must do so to get the best effect."

"But it doesn't drive you crazy that everything's not done?"

"What is truly worthwhile often needs patience."

"You have a lot of it, don't you?" She frowned. "I don't get that. My view is that you have to grab for everything as soon as you get the chance. You never know what will disappear and never come back."

He'd taken her hand again, and she found that she liked the sensation of his big hand swallowing hers. "Perhaps what's available for the grabbing isn't worth keeping," he said. "Slow is better."

Not to me, she was about to say when he opened the door to his—well, obviously not a garage. Tools of all sizes and descriptions were placed strategically around the floor or arranged on the walls. "Wow. What is all this?"

"The instruments of my trade. This," he indicated one that had a wicked saw blade sticking out of its flat surface, "is a table saw. That is a band saw, and over there is a lathe."

"What's a lathe do?"

"Do you recall the missing newels in the staircase? I'm replacing them with matching ones I turn on this."

"Really? How?"

He reached for a block of wood about three feet long and square. "I begin with this."

"I can't picture how that could become like the ones I saw. Would you show me? I mean, is it too much trouble?"

His eyes warmed. "Not at all. First put on these—" He handed her a set of goggles, then donned his own. "And these hearing protectors."

Once they were both armored, Jordan's own voice sounded odd to her as she stepped up beside him and watched him fasten the long piece at each end. Then his hands went unerringly to a tool with a wooden handle and a curved metal shaft. On the end, it was rounded.

"This is a spindle gouge." He pointed to a spot on the other side of the machine. "You stand over there. This—" he indicated a flat metal edge he adjusted to come closer to the block "—is called a tool rest."

When Jordan was in place, Will flipped a switch and the wood began spinning. He put the handle of the tool at an angle on the rest. With deft hands, he leaned the tool in and out, and wood shavings all but leaped off the block in long curls. Beneath his hands began to appear graceful curves she could never have imagined creating from a block of wood.

"That's incredible."

"What?" Will flipped the switch.

"Sorry." She stepped back, but she couldn't help wanting to touch. "I hope I didn't interrupt at a bad time."

He studied her and the hand that was rising by her side. "Come over here. You can help."

"Me? Oh, no, I couldn't—"

"Jordan, you're curious. There's no substitute for the feeling of the wood under your hands."

"But it's beautiful. I'll mess it up."

He shrugged. "I have more material."

She was torn between longing and fear. "I won't be good at it."

"Do you only do things you've already mastered, then? I think not. You were not born a lawyer."

"Some would say I was born to argue."

"And there I'd likely not disagree," he said with a smile. "Still, surely you've attempted the unfamiliar."

"I learned kickboxing," she admitted. "I'm really good at it—want to see?"

"Perhaps later. Just now, let's find out if there's a woodworker lurking within you."

"Okay." Truth be told, she really did want to try it. She assumed the place he indicated in front of him and tried to imitate his two-handed grip, one beneath and one over the tool, guiding it.

"Hold it firmly but keep your body relaxed." He arranged himself behind her, his big frame a comforting and disturbing presence all at the same time. "You'll need to be both flexible and vigilant. No piece of wood is uniform throughout. Its textures and composition differ from spot to spot. Keep the spindle gouge slightly loose in your fingers, but clasp it carefully enough so that the turning doesn't dislodge it. I wouldn't want to see a scar in this lovely exterior of yours. Notice the edges of the tool. They're wicked sharp."

"Maybe I shouldn't…"

"Here, place your hands in mine, and we'll begin together so you can acquire a feel for this."

She fought past her awareness of his big, warm

hands, of his hard body a shelter around her. She narrowed her eyes, staring hard and steeling herself.

Will kissed the side of her neck, jolting her.

"What was that for?"

"Don't tense up. Light on your feet, fluid in your motions."

Jordan inhaled one good, deep breath. "Okay, I'm ready." *I hope.*

Will flipped the switch and drew her hands with his closer until the blade touched the wood. Jordan gasped and jerked. The spindle gouge slipped, goring a crooked line in the wood before he pulled her hands back. "Sorry."

"You're doing fine. There's an entire forest lost to my learning. Now relax against me, and let's begin again."

Relax. Against him.

Yeah, right. But she tried, and he was a good teacher. Soon her fascination was great enough to overcome most of her extreme awareness of his body touching hers. She focused and watched the curves form under her hands—

It was *her* hands doing this, she realized with a jitter. Will had let go, though he still stood right behind her, his body big and warm and—

Another crooked groove. "Sorry." *Focus, Jordan.* She redoubled her efforts and moved the tool along the wood as she'd watched him do, weaving in and out and fashioning a curve not nearly as beautiful as his own, but not a total loss.

She pulled away and studied the piece still whirling in front of her. "Not bad, huh?"

Will leaned into her to flip off the switch. "Quite good, in fact."

"For a beginner?" she asked, turning toward him.

His eyes were hot on her mouth, then flicked up to her eyes. "Accept your due, Jordan. You did well."

Though her insides jangled, her rush of triumph overrode them, and she had to smile, throwing her arms wide. "I loved it!"

"Careful, now." He plucked the instrument from her hand, but just as she would have retreated, he took a step toward her, and she lost her breath.

She hastened to cover her intense reaction to him. "Can I do another one?" Then she experienced a moment of unfamiliar shyness. "If you can spare the wood, I mean."

Those blue eyes saw too much. As happened so often, she had the sense that Will Masterson understood her in ways that disturbed her.

Fortunately for her, he stepped away then, just before she could decide whether to yield to the kiss they were both obviously dying for or to run for her car before things got out of hand.

He turned back with another piece of wood. "All right. Let's try this one. It's oak, not pine. You'll want to pay attention to the difference in them." He went on to discuss those differences as he removed the turned piece and replaced it with the block.

And Jordan couldn't decide whether to be miffed or relieved that she'd dodged that bullet.

"WHY WOULD YOU NEED a wife?" Jordan asked much later after a delicious dinner. "You're a really good cook, on top of everything else. What can a woman do for you that you can't do for yourself? I can't believe you actually baked that bread."

Will settled beside her in the porch swing, looking down at her with a knowing grin on his face.

"Well, sex, sure, but you don't need marriage for that," she said.

He chuckled and rested his arm behind her. "Man was not made to live alone." He glanced over at her. "Nor woman, either."

"You're wrong. I prefer to be on my own." Jordan lifted a shoulder. "Some of us just aren't meant for the long term."

Will smiled indulgently, then set the swing in motion with a shove of one foot. "For an intelligent woman, you've a feather brain at times."

Jordan smacked him on the belly, but that didn't faze him. "Protest as you will, sweetheart, but you know I'm right."

"I do not." She frowned and glanced over at him again as the feel of his belly registered. The man had a six-pack, she would swear. Suddenly she really, really wanted to see him out of that flannel shirt and the T-shirt beneath.

"What has that lovely brow so wrinkled?"

"You. You weren't supposed to be sexy, damn it."

"What?" He did a double take, then guffawed. "How is one man supposed to keep up with that odd mind of yours?"

"You're big," she accused.

"I am. And what, might I ask, am I to do about that?"

"Nothing." She crossed her arms over her stomach and harrumphed. "My type is lean and dangerous."

Will sighed and set them swinging again. "You've no idea what your type is."

"I suppose you think it's you."

He captured her chin. "Now, why would I be wanting to make myself miserable, getting involved with a difficult woman like you, hmm? Last I looked, I'd not taken leave of my senses."

Stung, Jordan didn't respond. How could she argue? She was difficult. And, okay, maybe sometimes she was tired of being so on edge all the time, but… He was so not her type, she reminded herself. A man who worked with his hands, who gardened and cooked. Who wanted some country-girl type and had no taste for night life, for the dangerous edge of risk.

"What's going on in that serpentine brain?" he asked.

"Nothing. I should go," she said abruptly. "I never meant to spend the whole day here."

"Coward." His face was deadly serious.

"I most certainly am not."

He merely arched one eyebrow. "You know there's something between us, and you run rather than face it."

"Face what?" she scoffed. "You barely even kiss me. Who's the coward?"

His normally affable manner vanished completely. In a blink, he'd plucked her from her seat and settled her on his lap, sliding one big hand to cradle the back of her head.

And kissed the living socks off her.

For a second, she froze.

Then she dived in. To take control, she'd thought… but control wasn't in the cards. She dug her hands into his sides and felt muscles even more impressive than she'd realized. For all that Will looked stocky, he actually had great muscle definition. She'd had a fling with a bodybuilder once, and Will's torso and arms, not the product of steroids, she was sure, would have made that guy jealous.

Within seconds, she found herself surrounded by arms made of iron, snug against a big, warm body that felt like the haven she'd been seeking all of her life.

Will groaned and deepened the kiss, and Jordan followed him into a special, private place she'd never visited…never even imagined. She slid her arms around his neck and pressed closer against him, wondering if she'd ever kissed a man before who'd taken her on such a roller-coaster ride of emotions like this, spanning the spectrum in seconds.

But she knew the answer already. There was only one Will. And she didn't know what to do with him.

Finally, it was Will who drew away, and Jordan who whimpered and pulled him back. He resisted, though she felt his body's vivid response to her. He set her back a few inches, both of them breathing hard, and leaned his forehead against hers.

"Now, Will," she murmured. "Make love to me now."

Instead, he lifted her and set her on legs that wouldn't hold her, steadying her with his hands at her waist.

"No, sweetheart. Not in the heat of the moment."

"You want me. I know it, and you do, too."

"That's not enough."

"It's enough for tonight."

He looked at her sadly. "I'm beginning to think I want more than tonight."

"Do you always get what you want?" she whispered.

"I can't tell you. I've never wanted anything as I want you. I only know that when we make love, it's not going to be a whim, not one of your flings. You're still not ready, Jordan. And I can wait. Not easily, but I'll manage."

Her body edgy and aching, Jordan's temper spiked. She'd love nothing better than to stomp off and never see him again—except that wasn't at all what she craved to do with this excess of energy she was dying to spend in another fashion.

But he stood there looking at her, blue eyes sparking yet resolute, patient and seeing too much. Jordan had a sense that she was fighting a battle for her life. He would change her. This couldn't last—they were too different—and where would she be then? Who was she if not Jordan the Shark, with hot and cold running men?

"I can't be a Marly, Will."

He smiled. "I happen to like Jordan Parrish, saints preserve my black soul."

She relaxed enough to laugh. "You are certifiably insane, you know that?"

He shrugged. "I'll make coffee."

Jordan sighed. "It's a lousy substitute for sex."

"Ah, but that's where you're wrong, darlin'. Just consider it foreplay." He picked her up and strode inside with her. "Stay a little longer, would you?"

How could anyone remain angry at this man? She relaxed in his arms, enjoying an odd sense of freedom that the night would not, as all her others were, be about sex. He was the oddest person. He baffled her and enraged her.... "Can I keep my newel posts?"

He glanced down in surprise. "Of course." He didn't ask what she would do with them, didn't make fun of her for wanting them as souvenirs of a day she wouldn't soon forget. "I'm thinking that with a bit more practice, you could turn one that would fit exactly on my stairs."

She blinked, absurdly pleased at the notion. "Really?" Then doubt crept in. "I don't think so."

"Then I must believe for both of us." He seemed perfectly serious.

She stared at him and marveled at the kindness that was so integral to his nature. "What am I going to do with you?" she whispered.

He set her down on a bar stool in the beautiful kitchen he'd restored, trapping her between his arms and the counter, his eyes hot and blue and kind.

"Ah, but isn't that the journey we must take together to find out?" He pressed a kiss to her forehead, then drew away with an obvious reluctance that pleased her enormously.

"I'd best be making that coffee now."

Jordan swiveled to watch him, her greedy eyes following every move he made.

CHAPTER EIGHT

WILL HAD STAYED AWAY from her deliberately for nearly a week. Thankfully he had a lot of work to complete for David, and he was intent upon finishing the tiling in the master bathroom that was his concession to modernity. The original bath had been the size of a coat closet. He'd taken that space and a large chunk of the adjoining small bedroom and created a bathroom that would scandalize his family when they saw it. Their family of ten had shared one small bath and thought nothing of it.

One day they would understand that Will was here to stay. Surely when he had a family of his own, his mum and da and at least some of his siblings would relent and pay him a visit.

Though, he had to admit, the prospect of a family seemed further away than ever.

Because now there was Jordan.

Blast his black soul, why could he not simply see reason and walk away from her? Yes, there was more softness in her than anyone else recognized, but the distance between that and Jordan as a wife, much less a mother...surely the moon itself was closer.

What was it about her that drew him so? Was it, as his mum declared, only his weakness for the lost, the lonely? Jordan was lonely, of that he was now certain, whatever she might argue, and she did want to make love with him very badly. How much of that, however, was simply her competitive urge? He wondered if any man had ever said no to Jordan Parrish.

And why would they? Even a blind man, robbed of the sight of that tantalizing mouth, those endless legs, the sleek curves—that blind man would hear her husky, come-get-me voice and seek her out.

Yes, he wanted her to the point of distraction. But as lovely as her body was, it was Jordan's spirit that captivated him. A quick mind, a wry wit and, most of all, a wistfulness she normally hid well…there was much more to be discovered about Jordan.

And he wanted to be the one to do it. Only him and no other.

But she had not yet forsaken her playmates, he'd learned. In a moment of weakness, he'd driven downtown and nearly parked his truck, ready to climb her steps and be done with the waiting.

Then he'd spotted her walking down the street, tossing her head coyly and smiling at another man, one whose expression clearly spoke of anticipation.

Damn you, Jordan, he thought as he pulled into his driveway and parked. Finn came running, and Will wanted to brush past the dog, to throw something, to yell—

Horrified at the agitation he felt and how that turned him into someone he couldn't like at all, Will exhaled in one powerful gust and dropped to his haunches. "Sorry, boy." He gave Finn a good rubbing, then let his head sag while the dog licked his cheek and whimpered.

Perhaps he wasn't up to the challenge she presented. Gentling Jordan Parrish required too much. She bore not the faintest resemblance to the woman he'd fixed up this house for, the woman who would make him happy.

Will rose and stared into the growing darkness.

And tasted the bitter ash of defeat.

He should give her the freedom she demanded, let her waste her life however she might. It was her life, after all, as she never ceased to point out, he thought as he strode toward his back door.

As he passed his shop, however, he couldn't help remembering her childlike joy in turning newel posts, the shy pride when he'd said she could make one for his staircase.

He was so preoccupied as he ascended his back steps that he nearly toppled the package resting against his back door.

"Will Masterson" was written on it in a bold yet feminine slash he didn't recognize. Beneath it, in smaller letters, "You don't have to like this, but I thought of you when I found it."

"Jordan," it was signed.

He carried the bulky box inside, wondering how she'd managed it herself. He turned on the lights, then set it on his kitchen counter. What could the woman be doing? Carefully he slit the packing tape and dug through foam peanuts to a bubble-wrapped shape below.

Removing the mounds of cushioning required several more minutes, all the while his curiosity racing.

"Well, I'll be," he said to Finn when he reached the end. Will shook his head and glanced down at the dog. "She brought me a window."

It was the stained glass window he'd been seeking

to place above the front porch. Nearly two years he'd been searching, not sure exactly what he wanted and determined to wait until he had that figured out.

You don't have to like this, Jordan had written.

He'd thought he'd want to pick it out himself as he'd done with every last inch of this place up to now.

But somehow she'd known what he was looking for before he had. A Celtic knot, a lovers' knot in shades that would now determine his exterior paint choices at last.

Perhaps she couldn't cook, didn't know a weed from a tomato plant, couldn't sew on a button. No, she wasn't a Marly, nor did she have any desire to be.

But somehow, prickly, difficult Jordan Parrish understood him. Saw into his heart.

"Oh, but I do like this, sweetheart, very much."

Just then the thought of the man he'd seen her with earlier punched a hole in the pleasure he felt, but he tightened his fingers on the window frame and knew that she'd never done anything like this for any of those temporary men.

Patience. *You have a lot of it, don't you?*

"I'll need more, now, won't I, darlin' Jordan?"

Slow is better, he'd said to her. "You ass," he chided himself. "Too cocky for your own good."

Then he had to smile. He'd made himself scarce, and she'd come to him—with a present, no less.

His normal optimism returned. "You're mine, sweetheart, and it's only you who doesn't know it yet." He shook his head. "Not that I have the first idea what to be doing with the likes of you."

Will studied his window with greedy eyes.

And couldn't help laughing.

God save me, the woman does call a merry tune.

TWO DAYS LATER, ON Christmas Eve, Jordan toasted Jimmy Stewart with her eggnog. "Here's to sappy movies, pal. You made the best." The joyous faces and uplifted voices of *It's a Wonderful Life* shone from her TV screen, and she wiped away a traitorous tear. "What's wrong with you?" She hit the power button on the remote and the screen went dark.

She'd survived the inevitable argument with both of her parents in their separate calls, hadn't she? Why wasn't she in California instead of Texas? Why wasn't she married? Would she ever have kids?

She should be celebrating that triumph, not letting some stupid movie get to her.

She loathed Christmas more than any other holiday. It was all about families, and every avenue to escape it was closed. No stores open, no clubs to lose yourself in music and dancing and whatever else might ensue that would help you pass the time until the world got back to normal.

There might be a bar open somewhere, maybe, full of people without families, but she just didn't have the heart to go look for it. She could manage one night, anyway. Not like she hadn't done it before.

She padded across the loft in fuzzy socks to get more eggnog. Halfway there, her buzzer sounded, and Jordan glanced at the clock in surprise. Almost midnight.

The buzzer again.

She shrugged. "What the hell. Might as well see who it is. Probably just some curious drunk." She hit the button. "We gave at the office."

"Now, darlin', would that be any way to talk to a man bearing gifts?"

Will. "I'm not speaking to you. Go away." Where had he been while she'd been on pins and needles to know what he thought of her present? Giving him a window had been a stupid idea—hadn't she known that? "Why are you here at this hour?"

"Santa Claus has much territory to cover. I just finished sneaking off Marly's roof."

"You played Santa Claus for them?"

"I'm thinking that up there where you're warm is a better place to have this discussion, sweetheart. That is, unless you have company."

"I should say yes."

"Open up, sweetheart."

"Don't call me sweetheart." But she hit the buzzer. "You better mean that about gifts."

"Now, would Santa be coming to such a good girl empty-handed?"

His cheer made her grind her teeth—but even Will was a welcome distraction.

She heard his footsteps on the stairs and yanked the door open. "Where have you been? Why haven't—" She burst out laughing.

The transformation was amazing. His powerful frame made an impressive Santa, but he looked much plumper than normal. Friendly blue eyes gleamed at her above a snowy-white beard, and he brandished a large package. "Lovely to see you smiling, even at my expense."

Jordan stepped back and let him inside. "What's padding you? You're not that big."

Will waggled his fake white eyebrows at her. "So

nice that you've been paying attention. And here I was thinking you only noticed my handiwork."

She moved closer, and he stepped away. "Oh, no. No prodding and poking at St. Nick. Inappropriate behavior, Ms. Parrish. Only good girls receive gifts."

His good humor was infectious. For the first time in nearly a week, Jordan's heart lifted. "All right, spoilsport. So what's in the package?"

"Perhaps some child is waiting for this one."

"Uh-uh. You're too honorable. You'd never wave a package under my nose and then take it away. Now give."

"Now give," he echoed. "A cheeky bit of baggage you are. It's not Christmas morning. This will be going under the tree." He looked around the room, then back at her. "No tree?"

"A waste of resources." She jutted her chin.

"Not even artificial?"

One string of lights haphazardly draped over the bookcase, and a couple of poinsettias. For the first time, she saw how sterile this must look, especially if he'd just been at Marly's.

"Never mind that. Perhaps you'd be sharing a little of that eggnog with Santa?"

Jordan glanced back at him, peering closely for any sign of pity. If it was pity, he'd be back out the door before he could blink.

He smiled and sat down on her big overstuffed chair, setting the package to one side and patting his lap. "On second thought, why don't you come sit here, young lady, and tell me what you want Santa to bring you?"

"Santa as a dirty old man. Now, that's more my style."

Will shook his head, his gaze never leaving hers. "No, Jordan. It isn't. Now, come here and let me give you your present." He held out a hand in welcome.

She felt suddenly shy. "No eggnog first?"

"Not yet. I'm halfway to melting in this outfit."

More eager than she wanted to admit, Jordan approached. She had no idea what could be in the box, but she couldn't resist the unexpected treat. "But I don't have a present for you."

"A little elf delivered one to my back door."

"That was a housewarming gift. Did you—never mind." If he hated it she didn't want to know.

His gloved hand turned her face to him. "'Tis a beautiful window, Jordan. Perfect."

"So why—" She clamped her mouth shut.

"I needed to think," he said. "And I had something to finish. This is not the night to argue, sweet. This night all the world brims with love. We'll speak more of the window, but for now, end the debate and let me see your face when you open this."

At that moment, the child inside her that Jordan had long thought dead chose to make its appearance. Though she knew it was Will in the costume, that little girl wanted to sit on his lap and open the present, one she hadn't anticipated, hadn't begged to receive. A gift, in the purest sense of the word.

She pulled the box to her as she settled on his lap, feeling unaccountably shy but also supremely protected. Even more than she wanted to open the gift, she longed to cuddle against him, to lean her head on his shoulder and be a different Jordan than the world saw every day.

Nonsense. She hugged the package to her as solemn blue eyes studied hers. "Am I too heavy?"

"Not a bit. I'm thinking I could be happy like this for a long while."

Inside Jordan something eased, uncoiling when she hadn't even known she was tightly wound. "We're so different."

"Yes." He nodded, his smile solemn. "That's us, sweetheart. *The Odd Couple.*"

But she didn't have a sassy comeback this time. "Are we? A couple?"

His gaze never left hers. "I'm thinking yes."

"But why, Will? I'm—"

"Shhh," he whispered, placing one gloved finger across her lips. "'Tis useless to wonder the why of it, sweetheart. I'll gladly speak with you for hours of what I love about you, but it isn't your head you must be heeding—it's your heart that needs to be heard."

Love. No. "I don't let my heart call the shots, and you shouldn't either. You barely know me."

"Ah, but you, my stubborn sweetheart, cannot tell my heart whom to adore." He bounced her gently. "Now, will you open this present before I expire from the heat?"

"Sorry." She was surprised to feel reluctant. Once she started opening the wrapping, it would soon be over, this special surprise. "Maybe I'll wait until tomorrow, after all."

He shrugged. "You may wait…but I'll not be leaving until I see your face." He stretched and yawned. "Best be getting the sofa ready, Jordan darlin'. It's been a long day." But his smile was wide as if he was certain she'd crack.

She hugged it once more. "Thank you, Will. This is a wonderful surprise."

"As was my window." Pleasure beamed from his face. "I hope you like what's inside as much."

For the first time, she understood that he was nervous, and somehow that settled her. She began to open it carefully.

"Hmm. I always pictured you tearing into packages, ripping paper with abandon."

She shot him a glance, then grinned. "Oh, what the hell—you're right." She reverted to type and tore at the wrapping, eager to get inside.

Once she did, her heart stuttered. Lifting out the most exquisite wooden jewelry box she'd ever seen, Jordan gasped. "Oh, Will—this is beautiful." She pushed the wrappings aside and settled the gift on her lap, running her fingers over the silky-smooth edges, the tiny golden hinges, the beautiful carving of a Celtic design with her name worked inside the coils.

She glanced at Will, who watched her closely. "I've never seen anything so exquisite. You made this, didn't you?"

He nodded solemnly. "Don't you want to look inside?"

"I do." Barely able to tear her gaze away from his, she started to open the lid, but it didn't immediately lift.

"Here, press this." His gloved hand was too big, so he bared it, then pointed to a tiny recess.

Jordan marveled that those big hands could perform such delicate craftsmanship. With trembling fingers, she pressed against the recess and heard a click. The lid opened slightly, and she raised it to peer inside.

Jordan gasped again. Delicate as the air, a slender golden chain rested on dark blue velvet, a heart worked in hammered gold dangling from it, a blood-red ruby nestled inside the gold. She lifted it in her fingers and watched it catch the light, then darted her gaze to Will.

He looked less certain of himself than she'd ever seen him. Vulnerable. She thought she liked that, and she smiled.

"Do you like it?" he asked.

There was no way she could tease a man whose heart was in his eyes like that. No matter how much it frightened her or what accepting this might mean.

But she had to ask. "What does this mean, Will?"

"'Tis only a little trinket, nothing special." But his eyes told the lie.

"Will, I…"

"Let's see how it looks." He shed his remaining glove, then took the necklace from her. "Turn around."

Jordan obeyed, and he fastened it around her neck, then opened the top of the jewelry box wider so she could examine it in the mirror. The heart lay nestled just below the hollow of her throat, the ruby catching the light.

Will's finger traced around the heart, and his touch burned against her skin. Their eyes met in the mirror.

Jordan swallowed, her mouth suddenly dry. "Will, I'm overwhelmed. The necklace… I've never had anything so delicate. And the box is incredible.… I can't believe you made this. You shouldn't be building houses. You're an artisan. You could make a fortune on something like this."

"Ah, but a fortune isn't important to me, Jordan darlin'. I don't want masses of people buying work I completed in haste to satisfy a banker. Money is not the measure—it's the pleasure in the eyes of the recipient that's my reward. The hours I spend are precious to me, and I will not invest them to be paying overhead or keeping my attention on the bottom line. This work is my joy, and I only ask to be present to see the reaction when my work is received."

"Did you see what you needed tonight?" She couldn't imagine the hours this must have taken.

He held her gaze in his. "Yes, darlin', I did."

"I'm glad, because for once in my life, words fail me."

He chuckled softly. "Now, that in itself is a feat to trumpet."

"Want your thank-you kiss now?"

He shook his head. "I want out of this suit first." Will shifted beneath her.

"Wait—let me." Carefully, she laid the jewelry box on the side table. She removed his hat first, then his beard. Beneath them, his face was shiny with sweat, his shaggy hair matted down. She ran her fingers through it, lifting the strands and blowing through pursed lips to cool him. He closed his eyes and sighed in pleasure.

Then she began unbuttoning the jacket. "Good grief," she laughed. "No wonder you're sweating. Poor man—is this a down vest underneath?"

"I had to make it look authentic, and I couldn't gain fifty pounds in time."

She laughed, unzipping the vest, while he peeled off

the eyebrows. She stripped the vest away but stopped in midgesture at the sight of his muscular frame clearly outlined by a sweat-soaked T-shirt. "My, Santa, what nice muscles you have," she attempted to joke through a throat that had tightened with lust.

Jordan was touched to realize that Will was blushing, actually blushing. He leaned forward and pulled the jacket and vest from behind him and dumped them on the floor. When she started to rise, he used his other hand to pin her to his lap. "You're fine right here."

But she wasn't sure anymore. He'd played havoc with her heart for weeks now. The kisses they'd shared glowed in her memory like a beacon. And now he'd thrown gasoline on the fire with his gift.

She was so afraid he'd put her off again if she asked him to make love to her. She bunched her muscles to escape, but he stopped her once more.

"And would you be planning to renege on your thank-you, then?" His gaze pinned her, suddenly angry and fierce. "Is it because of the fellow you were with a few nights ago?"

"What fellow?"

"The one with the black leather jacket."

"You were watching me? Spying on me?" She reached for the clasp of the necklace. "Forget it. Take this back. Take all of it." She leaped from his lap. "Get out."

He rose, towering over her. "I won't. I wasn't spying. I'd had the thought to come see you because I missed you. But you were up to your old tricks, weren't you?"

"So what if I was?" But she hadn't been. Jordan had thought about it, yes, but only because she wasn't

ready to make Will any promises they would both regret down the road.

"How can you do that?" His expression was thunder-
ous. "You'd brought me a window—damn it, a perfect
one. Then you went out with some bloody oaf who's not
worth half of you because you're frightened of what's
between us?"

Not worth half of you. Even now he defended her.
She had to make him leave. She couldn't give in,
couldn't let herself— "I said get out. You don't know
anything, you, you *bloody oaf,*" she spat.

Those blue eyes speared into her, taking their time—
too much time, damn it. Studying her like some bug
on a pin.

Then a smile spread across his face.

"Don't you smile at me." She pointed at the door
again. "I said go away. And take your gifts with
you."

"You sent him packing, didn't you? But you won't
admit that because you're scared. Come here." He took
a step toward her.

She took a step back. "Don't touch me."

He didn't slow, and she couldn't seem to move. Then
his big hand was on her cheek, and he was examining
her too closely, seeing too much. "You fight yourself
as much as me, darlin' Jordan. Why are you so afraid
for me to love you?"

"You can't love me, Will. Don't." She closed her
eyes. "Please don't."

But it was too late. His lips were on hers. At first
gentle and soft, easing hers into parting, then sipping,
tasting with small, deadly kisses, each one crushing
her resistance with their tenderness.

"Jordan…" He groaned and drew her into him, that hard body that felt so much like a shelter in which she could hide. Where she could leave behind so much pain, so much sadness.…

His mouth cruised over her face, down her throat, stealing the breath from her as his hands untied her robe.

For a second, she stirred, aware of how unsexy her flannel boxers were.

"Shh. I'll never think of Yosemite Sam the same way again, darlin'." His soft chuckle faded as his mouth danced a new and devastating glissade over her skin. He bared her body as he was baring her heart, walking her slowly backward toward her bedroom, then impatiently, gloriously sweeping her up into his arms.

I can't promise, she wanted to protest. *This won't last,* she needed to warn him because he was so good, so kind, so…

Sexy. Sweet heaven, the man was driving her out of her mind, taking time—so much of it, too much of it until she would scream—to tease at odd spots on her body, avoiding the clearly sexual and in the process, driving her up and up and up.…

Until his hand covered the thatch of hair at her thighs, his touch both electrifying and somehow cherishing.

Jordan crested with a cry. Soared and floated for endless moments as she marveled that he'd made her come without ever even—

"Oh, dear mercy…" Was that her voice so high and thin as his tongue swirled around her nipple?

She felt his chuckle against her more than heard it. "Will…"

"Shh, sweetheart. Relax."

Relax? Then Jordan realized that he'd stripped away his own clothes. She watched that big, hard, warm body cover hers.

Oh, how good he felt. How much she relished the sensation of him—she, who was nearly always on top. Who preferred it that way. In control.

But Will was teaching her how little she knew as he continued his assault on her senses, devastating her every defense, dismantling them as though they were a child's building blocks. "Will, let me—" She was rising again as his fingers, his tongue, his heated breath… "Don't—"

"Again, darlin' Jordan." His voice was warm honey. Darkest velvet.

"Will, I want you in—" Then all thought fled again as her body came apart, as she flew higher still.

But for once, she wasn't alone. Will kept her safe as she flew. She rode on thermals like a hawk, an eagle soaring into the crisp blue air, the beautiful and welcoming sky.

In the piercingly sweet aftermath, she floated back to earth. "Jordan," he said, voice strained and taut now. "Look at me. Darlin', look at me."

Jordan opened heavy eyes to see his blue ones wide open, hot and beautiful and fierce. "I love you, Jordan Parrish," he said, and before she could voice the caution she knew she should—

With a bold thrust, he made them one.

Jordan's back bowed. Every cell of her body screamed with a freedom, a bliss she'd never before experienced. She was safe and she was flying and Will was with her and he loved her and—

Will found his release as she went sailing. Together they rode the night sky. Jordan clasped him tightly, pressing every inch of herself against him in fear, in ecstasy, in demand…longing…yearning…

I love you, he'd said.

Oh, I love you, too, Will.

But her heart wept, knowing she couldn't say it.

Because she could never love him as he deserved.

WILL AWOKE WITH Jordan's head pillowed on his shoulder. A slow, satisfied smile emerged as she whimpered at his movement, then curled more tightly against him.

God, she was sweet. Would anyone who knew her recognize the woman who'd given herself up to him again and again throughout the night?

I have you now, my Jordan. I know you as no one else does. Something very primal prowled inside him. *And they never will. You're done with playing around, sweetheart, whether or not you realize it.*

He'd been voracious—they both had, their love play at turns tender and bawdy, each one surrendering, each one conquering. Greedy and gentle, fierce and flirty, Jordan Parrish was what he'd been waiting for all his life.

He would, by God, have her. Though, he told himself with a wry smile, she wouldn't make it easy on him, of that he was certain.

She was his miracle, but that was not to say he expected prickly Jordan Parrish to magically turn soft overnight.

He chuckled quietly. *Or ever,* he hoped. Her spirit was half the appeal of her. She only needed showing that love was real. That he could be trusted with that frightened heart of hers.

Full of cheer and optimism, Will rose from Jordan's bed, energy coursing through him. He looked around him for clothing, then realized all he had was a Santa suit. *Ah, well, and didn't you plan this out poorly, my boy?* He shrugged on the red pants, cinching them up in gathers where the padding no longer took up space, then walked into her kitchen area. He was starving. Nothing like a good full night of loving to stimulate the appetite, now, was there?

A glance in her refrigerator had him sighing in dismay.

Right. This was Jordan, after all. Well, surely she'd be hungry, too. He began a pot of coffee, then strode toward her bedroom while it was brewing. For a moment, he simply stood beside the bed, enjoying the sight of her, all the hard edges smoothed off.

Prickly, yes. Quite likely always would be.

But enough gentling, and his cactus would bloom with the force of his loving.

For now, he was famished, and if he yielded to the temptation she presented, they'd be in that bed for hours yet, only to be found sometime later, victims of starvation.

A shower, then. *Keep your hands off her, boy. Let the woman sleep a bit.*

Will sighed and headed for the bathroom.

SUNLIGHT FILTERED INTO the loft, a soft whistling barely audible over the sound of the shower. Jordan frowned, then smiled and burrowed deeper under the covers as she remembered the night before. She missed the warmth of him, even as she groaned. Yes, Will was a morning person, apparently cheerful from the moment he awoke. She always had been, and always would be, a creature of the night.

Night. Oh, such a night. Jordan stretched in delight, recalling the hours just passed, the wonder of making love with Will.

I love you, he'd said. And not just once.

She sat up straight. No, it was too soon. Too… *Oh, Will. You think you love me, but…*

In the mirror across from her bed, the ruby at her throat winked in the sunlight. For a second, Jordan let herself feel how much she wanted all of this to be real.

Even though she knew her limitations in a way she wished Will would never have to.

Oh, give it a rest. It's Christmas. The day she normally barely endured suddenly glowed with fresh promise. They could take one day and indulge in the fantasy, couldn't they? After all, wasn't everyone else living in a dream world today?

Jordan sniffed the air as the rich scent of coffee drifted toward her. There could be real advantages to life with a morning person. Left up to her, coffee often had to wait until she got to the office.

Will's whistle stopped, replaced by song. Jordan stretched again, then smiled. Wide. With an unaccustomed energy, she leapt from the bed and padded toward the bathroom. Moments later, she pulled back the shower curtain.

Will started at the intrusion of cold air, followed by her undoubtedly cold skin against his back.

She snuggled closer, warming herself against him.

"And good morning to you, darlin' Jordan." Rinsing the soap from his face, Will turned to her, broad smile and dimples her reward. "Merry Christmas."

Jordan wrapped her arms around his neck. "Top of the mornin' to you, Tweety Bird."

He grinned, and she plastered her body against his.

His response was instantaneous. Strong arms wrapped around her and lifted her up for a long, heated kiss, his body's reaction to her as powerful as it had been the night before.

Jordan's own hunger answered his. She wove fingers into his hair and twined one leg around his muscular thigh. As though she weighed nothing, Will pulled her higher, wrapping her legs around his waist. Pressing her back against the wall of the shower, he thrust inside her in one powerful stroke.

"Damn, I love you," he gasped, then stopped any protest with his mouth as he took her once more to the refuge only Will had ever shown her.

Jordan's ability to think incinerated in the heat of her response to his hands, his lips, the feel of him inside her. Bliss roared through her veins and snuffed out all rational thought.

In the aftermath, Will held her tightly, his heaving breath against her throat triggering tiny aftershocks that sent goose bumps over her body. He was an assault on her senses, giving her both thrilling release and a sense of safety she'd never known. Jordan tried to remember why she was bad for him, but she could only feel the sweep of delight through her body.

Will pulled back and grinned, his eyes still dark with passion but sparkling with good humor. "You have a way with a shower, Ms. Parrish. I don't believe I've ever had my back scrubbed with fingernails before."

Jordan was surprised to feel heat rush to her cheeks. She pulled away slightly.

"Don't," he admonished, refusing to let her go. "Don't ever be embarrassed with me, Jordan. There's nothing forbidden to us, and it makes me feel grand to have you lose yourself so completely."

His good humor was infectious. "As if your monumental ego needs any stroking," she complained.

Crooking one finger under her chin, he pressed a gentle kiss to her lips. "Ah, but you make a strong man weak, love."

Her mouth opened to put him on notice to protect himself, but before she could, he sidetracked her with one more quick, hard kiss.

"Now, my Delilah, let us get washed up. You have not one decent morsel in this place, and I need my strength." He paused to waggle his brows at her. "As will you." His grin killed her, just demolished her. "We'll adjourn to my place, since there are no stores open. One of us, at least, has the sense to stock up on more than yogurt."

"I wasn't planning on company."

"But you had it, anyway, now, didn't you? Enjoyed it, too, eh?" His smile was smug.

"Some people just can't take no for an answer," she grumbled.

Will turned her under the cascading water and began to soap her up. "Someone wakes up grouchy, does she? As I've not yet done enough, apparently, to remedy that, let us see what tricks I might have up my sleeve."

"You don't have any sleeves. You're naked."

"And isn't that the handiest thing?" Will's hands slicked over her body, teasing and taunting.

Jordan laughed and set her own fingers to work.

CHAPTER NINE

"Is THERE ANYTHING you don't do well?" Jordan asked, prostrate on Will's sofa after devouring a trucker-sized breakfast.

"Let me think on that, darlin'." A quick, slashing grin. "But doing so might take a while, I'm warning you."

She burst out laughing. "Careful you don't scrape that monstrous ego on the ceiling."

"Ah, but 'tis not bragging if it's true, now, is it?" He lifted her feet and sat down, then resettled them on his lap and began rubbing.

Jordan was pretty sure her eyes rolled back in her head.

"There was the one time when my sister Brigid asked me to help her fix a dye job on her hair without Mum finding out what she'd done to herself."

Jordan smiled. "And how were you as a hair-dresser?"

He shrugged. "Was it my fault that I chose to be, shall we say, creative with the mixing?" His eyes twinkled. "Brigid wound up with purple hair."

"You did that on purpose."

"So she accused. Me, I'd merely claim it as her just deserts after all the times I'd been forced to play silly girl games with her when I wanted to be out with the other lads."

"I'd bet you played those games with her because you were a good boy."

"I'm thinking you've just insulted me. I am not a tame rabbit." Then he chuckled. "Anyway, I'd like you to be telling my mum that. She'd be of a different opinion. I was a hooligan, and that's a fact."

His eyes caught hers, and warmth spread through her, a sense of contentment she'd never before experienced.

It should scare the living daylights out of her.

In some ways, it did.

"What are you thinking, love?"

Love. *I love you,* he'd said in the heat of their joining.

Oh, Will, don't do that to yourself. I won't be good for you.

"Nothing."

"Somehow I doubt that." He lifted one foot and slowly peeled down her sock like a striptease. "But whatever is putting that frown on your face, let's see if we can change it." Never taking his eyes off her, he placed a slow kiss on her arch.

Jordan's nostrils flared. She couldn't help squirming in delight.

"That's more like it," he said smugly.

"You think you have me right where you want me."

He waggled his eyebrows, then turned and began to prowl his way up her body. "And do I not?"

Jordan closed her eyes. Drank in the feel of him

popping the snap on her jeans, lowering the zipper, micron by micron. "You're killing me," she said.

He bent his head, nipped at the curve of her hip. "Now, why would I want to do that, love?"

Love. "Will…" She had to warn him. "This is just… we're only…"

His jaw tightened. "Your protests grow tiresome, Jordan. You care, I know that. I feel it. I see it in your eyes."

But I don't want to. Can't afford to. "But…" she began.

He hushed her with a kiss.

Just then, his phone rang.

"Bugger that," he muttered and melted her bones with another kiss.

The phone soon stopped. He slid his fingers into her panties, and Jordan moaned.

The phone rang again.

Will dropped his head. "'Twill be my family." Blue eyes apologized. "I must take it."

She found a smile. "I'll be right where you left me."

His eyes were serious. "Will you?"

She made her smile bright. "Are you kidding? I'm not done with you, lover boy."

He examined her closely, too closely, then shook his head. "I'll be back. Stay right there."

Then he was gone.

Jordan felt too exposed, lying there half-dressed. Quickly she pulled up her jeans, refastened them.

Her sock, though, she clasped in one hand as if she could feel the warmth of him.

And maybe transfer it into her heart.

"Yes, Mum," she heard Will say from the kitchen.

"It's only midmorning here, you know. I've not yet had Christmas dinner, but I will."

A silence. "No, I'm not alone. As a matter of fact…"

No. Jordan tensed. *Don't do it.*

"There's someone special," he finished. "You'll like her."

Will, you can't…

Bits and pieces drifted in.

"She's a lawyer."

"No, Mum. She's not Catholic. I don't think."

"I doubt she wants to live in Ireland. It's too soon to ask that." Exasperation. "Mum, you'll meet her when she's ready, not before."

Will, don't do this to yourself. To me.

A sigh. "I love her. That's all you need to know."

Jordan jumped to her feet. Slipped on her shoes. Looked around for her purse, so she could get her keys and—

Will had driven her here in his truck.

She could walk. Or call a cab. Surely they operated on Christmas Day. But she hadn't brought her phone. She'd been so sated on sex she hadn't even noticed.

With mounting horror, she listened as Will exchanged greetings with others in his family, and she heard the homesickness in his voice. Cringed when she heard herself mentioned.

She had to make him stop. Right now, before—

"Yes, Da," she heard. "There's someone special now."

A chuckle. "Not exactly. She's…maybe not the type of girl you expected me to marry, but Da, she's exactly what I want." Another pause. "No, she doesn't—I don't know. I'm working on it."

Jordan chided herself for listening in, but someone had to look out for him. His family, who obviously adored him, was too far away. They couldn't prevent him from making this mistake.

This *huge* mistake.

She had to break things off immediately, before he got more involved.

Because she couldn't bear to disappoint him, and she would. Not intentionally, no. If anyone had ever tempted her to give love a try, to forget all she knew about how it could go wrong, how unrealistic the notion was…

Will was that person.

But it would come to no good end, and that big heart of his would suffer.

She was hardly an angel, and most times she didn't really care about the fallout of her actions, but—

This was Will. She had to be better, for his sake.

Jordan watched him pace the kitchen, sometimes laughing, sometimes with the saddest expression on his face.

She wanted to run, without a word. But if she did, she was positive he would chase after her, the thick-headed fool. He brought new meaning to the word stubborn.

She would have to break his heart a little now so that later, she wouldn't break it more by not measuring up to his cockeyed vision of her.

She knew who she was.

But Will—stubborn, blind Will—refused to see it.

So she stood her ground and waited for him to get off the phone.

WILL HUNG UP AND LOOKED out the kitchen window for a moment, picturing them all there together, one big, messy crowd. The kitchen would be full of women and wonderful smells. On the stoop would be his da and grandda smoking the smelly pipes that weren't allowed inside. Outside there would be children running around, dogs barking...

What he wouldn't give to be there in the thick of it.

And how horrified would the woman in the other room be if she could see it?

A wry smile curved his lips. It would be good for her, though. Jordan Parrish was the loneliest person he'd ever met.

He glanced at the clock. He'd been invited to the Prestons and knew she had, too. Though a part of him wanted her all to himself, they were her friends, and truth be told, being there would make up for some of what he was missing back home.

He turned and walked toward the living room. "We'd best be on our way if we're to make it to—"

Jordan was not on the sofa where he'd left her. Where she'd promised to remain.

She stood near the front door, stiff and waiting. "I need to go."

It didn't take a genius to know what had happened. "Eavesdropping?" He cursed himself for speaking his heart to his family. Hadn't he known she was far from ready?

"You weren't exactly whispering."

He leaned one shoulder on the doorframe, crossed his arms over his chest. "And I take it you didn't like what you heard?"

"I can't marry you. Why would you say such a thing to them?"

"Can't…or won't?" He kept his voice resolutely casual, his smile wide to hide his sinking heart. "Perhaps I should have waited—all right," he responded to the protest springing to her lips. "I definitely should have waited, but that doesn't change the fact of what's right for us."

"You are insufferable. You couldn't be more wrong."

He advanced on her. "Lie to yourself, Jordan, but don't lie to me. There's something between us, something powerful."

She lifted one shoulder. "The sex is great, I'll admit."

"Don't you dare cheapen this by making it about sex."

"Damn you, don't do this." Her casualness vanished.

"Don't do what?" He straightened as well.

"Don't you ruin what's happened. I'm not ready to let you go yet."

"Who says it's your choice? I'm going nowhere."

"You have to now."

"Perhaps you'd care to explain that." He stepped closer.

She jammed a finger into his chest. "Back off. I warned you, Will. You can't say I didn't. If you refuse to listen and get hurt, it's not my fault."

Fury simmered. "Now who has the ego? You're so sure I can be hurt so easily?" Deliberately he kept his tone lazy and amused, though he was anything but.

"Don't you patronize me. I told you I'm not the

marrying kind. Marriage is an obsolete institution. People who like each other, who have a good time, they get married and everything goes to hell from there."

Ah. "We're not your parents, love." This was fear talking.

"Don't be a simpleton. I'm not talking about my parents. Look around you—divorce is everywhere. Marriage is a hidebound tradition that doesn't work today. People need to be free to come and go as they please."

Anger sparked again. "And being with me would diminish you somehow?"

She lifted her chin. "Yes."

"How?"

"That's not the point."

"What *is* your point, exactly?"

"I won't marry you, Will."

"I haven't asked you yet, now, have I? You're frothed up for nothing."

"Frothed up? Don't be insulting. Look, I don't want to argue. We're too different, that's all."

"Because I'm not hysterical?"

"Hysterical?" Jordan turned around and headed for the door. "I do not get hysterical. This conversation is over."

Over, was it? Be damned if it was.

In her outrage, she didn't hear his steps behind her. He closed the gap, swung her off her feet and slung her over his shoulder. "Do you think I asked to fall in love with you?" he growled. "You are a spoiled, petulant child with no more vision than an old blind dog. You refuse to see what we could have."

"Let me down, you—you baboon." Jordan pounded his back, wriggling and kicking wildly. "I hate you."

"You do not." Will dumped her on his bed.

She scrambled to her feet, and he stepped in her way. "Don't push me any further, Jordan. You sit there and you cool off."

"You're insane. Haven't you heard one word I've said?"

"If I am insane, 'tis you who's driven me there. Yes, I'm listening, but all I hear is drivel and fear."

"Fear? Me? I eat guys like you for breakfast."

He looked at the ceiling and prayed for patience. "Of course it's not men you're afraid of. It's yourself. Your brain, Jordan darlin', is your worst enemy. You think too much. Love isn't reasonable or logical. The heart doesn't care if it makes sense. The heart wants what the heart wants, it's that simple."

"The heart is only an organ that pumps blood. Everything else is self-delusion. People want to believe in that fantasy because they're afraid to be alone. It's not real." She paused for a minute, and he waited to hear what would pour out of her next.

"Look, let's be reasonable about this. You and I are different, but we have a good time together. That doesn't have to go away if you can simply accept that's all this is. We can agree to disagree about sentimental matters." He could almost see her in court as she dared him to dispute the logic of her case. "Now, I'd like to go home, please."

"What about Marly and David?"

"I'll just tell them I don't feel well." Her chin jutted. "It won't be a lie."

"This is a mistake," he said quietly.

"It is."

He was certain they didn't mean the same thing.

"I won't come after you again, Jordan. The next move is up to you."

Her eyes were huge and dark and serious. "It doesn't have to be this way."

"Relationships have to grow…or they die." Couldn't she see what she was doing to them? What they could be? "Don't act like a child." *Please*. But he was sick to death of being the only one to believe.

Jordan watched him, and in her eyes, he thought he saw the stirrings of doubt, perhaps of regrets. "I wish I could make you understand," she said so faintly it was barely a whisper.

"What I understand is that you're going to let your fears win."

He saw her flinch from his words, but she didn't argue. Instead she put one hand on the doorknob. "Shall I call a cab?"

His heart was lead. "Very well," he said stiffly. "Suit yourself." He drew his keys from his pocket and reached past her to open the door for her.

The way a man did for the woman he loved, Will thought bitterly.

But he wouldn't beg for her to love him back.

CHAPTER TEN

FOR THE NEXT THREE DAYS, Jordan worked like a maniac.

But she also checked her phone obsessively.

Will never called.

Well, that's good, isn't it? She asked her reflection in the gym mirror. *It's exactly what you wanted.*

The ache in her chest weighed a hundred pounds.

She felt like a kid who'd given away her favorite toy. She hadn't understood how much Will had brightened her life until he was gone.

But she was the only one who understood that this could only end badly. She'd had no choice, once he started spouting foolishness about marriage, to end things before she inflicted damage he couldn't bear.

Because for all his great strength, Will's heart was soft and unprotected. She could live with most of what she'd done in her life, but she couldn't live with knowing she'd damaged that beautiful heart of his.

She'd done the right thing, Jordan knew that. What she hadn't counted on was how much she would hurt.

And the only person she wanted to turn to for comfort was the one she'd had to shove away.

Jordan ratcheted up the angle on the treadmill. She would get past this. She would sweat Will out of her system. She would get back in fighting trim, be back out in the game any day.

Fiona stepped on the machine beside her. "Hi— Wow, what's wrong?"

"What? Nothing."

"Then why are you crying?"

Jordan reached up, horrified to feel wet cheeks. "It's nothing."

"This is me, girlfriend. I can count the number of times I've seen you cry on one…actually, I've never seen you cry. What gives?"

"I don't want to talk about it."

"It's that guy, isn't it? Will?"

"I don't know what you're talking about."

"Oh, lordy." Fiona hit the stop button on both machines, then grabbed Jordan's arm. "Come on."

Jordan shook her off. "I'm busy."

"I don't care." Fiona practically dragged her off the treadmill. Once they were inside the locker room with no one around, Fiona faced her friend. "Spill."

"There's nothing to say."

"Sure there's not." Fiona studied her. She opened her mouth, then snapped it shut. Shook her head. "It has to be love. Nothing else makes a person so miserable. So do I need to kick his ass?"

"No!" Jordan subsided immediately. "The fault isn't his, it's mine." Misery swamped her, enough so she made a painful admission. "I'm not in love. I can't be."

"Why not?"

"Because I'll screw it up."

"Why do you say that?"

"I can't make Will happy. He needs a Marly. He

deserves one, damn it. I can't be like her." Her chin jutted forward. "I don't even want to." But she knew she was lying. If she could be a Marly, she would.

"Has he asked you to?" Fiona sounded enraged. "Because I'll march right over and read him the riot act. You're just fine as you are."

Jordan sagged. "That's what he said."

"Then what's the problem?"

"If you knew him, you wouldn't ask. He's this cheerful giant who works magic with wood, who deserves babies on his lap and gardens full of flowers and some little cottage with hand-braided rugs on the floor. That's not me, Fee."

She began to pace. "I'm a hard-nosed lawyer. I eat nails for breakfast. I party all night, and Will's up with the sun. I like bad boys and loud music. He talks like a damn poet. He's too patient, too cheerful. I'm bad-tempered and impatient, and I'm not going to change."

"Honey—" There was laughter in Fiona's voice. "That's it?"

"It's not a joke. Anyway, it's over and just as well. We're completely ill-suited. I wear Armani suits and he doesn't even own a tie, I don't think."

"Ah, so you're ashamed of him."

"Of course not." Jordan rounded on her. "I'm not a snob. I just…" Tears welled in the corners of her eyes. "I don't know how to fit him in, Fee. And I would screw it up, I know it. I'd feel like crap because he's such a good man, but I'd still do it. Sooner or later, I'd get restless and want to be out all night, and he'd be making hot chocolate and just want to rub my feet or something. He'd be miserable, and I'd never forgive myself."

Fiona put her hands on Jordan's shoulders. "My grandmother used to call what you're doing borrowing trouble. Can't you just see how this plays out before you declare it a disaster?"

"You don't understand. He came to my house on Christmas Eve dressed up as Santa and brought me a jewelry box he'd made himself. It's museum-quality stuff, Fee. And inside it was this necklace." She brought the piece out from beneath her old T-shirt. She should have taken it off, given it back…but she just couldn't.

Fiona touched it gingerly. "It's exquisite."

"He kissed me and made my toes curl. Made love to me until I lost my mind. But then he told his family he was going to marry me."

"Well, then. He obviously deserves to be shot."

"It's not funny."

Fiona rubbed her arm. "I can see that. What did you do?"

"I told him all the reasons why marriage is stupid. I mean, if even Marly and David can't make it…"

"Are you kidding me? Jordan, you're reading a lot into what Marly said. Marriage isn't a cakewalk, no, but they'll be just fine."

"She's not happy, and she's the most content person I ever met—well, except for Will, maybe."

Fiona shook her head. "She's going through a stage. We all do. People do—not just married people."

"But what if they can't fix it? Marly's ten times—a hundred times the woman I am."

"Honey…" Fiona stroked Jordan's hair. "You're smarter than this. So have you seen Will since?"

"No."

"Have you called him?"

"I don't want to talk about this anymore. It's over, the end. For once in my life, I'm trying to be noble. Leave this, Fee."

"Just answer me one question first. How does he make you feel?"

Jordan sighed loudly. "He's not just great in bed. It's not just the sex this time. He makes me feel so…cherished, so…special." Then she burst into tears again.

"And that's bad because…?"

"I'll ruin it. I won't mean to, but somehow I will. I'm not good at this, and Will deserves someone amazing." She shoved past her friend. "I don't want to talk about it anymore. Hard as it may be to believe, I'm thinking of someone besides myself for a change."

"Jordan," Fiona said. "Don't be an idiot. Don't walk away because you're scared."

"Too late," Jordan whispered as she gathered her things to go. "I already did."

"Jordan…"

But she rushed out before Fiona could say more.

ON NEW YEAR'S EVE at the Preston house, Will strummed his guitar dispiritedly out on the porch after just finishing a fast-moving set of Irish tunes he'd played for the assortment of guests.

The party resembled what people called ceilidh in his country—a gathering of friends and neighbors where music reigned, where everyone danced and brought food, where friendship and community was celebrated.

He'd never felt lonelier in his life.

Not that Jordan would fit in, he told himself. Oh, she cared enough about the Prestons that she'd pretend she was enjoying herself, but this was not her type of gathering. Most likely she was in some hot, crowded, smoky club right now, gyrating that beautiful body with one nameless man or another, teasing them, letting them put their hands on her, draw her close when they hadn't the first notion of how to care for her—

He gripped the neck of his guitar, seized by an unbearable urge to smash it on the porch rail.

"Will?" A sweet voice from behind him. *Marly.*

He exhaled. Eased his grip.

Jordan had said they were too different. Thought that she could simply walk away, that she could discard his love like it was nothing.

Then be damned to you, Jordan Parrish.

A small hand touched his shoulder, and he whirled on her.

Marly took a step back, and he was instantly ashamed. "I'm sorry." He set down his guitar and held up his hands. "I truly am—I don't—" Never in his life had he felt so out of control. So damned much pain.

Her eyes were soft and sympathetic as she approached him. "Are you all right? I saw you out here and you looked so…" She paused. "Is it Jordan?"

He looked away, unable to stem a bitter laugh. "'Tis my own fault."

"Why?"

"I—There's no point."

"Will…"

He steeled himself against her pity. "It isn't as though she didn't warn me, the blasted fool woman." His mouth twisted. "Though it's me who's the real fool."

"Are you?"

He glanced back in surprise.

"She's scared, Will, that's all."

"I know that, but—" Again he shook his head. "She's also right. We're nothing alike. She would hate my life."

"Does she have to live it?"

He frowned. "What do you mean?"

"Does it have to be your way or hers?"

Will stared at Marly. "The life she's living isn't good for her."

Marly's head tilted. "So Jordan's the one who has to change?"

He looked at Jordan's friend, but he was really seeing Jordan herself, remembering how she'd focused so hard on turning the newel post. How proud she'd been. "She would be happier."

But would she really? he asked himself for the first time. He thought about how little he'd questioned her about her work, how he didn't really know what she liked about her career or even how she'd come to choose it.

And being with me would diminish you? he'd asked, so certain that couldn't be the case, that he was offering her something far better.

He considered his conversation with his da on Christmas. *Son, only make certain that you respect the differences between you. Our way does not have to be yours.*

Hadn't he said that very thing to his family again and again? *I can't come back, Mum. I have a different life now.*

Yet he'd recreated most of his past life here on foreign shores, and he'd expected Jordan to fit into it. He'd told her he didn't expect her to be a Marly, but he'd never considered accepting her lifestyle for himself.

"She likes some of it," he defended himself. But how much of it would truly suit her? Was it only a changed Jordan he wanted? His own image of who she should be?

"What time is it?" he asked Marly.

"Just after ten-thirty."

Thirty minutes to get to her place. Less than an hour after that it would be midnight, and she could be in any number of clubs. Austin was a big town with endless venues for entertainment.

He wanted to be with her when the year turned. Needed to start the new year fresh, to tell her he'd been wrong, to see if there was a second chance for them.

Before it was too late.

Before her midnight kiss was with someone else, someone wrong for her.

And you've been so right for her, my lad?

He would be. Of that he'd make certain.

But where would he find her? How could he locate her in time?

"I have to go." He was desperate to find her before midnight. "Do you know her favorite clubs?" Shame on him that he didn't.

All he'd done was ask her to give up her life.

Marly gave him two names. "They're both close to her place. I'll ask Fee and our kids. Someone may know others. But check your cell, since the noise will be deafening down there."

He raced for the door, then abruptly stopped. Turned

and kissed Marly's cheek. "Thank you. Wish me luck."

"I do."

"I'll likely need it."

She smiled. "That you will."

He smiled back. "Whatever it takes, she's worth it."

THE MUSIC WAS HOT AND LOUD, just the way Jordan liked it. The driving beat of the drums vibrated through her body, the wailing guitar notes sizzled up her spine. All around her, people were having a great time, anticipation high as the midnight hour approached.

A new year. Ergo, a new beginning.

Why did everyone always believe that?

Most people kept going in their same old tracks, year after year. Their lives were no different on January first than they'd been at the end of December. So what made them hope? Simple delusion?

Your brain, Jordan darlin', is your worst enemy. Love isn't reasonable or logical.

Jordan halted in place, buffeted around by bodies on all sides.

Just answer me one question first. How does he make you feel? Fiona had asked.

Her so-called dance partner, a man she'd never seen before a few minutes ago, reached out to pull her close.

Jordan recoiled. When his grip tightened on her waist, she turned and used her elbow to get free.

"Hey! What the hell did you do that for?"

She could barely hear him and knew she couldn't make clear what she didn't know. All she was sure of was that she wanted out of here. Now. She turned to leave.

"Hey, wait!" he yelled behind her, but Jordan pushed her way through the crowd, her agitation increasing with every step. Clawing her way out, she felt as if she couldn't breathe.

Finally, she made it to the edge, gasping for air, her heart pounding wildly.

A lanky, pony-tailed biker appeared before her, eyes bleary. "Whassa matter, babe? Your date play rough? You can come with me."

She evaded his grasp. And tried to tamp down the thought that not long ago, she might have gone with him.

She had to get outside. Desperately. She couldn't think, could barely breathe, she needed—

Jordan suddenly stopped, her mind catching up with the frenetic whirl she'd been in since Christmas.

Will. She needed Will.

Outside the building, she leaned against the wall for a second, stunned. She could have been with Will tonight, but she'd closed the door on him at Christmas.

Because he'd said he loved her.

Because he wanted her to say goodbye to a life of easy conquests and meaningless encounters.

Because he'd asked her to belong to him.

But how could she be sure she could make him happy? Sure, she could try to change. And she would, for Will. But she was thirty-six years old, and people her age didn't change, not really. There was a purity in his heart that she'd tarnish if she ever got too close. She'd accepted it long ago—born to be bad.

So why didn't she go back to that club and dance the night away?

Because, she realized, she'd be less alone all by herself.

How she wished Will was with her right now—she'd love to just hear his voice. She'd let him sweet-talk her with that damned silver tongue of his. If anyone she knew had kissed the Blarney Stone, it had to be Will Masterson.

He might be at Marly's. She could try to call, but first she'd have to get where she could hear. Sixth Street was mayhem this close to midnight.

Her place was nearby. Jordan began running, darting through the crowd, skirting the drunks, avoiding the hands poised to grab.

Everyone wanted their midnight kiss. In years past, she'd shared many of them.

Every one meaningless.

Will, she thought. *I want Will.* If only she hadn't been so blasted stubborn. No, she wasn't right for him, maybe. And she didn't know how to believe in love.

But oh, how he made her want to.

How does he make you feel?

Amazing, she thought. Special. Like he can't see anything else when he's with me.

I love you, Jordan.

Oh, God. What had she done?

"Hey, baby—" Someone reached for her.

Jordan shoved him away, kept moving.

An ugly name followed her, but she didn't care.

Jordan sniffled, then realized her face was wet with tears. Damn him, damn him, damn him. What a way to start the new year, acting like some lovesick calf over a man who was her polar opposite, who didn't even care enough to come after her.

She smacked headlong into someone. "Sorry—"

Hands grabbed her. She shoved back.

"Jordan, darlin, it's me."

Her head shot up. "Will? What are you doing here?"

"Looking for you." But this was not the jovial Will she knew who stood in front of her now.

"Really? Why?"

He only stared at her for a long moment, then drew her off to the side. He said something but she couldn't hear him.

"What?"

He glanced up impatiently, searching the crowded street. One big hand locked around her wrist, he towed her along carefully until they reached the side street.

Halfway down the block, she dug in her heels. "Stop. What's wrong with you?"

He turned on her, his eyes anything but the cocky, cheerful ones she was used to.

"I should have listened to you."

"To me?" She went very still as the meaning of his expression sank in. *Here it comes. He doesn't love me. I've finally realized I love him just as he's accepted what I've been telling him about how wrong we are for each other.* Panic skittered up her spine. "Will…"

"What do you like best about your work?"

"What?" She stared at him in confusion.

"Tell me why you became a lawyer."

"Why?"

"I don't really know you."

Irritation stirred, and it felt much better than fear.

"That never bothered you before." She poked him in the chest with one finger. "I've said that again and again, haven't I? But you keep telling me you understand me better than I do myself." She stuck out her chin, waited for him to argue like always.

When he didn't, that worried her like nothing else. Her heart plummeted. "I don't want you to know all about me." She stared at her feet. "You won't want me then." And she wouldn't be able to bear it. She turned blindly to flee from the pain crowding her chest.

He grabbed her before she could escape. "What is it you want, Jordan? Answer me that."

She didn't know this Will. He looked so weary, so serious. She longed to stroke his face, to run her fingers through his hair. To turn him back into the arrogant, cheery giant.

To cuddle against him.

She shivered at his distant manner. "What I want doesn't matter. You know I can't be your Marly and—"

"I never asked you to."

She plunged ahead without listening. "—I would if I could, but— What did you just say?"

"I don't need you to be a Marly."

"But…" She frowned. "You're meant for someone exactly like that, someone who can do all those things like cook and garden and—" She burst into tears. "I'm not that kind of person. Damn you, I wasn't supposed to fall in love. I don't know how to be any good at it." She swiped at her runny nose. "This is all your fault," she blubbered.

Will reached in his pocket and brought out a hand-kerchief, wiping tenderly at her tears, then handing it to her so she could blow her nose. "What is?" he asked cautiously.

"That nothing fits anymore. That my loft is too noisy, that I don't want to dance with strangers, that—" She broke off at the sound of the crowd behind them chanting.

"Ten…nine…"

"Oh, no!" she wailed.

"What is it? What's wrong?" He moved closer.

"We— I— It's too soon!"

"For what?"

"I really, really wanted to kiss you at midnight, but now everything's a mess. And *you*—you want to *talk* about things," she spat.

She thought she saw his lips curve a little but still he didn't speak.

"Eight…seven…"

Desperation took over. "You know what? I don't care. I *am* all wrong for you and you're not my type, but—but—too bad. I love you, Will Masterson. Deal with it!"

He only stared at her, and dread ran roughshod over her fear.

"Six…five…"

"Okay, okay!" She threw up her hands. "I—I like the battle of wits with the opposing counsel. And I—I became a lawyer because, because…well, I really don't know why. I was just good at dissecting an argument. Not that you can tell that at the moment," she muttered. Then she glared at him. "Now would you please just kiss me?"

"Four…three…"

His lips twitched but still he didn't move. "You mean that? You love me?" he asked.

"Yes! What did I just say? Will, *please*—" Blast the man. Would he never—

Jordan reached up to take matters into her own hands.

Before she could, Will crushed her against him, then laid on her a scorching kiss, one that was everything she'd ever hoped to feel of home and welcome and beginnings.

Jordan's knees turned to water. *I didn't ruin it.*

She drew back to be sure. "I didn't ruin it, right?"

Will smiled wide and clear as he shook his head. "You never had a prayer of escaping me, Jordan darlin'."

"You arrogant—" She started to argue for form's sake, then thought better of it. They would argue again, probably often, but tonight…tonight was for lovers. For hope.

For new beginnings. And if that meant she was as delusional as she'd accused others of being, well, so what? Everything seemed possible now.

With bone-deep gratitude for stubborn Irishmen and second chances, Jordan rose to her toes and tightened her arms around Will's neck. He picked her up and twirled her.

"One!" the crowd screamed. Fireworks crackled in the sky. Horns blared.

But Jordan and Will were oblivious to anything but each other.

Far too busy laughing their way into midnight's kiss.

* * * * *

This story is for Jenn, because she gets me.

MIDNIGHT ASSIGNMENT

Victoria Dahl

CHAPTER ONE

"I'M NOT GOING TO LET you screw this up, Noah James, is that clear?"

Noah ignored the question and watched Elise Watson's sweet little backside as she walked ahead of him. Each of her long strides turned the gray conservative skirt into an intriguingly tight scrap of fabric before it relaxed into boring wool again. Then her next step would stretch it tight for another brief moment, cupping her muscles like a—

Elise stopped so suddenly that he almost crashed into her.

"I said, *is that clear?*"

By the time she'd spun toward him, Noah had forced his gaze higher, and he managed to meet her eyes with a cool glare. He, after all, hadn't been the one to screw things up the first time around. Elise had definitely been the one who'd caused that damage. She'd started the kind of trouble for him that had lasted two long years. Trouble that hadn't ended until he'd stolen the Denver job out from under her nose and gotten the hell out of D.C.

She was still pissed about losing the job, and her anger gave Noah an excuse to smile. "Whatever you say, Elise."

Her mouth tightened at his insolent tone. Her eyes

narrowed. Elise Watson was about to lose her temper, and the agents waiting ahead of them in the hotel lobby were cringing visibly in anticipation. When she lost her temper, heads rolled, and Noah knew she'd be pleased as punch if it was his head bouncing across the faded blue of the hotel carpet.

But hotel carpet it was, and he saw the moment Elise remembered they were in public. She couldn't scream and cuss and threaten death, or the hotel staff might suspect that they weren't really there for an emergency corporate meeting for a company called Workfire Industries. They'd already strained belief by holding their fake meeting two days after Christmas. If their supposed CEO started cursing like a sailor, punching Noah in the chest with her finger, suspicions would be raised. So her temper was thwarted. Noah was safe.

Plus, he reminded himself, he was armed. Surely one five-foot-seven-in-heels woman couldn't hurt him. Physically.

She leaned a little closer, her green eyes ablaze with violence, but before she could speak, someone else called out.

"Hey, Noah James!" Tex Harrison called. He was a forensic computer analyst, and though he looked like a scrawny seventeen-year-old boy trying to grow a beard, he was a genius. A perverted genius. Noah bit back a groan.

"Noah, I heard you got an invite to party with the flight attendant team from your flight. Where are they staying?"

Glaring, he gave a quick shake of his head, but Elise's eyes slid back to him and caught the movement.

"That's not true," he said, as if it could possibly matter to her.

She swept him with a scornful look. "The bank closes in five minutes. I want your team in place in four."

"Don't worry about my team."

"I swear to God you missed that flight just to make my life harder." The frustration on her face softened to compassion for a fleeting moment. "These people are about to have a very bad evening. The least we can do is handle this quickly and smoothly."

Noah clenched his teeth. "The flight was canceled. I briefed my team at the airport while we waited. If anything goes wrong, it won't be on our watch."

"You'd better hope not. Or you're going to regret the time you put into flirting with flight attendants instead of prepping for the job." With that, she swung around and stalked out to the tiny lobby.

Noah watched the rest of the team jump at some quiet word from her. She was sharp and exacting and one of the smartest people he'd ever met. She demanded excellence and expected miracles, and everyone on her team knew it.

She was damn good at what she did, and that made him crazy. After all, it would've been easy to get her out of his head if she weren't as sharp as a razor blade. That kind of weapon sunk deep and true. His only consolation was that since moving to Denver, he didn't waste so much time looking up whenever the elevator door opened, just in case it was Elise wandering down to his floor.

Noah followed the rest of the team toward the door, sparing a second to glare promises of retribution at Tex.

But Tex was busy hitting on one of the new girls and he only gave Noah a distracted wave in response.

Taking a deep breath, Noah looked down at his watch. Three minutes.

"It's time," he said, and his second in command stepped up to his side.

They both unsnapped the guards on their holsters but left the safety on their weapons.

Elise tossed him a glance. He gave a careful nod in answer and they both stepped toward the door, confident the other ten team members would follow. Ten more were assembled in the conference room, waiting for the signal to go, and two more teams were stationed outside the other two branches of the bank.

"Mrs. Smith!" a perky blonde receptionist called out as they moved past.

At the sound of the name she'd assumed for the case, Elise paused, her brown hair swinging forward as if she wanted to keep moving. "Yes?"

"Are you sure you guys want to go out in the cold? It'll be below zero by eight o'clock. We've got an arrangement with the local market, and I'd be happy to have dinner sent over. Maybe sandwiches or barbecue?"

"No, thank you. We're fine."

"Oh. Well... All right. It's just so weird to have a conference and no food service, but I guess, if it's an emergency meeting, like you said..."

Elise stared at the girl as if she were speaking another language. The girl's face turned pink, and Noah watched as Elise physically braced herself for the kind of polite talk people in places like Omaha expected. "Thank you so much for the offer, but we're fine. We'll have dinner out and then we'll be back for another meeting later, so keep the coffee brewing."

"Oh, I'll get some fresh cookies in the oven!" the receptionist responded.

Noah almost laughed out loud at the horrified expression on Elise's face. "That won't be necessary."

The men and women around her groaned.

"But…they're complimentary," the girl murmured in disbelief, but Elise was already walking away.

Noah rolled his eyes at her before following Elise out the door. "Make the cookies," he tossed over his shoulder, happy to needle Elise any way he could.

The frigid Omaha air hit him with a cruel blow as they stepped past the heated comfort of the lobby. He was used to the occasional arctic cold front, but Elise shivered as she raised a phone to her ear.

Noah listened while she checked in with each team. Behind her, downtown Omaha rose, huddled against the dreary twilight. The sight made the air feel colder, so Noah slid his eyes toward their target.

The main branch of the bank was directly across the street, though Noah would be making trips to the other two branches soon enough. This branch looked cozy and cheerful in the darkening evening. The desks inside were decked out in faux pine boughs and holly, and a few employees moved behind the glass, waiting for the clock to strike six and send them back home to their families. One of the tellers wore a Santa hat.

In a moment, Noah and all the rest were going to rush in and change their lives. He watched twinkling Christmas lights come to life in the plate glass windows of the bank. To Noah, the sight was the opposite of cheerful.

Elise snapped her phone shut. "All teams are in place. Is everyone ready? Let's go."

They were only a few hundred feet away, but they needed their equipment, so they slipped into two black SUVs and pulled out onto the street to drive straight across. The team in the conference room of the hotel wouldn't be needed for another five minutes, so they hung back.

Just as Elise slid out of the truck, the security guard approached the doors to shut the bank for the night. Elise reached into her pocket and moved forward. Ten feet from the door, Noah stepped into place beside her and signaled his men to stay close. The guard's eyes widened. He froze for a second, then swept his hand toward the lock on the glass doors, fear taking his mouth in a grimace that looked a lot like a smile.

Elise pulled her hand from her pocket and pressed the black square against the door. Metal clanked. The gold badge glinted its reflection against the glass. "Sir," she said so firmly that the man stood straighter, even as his expression limped toward confusion. "Please step away from the door."

The guard lurched back, Elise pushed open the doors, and they were in control of the bank. Just like that.

ELISE LOOKED AROUND at the frightened people and felt her gut clench, but she didn't let even a hint of pain show on her face. Yes, they were scared, but truthfully, they were better off now than they had been ten minutes ago. Platte Regional Bank had been teetering on the edge of collapse for months. Now the last tether holding them in place was about to snap, and Elise and her fellow FDIC agents were here to save this place from smashing into ruin.

"I'm Elise Watson, assistant director with the Federal Deposit Insurance Corporation. The FDIC has determined that Platte Regional Bank has become critically undercapitalized and is at immediate risk of collapse. In order to prevent this collapse, we have assumed control of the bank and all its assets and liabilities. As of 6:00 p.m., you are all employees of the FDIC."

Elise ignored the gasps around her and hurried on. "No one has lost his or her job. Your pay will remain the same until the new buyer takes control of the bank. And you do have a buyer. The new owner will be Simpson Finance, and they have assured us that once the riskiest assets are underwritten by the FDIC, the bank will be in sound financial condition and none of the branches will close. I know this is frightening news, but..." Her throat dried. Elise was at a loss, as she always was once she reached this part of the speech. She didn't know how to connect with people or offer comfort.

Unable to pull the right words from her brain, Elise turned helplessly toward Lara, the head of the human resources team. Lara stepped forward with a smile that promised comfort and understanding to all who walked near her outstretched arms.

"Most of you can go home in just a few minutes," Lara started. "The bank will open at its normal hour tomorrow, and your jobs will be here waiting for you. In fact, we can expect it to be quite busy. I'm here to answer any and every question you might have, but first I want to reassure you—"

Elise slipped toward the hallway on her right, knowing she'd left the employees in good hands. Lara was only twenty-eight, but she oozed assurance like a veteran mother hen. People loved and trusted her. People did not love and trust Elise. She knew about football and finances and accounting. She did not know how to make her face show the things she was feeling inside.

But she was good at taking control. She could run a team of fifty people with efficiency and confidence. She could choose the right people for the right positions. She was damn good at her job. And lately that was all she was good at.

Passing a large room filled with half a dozen computers and just as many agents, Elise raised her eyebrows in Tex's direction. He gave her a smile and sauntered over, letting his eyes drag down her body with a comically lecherous look.

"Cut it out," she said quietly, "or I'll write you up."

"God, you are so sexy when you lie."

He was right about the lying, unfortunately. She'd never write him up. He was her best source of comic relief on stressful trips. "You've got everything under control?"

"All clear here, boss. I'll let you know if we run into any trouble."

"Good." She moved on, totally comfortable with Tex's assurances. Hound dog, he might be, but she trusted him completely on the job.

Her last stop was the bank president's office, and Noah James stood straight in the doorway, his strong shoulders promising safety.

Noah was second in command at his branch office, but on this job, he was head of security, both physical and electronic, and he answered to her.

Despite their difficult history, she was glad to have him on the team. He was cool and calm and so smart he scared her. Or...he did something else to her that made her heart beat and her skin prickle and her breath come faster. To tell the truth, she knew it wasn't fear. She hadn't been the least bit afraid of him on their first job together.

Elise shook off that memory and took a deep breath before stepping into the office. She had to slide past his back to fit into the crowded room, and her arm tingled where it rubbed him. That tingle spread through her whole body, like fingers dragging down her skin, but Elise ignored it.

The chemistry was...a phantom. An illusion. Because true chemistry couldn't be one-sided and there was no doubt this was.

"All right, Mrs. Castle," Elise said. "Your staff is in good hands, and they'll all be back at work tomorrow morning."

The white-haired old woman behind the desk nodded, and when she smiled, half her skin seemed to disappear into the wrinkles. Elise had been shocked at her first sight of this frail old woman, and she only grew more surprised. The woman had to be close to ninety. Her son, standing behind her, was at least fifty-five. He put his hand on his mother's shoulder.

"Mother!" John Castle shouted.

Elise and everyone else in the room jumped in shock.

"Everyone still has a job!"

"Oh, that's good," she said.

Elise couldn't help the way her gaze slid over to meet Noah's pale blue eyes. He looked as dumbfounded as she did.

"Except us," the son sighed.

Elise cut her eyes toward him and then back to Noah. He gave a barely discernable nod and turned toward the vice-president of the bank. "Mr. Castle, can we speak in your office? There are some questions we need answered."

The man's shoulders slumped. "Of course."

When Noah left with Mr. Castle, it was just Elise and one other agent left with the bank president, Mrs. Amelia T. Castle.

All the documents indicated that Mrs. Castle still ran the bank. She'd been president since 1971 when her husband had died. Her signature appeared on every important document to this day. A stack of papers sat in the middle of her desk, and as far as Elise could tell, the woman had been in the office all day.

But Elise was having a hell of a time accepting that Mrs. Castle could have had a hand in deciding to pursue the high-risk loans that had eventually crumbled the foundation of the sixty-year-old bank.

"Mrs. Castle?" Elise cleared her throat and tried to speak more loudly. "Did you understand what I told you earlier about the auction?"

"Of course I did, dear. Would you like a piece of candy?" She held out a bowl filled with the kind of old-fashioned ribbon candy they used to sell at general stores.

"No, thank you. I just want you to be aware that on

January 4 the bank will have a new owner. Simpson Finance."

The woman's eyes closed for a moment, and her smile finally faded. "Yes, I know. Simpson Finance. They took over a bank in Lincoln last year, and they're still up and running. It'll be fine, I suppose. It's time for me to retire. I just worry about my little Johnny."

Little Johnny? "Yes, well… I'm sure he'll land on his feet. He seems like a smart…boy."

"Oh, he is."

A smart boy who was old enough to be a grandfather himself. Elise straightened her spine. This woman was the president of the bank and there were rules to be followed. Ninety years old or not, Mrs. Castle was going to get the spiel.

"Starting tonight, our forensic accountants will begin reviewing every account at this bank in an attempt to give the purchasing financial institution the most accurate account of bank assets—"

"Oh, I should hope so."

"I should warn you…" Elise swallowed the sour taste in her mouth. She felt like she was threatening someone's nana. "That any serious discrepancies will be turned over to federal prosecutors for further investigation and possible criminal charges."

"Well, I've nothing to worry about there, my dear. Of course I don't."

"Your customers' accounts are safe, up to and including the maximum amounts insured by the FDIC, and we will be here from 8:00 a.m. to 6:00 p.m. to assure every one of your customers of the safety of their deposits. However, once you are escorted from the premises, you will not be allowed to return unless you're under the supervision of Mr. James or one of his team."

She paused and searched Mrs. Castle's face for some sign that she understood the permanence of all this. But Elise could make out nothing beyond the powdered, papery skin and the deep lines that framed her mouth and eyes.

A small, tasteful Christmas tree glowed behind her, the halo of white lights making the whole scene that much more surreal. Just as Elise decided that nothing was getting through to her, Mrs. Castle sighed.

"I suppose you'd better find me a good box, then. I've got to start packing."

Hoping the woman's gray eyes were simply watery with age and not grief, Elise nodded as she stepped out into the hall to call for a box. In the relative quiet of the hallway, she took a moment to remind herself that this was one of the happy endings. Yes, she was firing this sweet old lady, and John Castle would lose his job, as well, but the rest of these people would start the new year with a paycheck. So when a junior team member hurried over with a box, Elise forced herself to walk calmly into Mrs. Castle's office and help her begin to pack. She could do this for her, at least.

Then the long hard work of combing through the accounting would begin.

CHAPTER TWO

IT ALWAYS FELT GHOULISH taking over someone's abandoned office. Elise had refused to take Amelia Castle's office, so she'd been left with John's instead.

Seven hours into the takeover, she was too tired to sit down, so she stood at the black window and stared out. The cold glass poured icy air over her face, helping to rouse her a little. Blinking lights lit up the neighborhood beyond the parking lot. Wreaths hung on the doors. Most of the windows were dark now, but the houses still looked cozy.

Families were in those homes, exhausted from the holidays. Happy and tired. Elise wished she were at home. Better yet, she wished she could go back two days to Christmas itself and curl up on the chair in front of her little fireplace. Or best of all, she'd return to a previous Christmas where she could be with her dad. She missed him so much.

The one place she didn't want to be during the holidays was here, at this bank, stuck in close quarters with Noah James.

"Someone's funneling money out of this bank."

She jumped in shock and knocked her head into the glass. "What?"

"Are you okay?"

She waved an impatient hand as she turned toward

Noah. He stood in the doorway like an avenging financial angel. Hopefully he couldn't see the forehead print of makeup she'd left on the glass behind her. "What did you say?"

"There are discrepancies. They're small but consistent."

"Seriously? Someone's embezzling from *this* bank?"

"Money is missing."

"How much?" she demanded.

"The individual amounts are small enough not to draw attention, but I don't have a definite figure yet."

"So, not a lot. Come on, Noah. Even I can tell these people are apple-pie, small-town folks."

"Small-town folks are no different than you big-city types, Elise. Some are good, some bad."

"Do *not* try to tell me old lady Castle is a bad seed. For God's sake, I thought she was going to make me a sandwich!"

He shrugged, the hardness of his face not even hinting at softening. "If not Mrs. Castle, then her son. You don't really think she's been running things, do you?"

Elise frowned down at her coffee cup, feeling suddenly exhausted. She liked these people. The old woman who still came to the office every day. The son who'd come in to help carefully pack up his mother's office. They were real people. Good people. Elise *needed* them not to have dark, hidden sides. It was just too damn close to Christmas to deal with that kind of crap. "She claims to still be in charge of day-to-day operations."

"John Castle says he started taking over some responsibilities in 1998."

"Regardless, I don't believe the Castles were stealing money from the bank."

"When did you grow a heart?"

She snapped her head up and glared. "Excuse me?"

"And a soft one at that."

"There's never been even a hint of suspicion about their business practices. They've filed every report we've asked, taken every measure we've suggested and—"

"There's a hint now. I'm heading over to the other branches to make sure everything is running smoothly, but when I come back, I'm going to concentrate my efforts on those missing funds."

"Fine." She closed her eyes. He thought *she* was heartless? He was an ice-cold bastard and always had been. "But you're wasting your time." *I hope.*

"Wanna bet?"

She rolled her neck, trying to ease some of the strain from it. It was one in the morning, and though she'd started sending team members back to the hotel in shifts, she was going to be here until 6:00 p.m. the next day. "Sure. I'll take that bet, if only to teach you a lesson in humility. And *heart*. How much?"

"Oh, I didn't say anything about money, Elise."

Her weariness vanished like a popping bubble, and her head snapped up. He'd said her name like a dare, as if he meant to demand something from her. A forfeit. A prize. A kiss.

Ridiculous. His face didn't hint at anything more than anger.

His gaze dipped for a split second, brushing over her mouth.

"Um…"

He just stared, ignoring her uncomfortable squirm.

"Not money?"

He raised his eyebrows. "No."

This uncertainty pissed her off. Elise set her jaw. "What, then? Are you going to lay your manly pride down on the table as a prize?"

His eyebrows lowered. Two spots of pink burned into his cheekbones.

Oh. Elise took a deep breath and replayed her words in her mind. She couldn't stop her face from heating. "I mean…not your…I meant…"

"My pride, huh?" he said roughly. His gaze slipped down her face, and for one frightening, exhilarating second, she was sure he was glaring right at her mouth. Then he smirked. "Yeah, sure. Why the hell not? I've managed to restock. Pride, it is."

Elise's mind spun, and by the time she'd righted herself, the doorway was empty and Noah was gone. She pressed her fingertips to her mouth and cursed. Kissing that man had been a horrible, awful mistake. Even two years later she couldn't quite believe she'd done it.

This was going to be one hell of a long week, and with Noah James around, she wouldn't get one second to relax. He'd make sure of it.

CHAPTER THREE

EXHAUSTION FELT LIKE anger. At least it always had to Noah. He'd been working for more than twenty-four hours without a break, and he'd been awake much longer than that. Now as he stared at the man standing before him in the parking lot, all Noah wanted to do was yell.

He didn't.

"Sir, the bank is closed for the evening, but it will open again at eight tomorrow morning, just like always. I promise you that your money is safe."

The middle-aged man waved a pillowcase around and screamed that he wasn't going to let the government steal his hard-earned cash. Noah tuned him out and watched the tirade turn to clouds of white in the frigid night. Man, it was cold. His own breath froze against his lips like dry ice. He wanted to be anywhere but here, being yelled at by a stranger.

Maybe exhaustion wasn't anger, maybe it was just a need to escape. Or maybe it was irritating intro-spection.

He stifled a yawn.

A security guard approached the door from inside the bank, and Noah waved him off before returning his attention to the irate customer. "Sir, I understand your frustration, but the bank closed two minutes ago. Not because we're shutting it down, but because of normal business hours. If you'll—"

The bank door opened, and Noah turned to snap at the security guard, but found himself scowling at Elise Watson. Well, what the hell. She deserved a scowl too.

"It's all right, Mr. James. Let him in."

"You're sure?"

"Yes." She must be as exhausted as Noah. The rest of the team worked in shifts, but the team leaders often refused the breaks. She'd ordered Noah to take a break at 10:00 a.m. today. He'd ignored her. And he knew for a fact that Elise hadn't let up once.

Unlike Noah, her weariness didn't look like anger. As the muttering, hunched customer pushed past her without a word of thanks, Elise's face looked soft and sleepy, as if she didn't deserve a scowl at all. Damn.

She held the door open and Noah slipped inside before locking it behind him. A glance at the teller line showed Lara smiling and speaking calmly to the man, but he shook his head and waved his pillowcase around. The teller began counting out bills.

"He called a half hour ago," Elise explained quietly. "Told us to have his money ready to go. It's only seventeen hundred dollars. I don't want him losing any sleep over it."

"Or God forbid, taking his story of government hooligans to the local news."

When she tilted her head up and met his eyes, Noah felt his heart stop. And when a slow, tired smile crept over her face, his heart started again with a crazed rhythm.

"Exactly," she said softly. An innocuous, everyday

word that sounded impossibly sexy coming from Elise's mouth.

For a long moment, Noah couldn't recall what the hell they were talking about. Then her smile faded and she looked tired again.

"You should go back to the hotel," he said. "Get some rest."

She shook her head. "The team…"

"There'll be here for another two hours, and they've already had a full night's sleep."

Her eyelids moved slowly when she blinked, but she glanced around and shook her head again. Noah didn't know why he felt protective. Elise could take care of herself, and this wasn't the toughest case they'd ever worked. But she looked so…vulnerable.

Elise Watson, *vulnerable?* Man, he really was tired.

"Come on. We'll both call it quits," he offered. "Have you eaten dinner?"

She shot him a guilty look.

"Lunch?" The last customer scurried past, still glaring with righteous suspicion, despite the fact that they'd willingly handed over his money. "All right," Noah sighed as he locked the door behind the man. "Grab your stuff. We're leaving in two minutes."

"But I need to—"

"They've got your cell number, Elise. They'll call if they need you."

The lobby hummed with quiet work as the last two tellers counted out their money drawers. Lara laughed at something one of the loan officers said. There were no crises in the offing. No swelling tension.

"I'll buy you a beer," Noah said.

"Two minutes," she said over her shoulder as she hurried away.

The surge of triumph and anticipation that flooded his blood was something Noah chose to ignore, because he did have his pride, damn it, even if it had been so thoroughly battered and bruised by Elise two years before.

He checked in with the guys working the computers in the back room. He called the men in charge of supervising security at the other two branches. He looked over the latest numbers in the forensic investigation. And his heart never once settled back to its normal beat.

Exhaustion made him angry. Or maybe it just made him need...something.

"OH, MY GOD," Elise groaned. "Oh, God, that is so good." Pleasure swarmed over her in little pinpricks of relief. Eyes closed, she moaned as she pressed the bottle of golden joy to her cheek.

Noah cleared his throat. "You really needed a beer."

"You have no idea." She took another long draw of the bottle, but she was already anticipating the margarita she was going to have next. It wasn't her fault. She'd settled on a chile relleno, so the margarita was required by federal law.

She let her head fall back to rest against the booth. They were alone here for all intents and purposes. The only people staying at the hotel were working for her, and at the moment they all seemed to be either working or winding down in their rooms. If there was anybody else here, they were hidden by the six-foot-tall walls of the booths.

"Thank you so much for pulling me out," she sighed. "Sometimes when I get tired, I just get more and more focused, until I can't see at all. That's probably what happened in Madison...." Elise regretted the word before it left her mouth, but Noah didn't seem to notice her hesitation.

"That was a tough job." He took a swig from his own bottle. Elise watched the muscles of his throat work, strangely fascinated by the rough look of his jaw. He needed a shave. His light brown hair was sticking up where he'd run his hand through it. He looked more like a bank robber than a federal employee. It didn't help that he'd slipped off his jacket and loosened his tie. As she watched, he began to roll up the sleeves of his plain white shirt.

She wouldn't stare at his hands. She wouldn't. Lusting after his hands had gotten her into trouble that first time. His fingers were long, but not slender and pretty. They ended in blunt lines and square nails, and his hands were so *wide*. Something about the sight of them made her weak and stupid.

She dug a fingernail beneath the label on her bottle, determined to distract herself. "You know, that was my first takeover."

"I remember. It must have been an awful way to start. That one was hard even on the veterans."

Lately, she'd been thinking a lot about Madison, and it wasn't only because she'd worked closely with Noah on that trip. The Madison job had been close to Christmas, too, and the weather had been brutally cold. But there the similarities ended. The Madison bank had been too far gone. There hadn't been one interested buyer. And Elise and Noah and the rest of the team had been in charge of laying off ninety-three people only two weeks before Christmas. Some of the employees had been angry, but most of them had been terrified.

One of Elise's most vivid memories was locking herself in the bathroom stall to cry. The other one involved Noah James and his hands. And that straight, unyielding mouth of his. It was softer than it looked. That knowledge only added to the general feelings of sorrow that still clung to her thoughts of Madison.

She sighed hard. "Do you remember the senior teller? She'd just bought her first house. She kept whispering 'What am I going to tell my kids?'"

"It was bad," Noah said softly. "But this trip...this trip is better."

"I'll drink to that," she answered, clinking her bottle softly against his and averting her eyes from his fingers curved around the glass. They both finished off their beers just as their dinner arrived.

"Two more beers?" the waitress asked with a wink.

Noah nodded, but Elise shook her head. "A margarita on the rocks for me. And..." The tension still shrieked in her shoulders. "Two shots of Patrón?"

Noah raised his eyebrows in a challenging look, but he didn't say no. She hadn't planned on anything more than a tension-breaker, but she was now wondering what Noah James would be like after a few drinks. She couldn't quite imagine it. A picture of him loose and happy flashed through her mind, and Elise couldn't stop her snort of laughter.

He'd just opened his mouth to take a bite of his bacon cheeseburger, but he lowered his food. "What?"

"Nothing."

Frowning, he muttered something like "Nothing, my ass," and Elise had to stifle another snort.

Then the drinks came. And the shots.

Half an hour later, Elise was laughing so hard that tears leaked from her eyes. "Shut up," she gasped.

"And the last ones out of the hotel were Tex and some woman twice his age—"

"No!"

He put a hand over his heart. "I swear to God, he stood in the parking lot wearing nothing but his boots and a pair of boxers, completely unselfconscious. As soon as the fire alarm stopped blaring, he started introducing everyone to his 'friend' Jeannie, who, by the way, was wearing a bathrobe and a wedding band and not much else."

"Who was she?"

"I have no idea, but she raced back in with Tex as soon as the fire department gave the all-clear. And that was our trip to Lubbock. Those Texans really know how to run a bank into the ground."

Still smiling, Elise sipped the last dregs of her margarita and resisted the urge to order another. The shot had been too much. The second round of tequila had been way over the line. She needed some sleep. She needed to regroup. What she did not need was to get sloppy drunk with Noah James.

But she had found out what Noah was like under the influence…he was exactly the same: controlled, quiet and handsome as hell, though he did smile a little more.

Those occasional smiles were killing her.

She remembered now what had led her to kiss him in the first place. Watching his hands. A few drinks. A few of those rare smiles and she'd been melting all over. Just like she was now.

But at least now she knew better. A few smiles did *not* mean that Noah James wanted to be jumped. What a shame. It was the least he could offer for being so stubborn on every single job.

The last time they'd worked on the same team, he'd publicly defied her orders that he discipline one of his team members. They'd fought that out in her office and reached a tentative truce, but...

Elise frowned. "Hey, did you tell Michael Valdez he could fly home tomorrow?"

"Yes. The bulk of his duties are over and his mom is having surgery."

"Don't you think you should've at least run it by me?"

"I meant to. I got distracted by the embezzle-ment."

"The embezzlement." She rolled her eyes. "Why are you always such a pain in the ass?"

"Why do you think I'd make up missing funds?"

"That's not what I meant. It's just...everything. I feel like you're always fighting me, and I don't know why."

"The flight was canceled, Elise. I had nothing to do with that. What should I have—"

"You stole my promotion," she bit out. Silence fol-lowed her words. Even the quiet music playing in the background seemed to pause. Elise held her breath as Noah leaned back and picked up his empty beer bottle.

He rolled it in his hand. "That was a lateral move, not a promotion."

"It was *my* job." She leaned forward to glare at him, but her anger only made him smile.

"Obviously it wasn't."

"Everyone knew how much I wanted it."

He shrugged one shoulder. "I didn't know anything about it. I just knew I needed to get the hell out of D.C."

She rolled her eyes. "Oh, so it had *nothing* to do with me?"

His gaze flew up to meet hers, and her breath hitched at the brightness in his pale blue eyes. Hot emotion flamed in their depths, but she couldn't decipher it. "Nothing at all to do with you," he murmured.

He was lying. He was lying, but she didn't know what she'd done to make him so mad he'd interfere with her career. "Damn it, Noah. I don't know why you did it, but I *needed* that job."

"You didn't need it as much as I did." His jaw was so tight that his mouth hardly moved when he spoke, and Elise was tumbling through anger and confusion. What had she ever done to him? She was the one who'd left Madison humiliated.

"I needed it," she said again, "because the rest of my life was going to Colorado. My boyfriend took a job in Boulder in June. Or should I say *ex*-boyfriend? He broke up with me because I couldn't move with him!"

Her words rang in the small confines of the booth. She'd raised her voice. Maybe she'd even yelled.

Noah's eyes narrowed slightly. He cocked his head and studied her face while she tried to control her breathing. "So," he said thoughtfully. His eyes narrowed further. "Was this the same boyfriend you had when you kissed me two years ago?"

Elise gasped and sat up so quickly that her elbow banged hard into the edge of the table. "Excuse me?"

"Because he didn't seem that important to you then."

"You... I can't believe you'd bring that up. I—"

"And since you were both willing to choose a job over the relationship, I can't pretend to be prostrate with regret. Sorry, Elise. I guess that relationship wasn't meant to be."

Her mind spun like a top, buffeted from all sides. She was outraged and insulted and hurt. But she was also reeling because he was throwing her own lie back in her face and she didn't know how to respond. She hadn't had a boyfriend when she'd kissed Noah. She'd made that up to save face, but now it seemed like a juvenile response to an adult situation. *Oh, sure, I'm dating someone, too.*

So on top of everything else, she now felt stupid and small.

Elise grabbed her purse and slid out of the booth. "Charge it to Room 207," she growled.

"Elise," he said, but his tone was half-hearted. She kept moving.

Unbelievable. They'd been having a meaningful conversation, and then he'd pulled *that* out. Her stomach burned as if he'd stabbed her with a real knife instead of a metaphorical one. He'd dismissed everything she'd built with Evan as if it had been nothing.

Almost the same way Evan had dismissed the life they'd built together. The way he'd so simply proven that work was more important than love to both of them.

Elise was such a failure at love that *everyone* could see it, from inside and out.

She wiped a tear from her cheek before she stepped out of the dimness of the bar and into the bright hallway that led to the elevator. She was terrible at relationships, but she was good at her job, and she'd be damned if she'd let one of her people see her crying like a little girl.

Her father and her uncles had raised her to be tough. Once she'd turned five, her dad had told her she wasn't a baby anymore, and she'd agreed. She'd lived for her dad's pride and approval, and even when she'd broken her arm playing peewee football, she hadn't cried. But being a woman was so much harder than being a kid. Kids were allowed to throw themselves into situations and fall flat on their faces if they failed. But as an adult…she had no idea how to navigate relationships. Throw yourself in or hold back… She'd tried it both ways and neither had worked.

But she was thirty-one years old. She had to figure it out soon, or she'd live her whole life lonely. That was another reason she'd been so desperate for the Denver job. She needed a big change in the worst way. Most of her Saturday nights over the past year had been spent with her uncles. Elise was turning into an elderly man.

She slipped into the thankfully empty elevator and tipped up her head to keep more tears from falling.

God, she didn't know what was wrong with her. The holidays or the weather or…the *tequila*.

Elise immediately felt better. The tequila had exposed her maudlin side. She could not fall into the trap of drinking with Noah James again. The man was a menace, sliding past all her defenses like an assassin. Did he have this effect on other women?

She'd never heard a word about an office romance, and she'd damn sure been paying attention. The man drew her eye anytime he was near.

In Madison, she'd been emotional because of the layoffs, and Noah had been right there, solid as granite. But that wasn't right. Not like granite, because sitting next to him at the bar, she'd been able to feel the warmth coming off him. And—she'd thought—sparks. Sparks like little bits of fire floating through the air and landing on her skin. Sparks that had made her nerves shiver…

She'd sat there with him, forcing herself to breathe and smile and talk, but all she'd wanted was to turn and press into him. And finally she had.

The tears overflowed then. Elise rushed blindly toward her room, praying none of the other doors opened before she could get there.

Sadly, her assault on Noah James had been the most alive she'd ever felt. Powerful and feminine and recklessly *alive*. Sad, because despite her initial certainty that he'd been responding—really responding—Noah had pulled away. Sad, because she'd followed him and he'd been forced to push her back.

All those sparks, all that chemistry…it had only been Elise. He hadn't felt it at all.

Another romantic failure. She moved through her

love life like an awkward, gawky teen, lurching from one uncertainty to the next.

But at least she was good at her job. She liked being in control. She never let a goal slip from her grasp no matter what else she was juggling. As long as her goal wasn't Noah, anyway.

Elise's jaw was set as she let herself into her room, determined to put these messy emotions behind her. She'd have a shower, sober up, and crunch some numbers on her laptop. Then she'd take a quick nap and get back to work.

Elise started the shower and tossed her dirty clothes onto the closet floor. When she stepped back into the bathroom, it was already foggy with steam. She stood under the hot spray for a long time, cocooned by the wet heat that quickly filled the entire space. Forcing the rest of the world to fade away, Elise let herself think of that kiss. She took out the memory on rare occasions, handling it like a keepsake.

There had been a few awkward silences in their conversations that night, moments when they'd meet each other's eyes and then look away. Elise had still been holding her breath after one of those moments when she'd slipped away to flee to the bathroom. There, she'd checked her makeup and fixed her hair and smiled nervously at her own reflection. Noah James was handsome and intimidating and out of her league, but she wasn't going to let that stop her from hoping. He might make a move. He might offer to walk her back to her room. And even though they worked together…she'd let him.

Heart beating hard with excitement at her own pep

talk, Elise had stepped into the dim hallway at the back of the bar… and right into Noah.

Eyes wide, he'd reached out both hands to steady her, and that touch had done something to her. Made her bold or brave or incredibly stupid. Elise had stepped forward, and he'd stepped back. There was no give in the narrow corridor, and when his back hit the wall, she'd stepped forward again, pressing her body to his. When his hands had tightened on her upper arms, she'd mistaken the emotion and risen on tiptoes to kiss him.

Wincing at the memory, Elise dipped her head and let the shower drown her in a curtain of hot water.

Despite her humiliation and embarrassment, she'd never been able to nullify the pleasure of that moment. The perfect taste of him, the incredible heat. She'd swept her tongue into his mouth and shivered when he'd responded. And he *had* responded, hadn't he?

He'd opened his mouth, after all. He'd sighed. He'd rubbed his tongue over hers and slanted his head to delve deeper.

The kiss had seemed to last a thousand heartbeats, but it must have been just a few seconds. Still, it had been enough to wake something desperate inside her. Something strong and relentless and demanding to have its way.

Her moan must have startled him. Or the way she rubbed her body closer to his and wrapped her arms around his waist. Whatever she'd done it had spooked him, and while she was still trying to get inside him, Noah had broken the kiss and raised his head.

That hadn't been enough of a hint. As his grip had tightened on her arms, Elise had pressed kisses to his jaw. She'd dragged her open mouth down his throat, sighing against his skin, pressing her teeth to his flesh.

"Elise," he'd said.

"Noah," she'd whispered back. "God, you feel so good."

"We can't do this."

She'd been nodding when he'd finally forced her off. "Not here. My room."

Her lust had kept her from seeing the horror in his eyes, but she couldn't help but notice when he'd started shaking his head. "No. I can't do this."

"Why?"

"I have a girlfriend. I'm sorry. I shouldn't have let you think…"

The power coursing through her had taken a moment to dissipate. She could picture how lust-dazed she must have looked as she stared in confusion. His taste had still been on her tongue.

"Oh," she'd finally said. "Oh, of course." Yet her arms had still circled his waist, her knee was still thrust between his. Disentangling herself had been the single most awkward moment of her life.

"I'm sorry, Elise. Really, but I don't want to—"

"No big deal! I understand. Really. Sorry about that."

Unable to take the hot water or the memories anymore, Elise reached blindly for the faucet and shut it off. The steam still surrounded her in a comforting blanket, so she wasn't the least bit cold as she stepped out. The little bathroom felt like a dream world, so she didn't bother to wipe off the mirror. She liked the white blankness of it as she dried off and rubbed lotion into her skin. She didn't want to watch her reflection and worry over the same imperfections that every woman did. Too much here, not enough there. Screw it. Her body had nothing to do with her romantic problems. It was her awkward tomboy insides that threw everybody off balance.

She didn't know how to dance or flirt or make men feel strong and steady. She wasn't soft or comforting. Whatever women like Lara had, Elise had gotten none of it. She had confidence and control and a hell of a fake on the basketball court, but her best efforts at being feminine were shaving her legs and wearing mascara. Those two ploys had been enough to fool Evan into dating her, but not enough to coax a man into *truly* wanting her. Certainly not a man like Noah.

But maybe that was for the best. Love was too fleeting and delicate and easily lost. Even the kind that was supposed to be permanent…like a father's love. That left too, because there was no way to hold on to it, even if you tightened both your hands until the nails dug in hard enough to make your palms bleed. Even then, your dad still died, and his love left right along with him.

Elise bent slowly forward, watching the bloblike outline of her reflection grow larger. She pressed her forehead to the cool, wet glass and closed her eyes. She didn't cry. It had been ten months; she was all cried out. But the cold felt good and she held herself there for a long moment.

She still had her uncles. She still had her job. And maybe someday she'd build a bigger life with a good man who didn't mind that she wasn't cozy and warm and comforting.

"Forget it," she muttered, so tired that the words

were more a whisper than a curse. Apparently tequila made her feel maudlin *and* hopeless. Next time she'd stick to beer. And she'd find a table that didn't come equipped with the hot guy she'd mauled two years before.

Elise pushed herself off the glass and flicked the switch that started the fan. She brushed her teeth and combed out her hair. As she dried it, her ghost self became solid in the mirror, and eventually, it was just her. Looking clean and exhausted and typically grumpy.

But when she switched off the hairdryer, the high-pitched whine faded away to expose a new sound. Banging. Frowning, Elise switched off the fan as well, and then there was no question about the source of the sound. Elise met her own wary eyes in the mirror and considered who could be knocking.

It's not Noah, she told her galloping heart. *And you're a fool to be excited by the thought.*

Angry in the face of that hope, Elise wrapped a towel around her body and stalked out of the bathroom. A tiny shiver coursed through her at the change in temperature, but she refused to feel vulnerable as she put her eye to the peephole and squinted.

It's not Noah, her brain was still repeating. But it was. And her heart slipped so quickly into a downward lurch that Elise only got angrier.

She yanked open the door and glared.

"WHAT THE HELL do you want?"

The voice sounded like Elise Watson. The words fit her perfectly. But the woman standing in front of him did not complete the puzzle. Elise Watson did not have hair that cascaded in dark, shiny waves down bare shoulders. She didn't have cheeks that glowed with pink innocence. And she didn't have so much skin, surely.

"Uh," Noah managed.

"Get over it," she snapped. "I don't sleep in business suits, regardless of what you might think."

Actually, she'd never worn a business suit to bed in any of his unwanted fantasies about her. He stared at the dewy skin just above the confines of the towel. She'd wrapped the towel firmly around her. It looked perfectly secure. It also squeezed her breasts so tightly that they mounded above the fluffy cotton. She looked so...warm. The scent of her soap wound around him.

Elise shifted, her hand touching the edge of the towel as if to be sure it hadn't moved. "Did you come to apologize?"

Right. That was why he'd banged on her door for the past two minutes. Noah forced himself to snap from the daze of nearby nudity. "Yeah. I didn't—"

"Apology accepted," she growled and started to push the door closed.

Without any signal from the conscious part of his brain, Noah's hand rose to stop the door from shutting him out. "I shouldn't have said what I said. Can I apologize and blame the tequila at the same time?"

"You can do anything you want." She glanced down at his hand. "Just not in my room."

The sentence got all mixed up in Noah's brain, even as he shook his head against it. *Not here,* she'd whispered two years before. *My room.* And now: *You can do anything you want.* But that hadn't been what she'd said. It wasn't what she meant.

His eyes swept down her body to the fascinating

amount of thigh that showed beneath the hem of the towel. She tensed and those thighs turned from softness to muscle, and Noah's body responded in full.

Mistake or not, *she'd* kissed him two years before. She'd felt it too, the aching need that arced between them. The tension that made them snap at each other whenever they were in close proximity.

But Noah didn't feel like snapping now. He felt like touching. And kissing. And tumbling into bed with her.

Elise crossed one arm over her chest and pulled the towel tighter. "I'm not decent," she said, vulnerability rounding the edge of outrage in her words. "We'll talk later."

"We never have time to talk. You're too busy bossing me around."

Her eyes narrowed. "That's my job. Screw you if you don't like it."

He cocked his head. "Who said I didn't like it?"

That surprised her so much that she took a step back. Noah stepped forward, sliding his body through the space she'd opened in the doorway. But he stopped, half in, half out, and waited for her to regroup. Shocking her was fun. Scaring her wouldn't be.

Her grip tightened on the towel, but instead of making it more secure, she pulled the edge down an inch. His fingers curled in response.

She shook her head like she was tossing off her reaction. "I can't be sweet and cuddly and still do my job."

"No," he answered. "You have to be strong. And hard. And sharp as a blade."

"Yeah." But she didn't look like a woman who'd won

a debate. Her face tightened with hurt for the briefest moment. Her gaze fell, hiding her thoughts.

"You can't be soft," he continued.

She raised her chin and hardened her expression, but her eyes still glinted with sadness. "Good, because I'm not."

He swept his gaze over her body again. She looked soft as all hell right now. "Sometimes," he murmured. "Sometimes you are."

Panic flashed over her face and she put her hand to his chest to shove him. "I'm not!" She proved herself by pushing him hard, but his back was against the doorjamb and he didn't move an inch. She, on the other hand, leaned into him with the effort.

Instead of sliding out the door, Noah slid his hand beneath her hair. He held her neck still, and he kissed her.

There was no softness for a moment. Elise was still straining, pushing him harder to the wall, mouth tight under his. She made a little noise of shock that was neither pleasure nor horror.

She'd said kissing him was a mistake, but she *had* kissed him, damn it. So he waited out her surprise. He tightened his fingers and stroked his thumb down her neck and brushed his mouth over hers. And he waited.

"Mmm," she murmured, still not offering a hint of what that sound might mean.

But he'd waited two years, a few more heartbeats shouldn't matter....

Her fingers ceased pushing and curled into his shirt. Her lips parted and her breath sighed over his mouth, spreading the faintest of pleasures. Noah chased that pleasure with his own mouth, opening her, tasting her. Her quick intake of breath was no neutral noise this time. The hitch in the sound coincided perfectly with the first touch of his tongue against hers.

Two years he'd waited to slide inside her again, and Noah growled with the satisfaction of it.

Her hand tugged him closer, and Noah let himself be pulled all the way into the room. He slammed the door with his heel and put his hands on Elise Watson.

Despite both their words, she *was* soft. Her neck was soft, and her shoulders, and her back. Her skin felt delicate as butterfly wings, despite the strength of bone and muscle beneath it. For a moment, he meant to be gentle, but then Elise curved her hand to the shape of his skull as she pulled him tighter to her. She wasn't delicate. She was hard and strong and ruthless, and that strength had been the cornerstone of all his fantasies about her, so Noah shoved the gentleness away and kissed her harder.

Her nails slid down his neck, sending sparks shivering down his spine.

He tipped her head back. She panted as her mouth lifted from his, and Noah's blood surged in response. He kissed her chin and the tender skin of her neck. "You're soft here," he murmured. She shook her head in denial. "And here." He shaped her shoulder, edging his thumb over her collarbone. Her growl was almost a sigh.

He shouldn't do this. He'd spent two years avoiding her so he wouldn't step across this line, but the line had disappeared when she'd curled her fingers into his neck. And she was single, finally, and Noah hadn't had a girlfriend since that night in Madison.

His mouth slipped lower, sucking at the place where her neck curved into her shoulder, pulling her head farther to the side. She didn't fight him. She didn't say no.

When he slid his hand down her chest, her skin rubbed heat into the palm of his hand. He felt her shivering as if it was his own.

"You're soft for me, aren't you?"

"Yes," she moaned, and her moan turned to a little sob when he tugged her towel away.

The sight of her naked body weakened him for a split second, and Elise pulled free. Her hands framed his face and she kissed him again—her mouth was as hungry and desperate as his, like they were fighting to get more from each other. The idea inflamed him. He turned their bodies and eased her back against the door before dropping down to kneel before her.

"Noah," she gasped, "what…?" Whatever she'd been about to say, she forgot it when he closed his mouth over her nipple.

"Oh," she sighed. "Yes."

Noah couldn't count the number of times he'd imagined a scene like this, and Elise was everything he'd fantasized. One of her hands clutched his head. The other pressed his hand as if to keep him from letting go. Noah ached with want at the way she tried to control him even as he gave her what she wanted. He bit her nipple, gently, then he swirled his tongue around her. Her whole body jerked against him. For a moment, he worried he'd hurt her, but then she moaned and her fingers slid between his. She dragged his hand up, away from her breast, sliding it over the skin of her chest and her neck.

Noah noted this with only the barest attention. He was too busy shaping his other hand to the naked curve of Elise's hip and considering which of his fantasies to indulge. But before he could decide, she pulled his hand all the way to her mouth and closed her lips around his index finger.

"Oh, God," he whispered against her nipple. All he could think was that this was *Elise*. Noah had lost his mind.

HIS FINGER SLID FROM HER MOUTH. Elise grabbed his wrist to try to keep him where she wanted him. She'd waited a long time to act out her fantasies.

But here was a new fantasy. Noah rising to his feet, face beautiful in its intensity. She felt so vulnerable, standing naked before him. She felt…soft.

She closed her eyes against the vulnerability, and then Noah was kissing her again, his hands roaming over her shoulders and her breasts and her hips. The door pressed cold against her naked back, but Noah was all heat against her front. She couldn't keep track of his hands. They were everywhere, everywhere…and then her awareness focused on one spot. On one hand. On one pair of fingertips that edged down her stomach with the faintest pressure.

His fingers dragged down, torturing her, and finally they slid over the most sensitive spot on her body. Heat bloomed in a fiery rush over her skin. Her need felt almost violent, it built so quickly inside her. And Noah…Noah was still completely dressed in his suit and tie, while she wore nothing at all. Trembling at the pleasure that raced through her at every circle of his fingertips, Elise reached for him and jerked his shirt free of his pants. She caught a flash of tanned, flat stomach before she slid her hands beneath the cotton and touched his body for the first time.

He felt strong, his skin stretched like a sheet of pure heat over hard muscles. Those muscles jumped as she explored him. Before long, Elise had tilted her hips toward him and used his belt to pull him closer. She wrapped one leg around his hips and pulled him tight against her. When he pushed her hands away and finished unbuckling his belt, she looked up to his face and shivered.

Noah James looked desperate in his need. He watched her like he'd spent two long years wanting nothing more than this, just as she had. Two years of need did not make for soft wanting on her part. She *needed* him.

His belt opened with a clink. Her heart pounded so wildly she couldn't hear the zipper, but she watched as he pulled a condom from his pocket and tore it open. She helped him slide it on, frantic to have him inside her. And when he lifted her and braced her against the door, Elise wrapped both legs around his waist and took him deep.

So deep.

It was perfect. Unforgiving and delicious.

She curled her arms around his neck and pressed her face to his shoulder. "Noah," she whispered. "Noah." Every breath she drew was filled with the scent of his skin. He filled every corner of her body.

It had only been a few months since she'd had sex, but it felt like she'd been empty for years. Noah's strokes took on a slow, brutal rhythm.

She was going to come already. Gravity pushed her

hard against him, rubbing her in just the right way. Sweat trickled down his neck, and Elise pressed her open mouth to his skin. He was sweating for *her*.

This was a dream. It must be a dream.

She clutched him tighter as her body squeezed him. Noah cursed. She felt his hands shake where they gripped her. "Oh, God," she whispered into his damp hair. He slid against her one last time and her nerves stretched to the breaking point then snapped.

"No," she moaned, but it was too late. Her body had betrayed her and all she could do was ride the ruthless waves of her climax.

She sobbed his name and held tight to his shoulders when he came with a strangled groan.

Gradually, the world returned, bringing with it a strange silence. Her heartbeat slowed, and she could hear the sounds of both of them panting, but all the rushing emotion that had taken her over was gone. It was just Noah and her, alone. The door was ice against her back. The frame of the fire-escape plan pressed into her shoulder blade.

Noah's breathing slowed, but Elise suddenly felt like she might be drowning.

"Oh," she said softly as she carefully lowered one leg and then the other to stand on her own once again. Before she could start babbling excuses or questions or horrified exclamations, he took a deep breath and said, "Hold on a sec." He disappeared into the bathroom.

Seconds later, just as it occurred to Elise that she was stark naked, Noah stepped back into the room. One quick zip of his pants, and he was fully dressed again, if a bit rumpled.

Something tingled under her breastbone and spread

out from there. A fizzy mix of mortification and joy and sheer disbelief. Just as she was reaching to cover herself, Noah met her eyes, and the seriousness in his gaze stopped her words.

"We're both exhausted," he said, slipping off his suit jacket. "We'll figure this out later, all right? For now, we need sleep."

Elise glanced at the clock. It wasn't even seven, but it felt like two in the morning. For a few long seconds she was frozen by the door. How could they not talk about this now? How could she get into bed with him without knowing what was going on between them?

Panic tried to rise up in her chest, but Noah was pulling his tie free of its knot and toeing off his shoes, and her body felt weak and heavy. Her muscles yearned beneath her skin, swaying her toward the bed. "All right," she whispered, ignoring the fact that her voice was downright *soft,* and she rushed for her suitcase.

She'd just had sex with Noah James, and the very fact that she wanted to cuddle up naked with him was enough of a reason to pull on panties and an old T-shirt. Sex was one thing. Cozy, sweet cuddling was another. That was an intimacy she could not grant.

When he spied her pajamas, Noah raised an eyebrow that implied she was a coward, but he stripped down to his boxer briefs and stopped there.

Elise slid beneath the covers and stayed solidly on the left side of the bed, but Noah's respect for her boundaries ended with underwear, apparently. He turned over, pulled her close, and kissed the top of her head. "Mmm," he murmured. "You're even softer now."

"Shut up," she snapped.

He chuckled against her hair, but her words worked. He

stopped talking. His body lay heavy against hers, making her feel small and feminine. "Noah—" she started, but he shook his head, his lips brushing her temple.

"We'll talk, Elise. But give me a little while. I've been up for two days and I just had a mind-blowing orgasm. My brain isn't in top form. We'll be okay for a few hours."

She should make him leave. She should've never let him in. This had been an awful mistake, and letting him sleep in her room would only complicate the issue. But in the end, she spent too much time thinking, and his breath grew even and deep against her. And he smelled so good, and his arm was so warm across her waist.

Elise closed her eyes, then she carefully curled her body so that their skin touched in as many places as possible. He'd never know, and she was too tired to pretend anymore.

CHAPTER FOUR

"Ms. WATSON!"

Elise drew a deep breath of spiced air and purred with pleasure. She'd been dreaming of Omaha and snow-swept plains, but now she was so warm. As if she were stretched on the sun-heated sand of a tropical beach. "Mmm," she sighed. The beach curved around her and eased her into a hill of hot sand.

Somebody rudely pounded on the door that stood next to the coconut palm. But why in the world was there a door standing on the beach?

Her eyes popped open. A chest came into view, dusted with dark hair. She squinted at a flat bronze nipple.

"Ms. Watson?" a muffled voice yelled.

"Holy crap!" she yelped, lunging upright.

Noah's eyes opened, but they were heavy with sated exhaustion. "Good morning, beautiful."

"Oh, crap," she cursed, her gaze sliding toward the door. "Just a second!" she screamed.

"Ma'am," the voice said from the hallway. "I'm sorry to wake you, but the security team had a small issue and we're unable to locate Mr. James."

Her eyes slid back to Noah's naked chest. And stomach. And the hair that trailed down muscled abs to disappear beneath his underwear. What the hell had she done?

As she watched, Noah frowned at the door and reached for the phone he'd set on the bedside table. "Dead," he muttered. "I guess two days is its limit."

Shaken to the core, Elise jumped from the bed and rushed for the dresser. Where the hell was her phone? "Um... I'll track him down," she called, still trying to place the voice. "And, uh...Miller?"

"Yes, ma'am?"

Okay. Good. She still had this under control. She looked at the clock and let out a sigh of relief. It was only six-thirty. "I'll meet you in the conference room in ten minutes."

She finally found her cell phone, left on the bathroom counter and emitting an occasional plaintive beep from beneath the towel she'd used to dry her hair. Clutching the phone tightly in her fist, she caught sight of her own crazed eyes in the mirror. She'd gotten drunk, argued with Noah James and then had sex with him against a hotel-room door.

A one-night stand with a man who could barely tolerate her. Things had been tense between them before. Now they'd be...

"Oh, God," she whispered.

It had seemed like a good idea last night when she'd been tipsy and half-naked. But no...that wasn't true. It had seemed like a really bad idea, and that had only added to the excitement of being shoved up against a wall and shagged like crazy.

"Oh, God." Her cheeks burned at the memory. He hadn't even taken off his *shoes*.

"Elise?"

She whirled around in time to see him throw the sheets aside and stand up. Oh, *God*.

He wore gray boxer briefs that left nothing to the imagination. But she didn't need her imagination, did she? She'd seen it all last night....

"What's going on with my team?" He ran both hands through his hair and stepped toward her.

"I don't…I don't know. It's…"

"Did they leave you a message?"

"Oh. Probably. Let me…" He was right in front of her now. If she raised her hand, she'd touch his broad, muscled chest. Or that enticing bulge in his underwear. Elise blindly pushed a button on her phone and forced her eyes to the screen.

When he brushed past her, Elise jumped out of the bathroom as fast as she could. Water rushed behind her when he turned on the shower. *Her* shower.

She'd fallen down the rabbit hole.

The room spun around her.

The toilet flushed and the shower curtain rattled. "What's going on?" he called past the noise.

Elise shook her head and made herself focus on the phone. "Messages," she muttered, frowning over the password she'd used for eight years. Finally, she accessed the five messages and listened to them with her eyes clenched shut, one hand pressed to her mouth.

The first message was just a routine check-in. The second was a calm inquiry into whether or not she'd seen Noah James after he'd driven her back to the hotel. The last three were increasingly frantic messages from various team members. No one could find Noah James, and by six in the morning, they'd finally registered that no one could reach Elise either. The security question, it turned out, was rather inconsequential, especially in the face of two missing senior team members.

"No, no, no," she whispered. They'd all figure it out now. Every single one of them.

"Elise!" Noah shouted.

She shook her head frantically, rushing for the bathroom just as the shower cut off. "Shhh! Be quiet! There's nothing going on. One of the satellite branches lost power for a half hour, that's all. But now everyone is going to know! You've got to—"

"Know what?"

"That we—" Elise snapped her mouth shut and glared. Not an easy accomplishment. Noah had pushed back the curtain, and he casually toweled himself off as he watched her with raised eyebrows.

"You know exactly what I mean. You've got to get the hell out of my room. But what are you going to tell them? What will you say?"

His brow snapped down. "I'm going to tell them my phone ran out of power."

"They went to your room, and you weren't there. Then they couldn't find me and… This is a disaster!"

"Elise—"

"Wait! I've got it. I know where you were last night. You met up with those flight attendants. It's perfect!"

Noah stepped out of the shower, his deliberate movements giving him a menacing look. Or maybe it really was a menacing look. "What are you talking about?" he growled.

"Last night," she said simply. She very carefully kept her eyes on his face. "We were tired and…the tequila. It was a mistake. I'm your supervisor—"

"A mistake."

Something dangerous glinted in his eyes. Elise swallowed and told herself she was backing out of the bathroom again only because he was stark naked. And damp. And ten inches away. She hid on the other side of the door. "Hurry up!" she hissed.

She needed a shower too, but it would have to wait. Elise faced away from the bathroom as she switched her T-shirt for a bra and clean blouse. When she turned around, she was confronted with Noah standing there, towel around his waist. Stupidly, she reached down to cover the sight of her underwear with her hands.

Noah's gaze slid down to the shield of her fingers, and when his eyes rose to meet hers again, she read disappointment in the pale blue depths. "Unbelievable."

"What?"

"You're doing it to me again. But this time..." He threw a hand toward the bed.

Panic finally exploded in her chest. What had she *done?* No, she hadn't jumped on him this time, but she'd opened the door with only a towel around her. She'd let him in. He was a man, and she'd presented him with a little free action.

"No one can know, Noah. Please. My job!"

"Sure. I understand. Want me to go out the window?" He snapped his towel off and spun back to the bathroom, leaving Elise with a brief but thorough glimpse of his taut behind. Her knees weakened, but that was probably lack of oxygen. Her lungs were working too hard, too fast. She dressed herself while Noah stomped around, snatching his wrinkled clothes off the floor. She tried to keep from hyperventilating.

"Noah," she said when he reached for the door. He froze, back tense, neck tight. He waited, and she realized she didn't have any idea what she meant to say. *I'm sorry* or *Did you mean it?* or *I've wanted that for so long.*

She couldn't manage any of them. In the end, she just said, "Make sure no one's in the hall."

His shoulders rose higher, as if he were protecting himself from a blow. He took a deep, quiet breath. And then he left.

She didn't feel better. She felt worse. The panic swirled inside her chest, more like heartache and sorrow than pure fear.

But this was work. Nothing more or less than that. So Elise brushed her teeth, fixed her hair, and dusted on powder and blush. And then she went back to work, ignoring the ache in her muscles and her heart.

"HEY, MAN," Tex Harrison drawled from behind Noah's back as he poured himself a coffee in the bank's break room.

"Yeah?" Noah's tone wasn't polite, but he marked it as a great triumph that he hadn't actually punched anybody in the two hours since he'd gotten out of Elise's bed.

"I heard you were a naughty boy last night."

Coffee sloshed over the edge of Noah's cup, burning the tip of his thumb. He didn't notice the pain, because he was busy trying to stop the movie playing in his head. Elise, against the door, both legs wrapped around his waist as she tilted her hips to take him deeper... Noah cleared his throat and squeezed the mug tighter. "Excuse me?"

"The flight attendants? Dude, everyone is talking about it. You're a rock star. Listen, can I go with you tonight? I don't mean for some sort of group scene, but surely you can't handle another night of all three—"

Noah spun around and stalked from the break room. Behind him, Tex muttered, "Jeez, I'd think you'd be in a good mood."

He did not turn back and throw a roundhouse at Tex's jaw. He did not slam the door of his temporary office. He didn't do anything except sit down in the chair, place the coffee slowly on a coaster, and force himself to breathe in and out. In and out. Calmly.

She'd done it again. Made a fool out of him. Apparently Elise Watson's attraction to him only kicked in after a few drinks. Tequila made him palatable, but the cold light of day reminded her of her real feelings. She didn't like him.

At least this time he hadn't broken up with his girlfriend for her.

He breathed. In. And out.

This time, the outcome was bad, but less complicated. They'd had a one-night stand. People did that all the time. He should be happy. It *had* been mindblowing. Enough said.

Except there were all those unsaid things, wrapping strings around him, pulling so tight they cut. The sweetness of her skin. The heat of her mouth. The way she'd curled into him in the night, a tiny sigh drifting past her lips when he'd stroked her back. There was the sound of his name in her breathless voice, and the strangled scream of her climax. And there was the fact that he'd fallen hard for her a long time ago, long before she'd kissed him in that crappy little bar.

He'd thought Denver would be far enough to free him, finally. He'd been wrong.

"Damn it," he said softly.

She'd said it was a mistake. Again.

Noah should've known better.

Her voice drifted down the hall, and he held tight to his anger so as not to expose any other emotions.

"Flight attendants," he cursed, hitting the computer mouse too hard. Now he had to put up with the winks and nudges of half the team, as if he were a member of a fraternity instead of an important financial institution.

At least the job was almost over. As soon as he discovered the source of the discrepancies, they could turn the bank over to its new buyer and be on their way. Two days, tops, and he'd be free of Elise Watson. Again.

CHAPTER FIVE

TWO DAYS LATER, ELISE still blushed every time she
came face-to-face with Noah. But she'd made progress.
This morning, she'd finally stopped burning in imagi-
nary flames each time his name was mentioned. She'd
expected someone to figure out the lie just based on the
signals her face was sending, but the flight-attendant
story proved too delicious. People were too busy grinning at each other to notice that their team leader was
flustered and nervous for no reason at all.

But she had to stop reacting to him. Noah's attitude
toward her hadn't changed at all, and she'd do well to
take that to heart. They'd slept together. No big deal.
They were both adults. They were away from friends
and family and staying in a deserted hotel. These things
happened.

He wasn't the least bit fazed by it, and she wouldn't
be either.

Despite her internal monologue, her heart wasn't
interested in staying calm. When she stepped through
the door of his office, her pulse careened into a jagged,
frantic pace.

Noah's eyes flickered up, then just as quickly returned to his computer. "Yeah?"

"We can't drag this out forever."

His jaw jumped and his gaze slowly rose to hers.

"It's New Year's Eve. Everything is in order. The new bank takes control on Monday. They don't care about the discrepancy."

His mouth flattened in frustration. "Of course they don't. You know as well as I do that the discrepancy will be our liability, not theirs."

"Half the team has gone home and almost everyone else is leaving this afternoon. How long are we going to stay here just so you can solve a riddle?"

He put his hands carefully on the desk. "Are you ordering me to drop it?"

Christ, he had problems with authority. "No, I'm not ordering you to drop it."

"Good. Because I don't like to make mistakes, Elise."

She swallowed hard, and assured herself that hadn't been a swipe at her. "The acquisition team arrives on Monday, along with the people from Simpson Finance. You have until then. If you can't figure it out by Monday, you'll have to take the mystery home with you."

"Who do I get to keep?" he asked.

"You can have three people. Who do you want?"

He named Tex, a forensics accountant, and an asset specialist.

"They're not going to be happy about spending New Year's Eve in Omaha."

"I'm not exactly thrilled either," he snapped.

Elise left, tight with anger. Nobody seemed concerned about *her* New Year's plans. The fact that she didn't have any only made her more irritated. Yes, New Year's in Omaha would be the same as New Year's in D.C. for her. Take-out dinner. Ball drop on television.

In bed by 12:02. And in the morning, she'd wake up too early and sit in her bed reading case files.

But the fact that Noah would be only a few doors away made it all more pitiful and lonely.

As much as she'd resisted postsex cuddling with Noah, it had been…beautiful. Sweet and so meaningful. Because it had been Noah, whom she'd had a crush on from the moment they'd met. Noah, who was serious and strong, whose occasional grins made her heart hurt. Noah, who seemed so far beyond her reach that she could still barely believe she'd slept with him.

Noah, the man who was even more distant than he had been before they'd had sex.

Elise swallowed her hurt like a dose of medicine. She'd slept with him. That was all. He lived in Denver. He'd never be her boyfriend. "Get over it," she whispered.

Before she could descend into crippling sorrow, Elise picked up the phone and called the head members of the two satellite teams to clear them for the return home.

Then she called in each member of her crew and gave them the good news. Lastly, she called in the three employees Noah had asked to keep on, and gave them the bad news. Not only would they not make it home tonight, but since New Year's Day was a Friday, they'd have to stay the whole weekend.

None of them looked honored to have been hand-picked by Noah to hang around, but they should've been. He had high standards, and his approval wasn't easily won. She should probably tell herself that and be happy with one good session of animal lust.

"Ms. Watson?"

Startled from her thoughts, Elise jumped a little at the tentative voice. The head teller smiled nervously from the doorway. "Sorry. I didn't mean to interrupt."

"It's no problem. Come in. You're Marie, right?"

"Yes, ma'am. Marie Rea. I just wanted to thank you. I already talked to Lara, and… The day before you came, Mr. Castle had warned me that there were going to be layoffs. He hinted that I should prepare myself and… Well, Lara tells me that there won't be any layoffs in the short term, at least. So I wanted to thank you on behalf of all of us."

"Oh. It's not… The FDIC decides…" Elise pictured herself saying "Just doing my job, ma'am" and forced herself to stop stammering. "You're welcome," she said slowly, uncomfortable with the gratitude. It was the FDIC higher-ups who decided when to pull the trigger on a takeover, after all. But even Elise knew that would sound rude to say aloud. Maybe she was getting better at this.

But the woman looked like she was waiting for something more. Sweat tickled Elise's hairline. What was she supposed to say? "Um. I'm really glad we got here before anyone was let go."

"So are we. Have a happy New Year."

"You, too. Happy New Year." She wanted to slump with relief when the woman left. Why in the world was she so bad at this? She could speak in whole sentences. She wasn't a mean person. But small talk defeated her. All she could think of was what she was supposed to say, and what she really had said, what the other person must be thinking about her and… With all those thoughts pin-balling inside her skull, there wasn't any room for actual conversation.

Did other people feel like this? She supposed she'd never know, because if there was someone like her in the same room, they'd be the last two people to talk to each other.

The best part of her job was knowing that she'd taken a bank on the verge of collapse and propped it up long enough to save it. And the best part of that was knowing people still had jobs. Yet she couldn't even accept a simple thank-you with grace.

Maybe she'd have been different if she'd been raised with a mother. Or maybe not. Each of Elise's brief interactions with her mother's family had been awkward and halting. They seemed just as bad at making connections as she was.

But the last time she'd called her aunt, the woman had assured her they'd welcome "a nice sit-down" if Elise ever made it out to western Kansas. They were only three hours from Denver. She tried not to think of that now.

Hoping the day was almost over, Elise looked desperately to the clock. She was shocked to find the day actually *was* over. All those employee briefings had chewed up the time. It was four o'clock. The bank was closing early for New Year's, and she would be back in her empty room within the hour.

Through the shared wall with the break room, Elise heard laughter. She recognized Tex's voice as he loudly made plans with his two coworkers for the night.

A moment later a hand slapped her open door hard. "Hey, boss lady."

"Tex," she said, purposefully not smiling at his

flirtatious drawl. Not an easy task now that she could imagine his skinny body in boots and boxers.

"I hope you brought your dancing shoes."

"I did not."

"Well, get your hands on some. We're going out. I have it on good authority that there's a honky-tonk at the edge of town with a huge dance floor and a mechanical bull. Have you ever ridden a beast like that?" He wiggled his eyebrows in case she missed the blatant suggestion in his tone.

Elise sighed. It actually sounded like fun, but nobody wanted their boss along for a New Year's Eve party. Nobody but Tex, anyway, and he wasn't going alone. "No, thank you," she answered.

"We're all going out. Even Noah."

Drinks with Noah? "Nope."

"Aw, come on, Elise. I want to see you let your hair down."

"My hair doesn't come down," she lied. Honestly, she would've loved to ride that bull. When would she get the chance to do *that* again?

Tex narrowed his eyes at her as if he didn't believe her.

She smiled tightly. "Take a cab, all right? You can expense it."

"Really? What about—"

"And your meal, but you'd better not turn in a receipt for any other refreshments."

"Deal." He winked. "Happy New Year's Eve, beautiful."

Elise was left staring at an empty doorway, her lips parted in shock. She'd forgotten that moment, when she'd awoken to find Noah in her bed. "Good morning, beautiful," he'd whispered. As if he were happy.

But of course he'd been happy. He probably said that to every woman he woke up in bed with.

She heard the muffled rumble of cars pulling away from the parking lot. Most of the employees were on their way. Her team would be leaving in a few minutes, but she'd decided not to go. Elise closed her door and settled in for a couple more hours of work.

At least her New Year's resolution would be simple: get a life outside work. And try not to screw it up so badly this time.

CHAPTER SIX

HER PLAN HAD BEEN SIMPLE. Take a ridiculously long shower. Order room service. Go to bed early so she wouldn't hear the team coming back drunk and late and maybe with new friends in tow.

But after that freezing-cold walk across the street, dodging iced-over puddles and cars with wreaths wired to their bumpers, she'd sprinted up to her room, turned on the hot water, and found that she couldn't stop thinking about Noah. In her shower. Naked. Her thirty-minute shower had ended at five minutes.

Room service had offered more bad news. Two employees had called in sick, and the food wouldn't arrive for at least an hour. Stomach grumbling, Elise had stared down at the bed for a long time. Finally, she'd given in to fate and pulled on jeans and a sweater to eat downstairs.

Then disaster had really struck. With an hour wait for the food, she'd expected to walk into the hotel bar and find it packed with partiers. But just the opposite was true. The place was deserted. Not even a bartender stood behind the bar. If it hadn't been the dead of winter, crickets would've chirped.

Defeat curved her shoulders down.

A throat cleared from somewhere to her left. Elise turned to see Noah James sitting in the closest booth.

The quiet of the room suddenly had weight, and lots of it.

He cleared his throat again. "The cook is coming back in a few minutes to take my order. You're welcome to join me if you like."

"Oh. I see." It would be very strange not to sit with him. If she demurred, he'd know she wasn't as okay about their night together as she pretended to be. He'd know her nerves twisted into jumbled chaos each time she saw him.

She had no choice. Elise slid into the booth. "I thought you were going out with your team."

"I'm not really the line-dancing kind of guy." He raised his beer. "Domestic is on the house tonight. I think the cook just doesn't want us bothering him, so he pointed me toward the fridge. Can I get you something?"

She looked at the bottle, worried even a few sips would turn her into Noah's love slave again. But it was New Year's Eve, damn it. "I'll have the same. But just one."

"Got it." He walked around the bar and grabbed a beer while Elise watched him past her lashes. Like her, he was dressed down in jeans. He wore a faded T-shirt that made him look closer to twenty-five than thirty-six. It clung to his shoulders, reminding her of their strength. As if she'd forgotten. She knew the smell of his skin, after all.

He delivered the bottle, and Elise closed her eyes and took a long draw of the ice-cold beer, wishing once again that she was somewhere else. Christmas past.

Neither of her uncles had ever married, so it had always been just the four of them. Elise, her father,

Uncle Robbie and Uncle James in the little house her dad had bought decades before. Her dad had cooked the turkey. Robbie had made mashed potatoes, and James had brought store-bought pie. Every year, the same thing. A college bowl game on the TV. Beers in hands. Sweats and T-shirts all around. Lots of shouting and laughter. Robbie would drink too much and sleep on the couch. Her dad would give her a new Christmas ornament that she'd add to the box she kept in her closet.

This year, she'd finally put up her own tree, and hung all thirty ornaments up. Whenever she looked at it, all the happy times with her dad enveloped her heart. Maybe she'd leave that tree up forever.

"Are you okay?" Noah asked.

Elise forced her eyes open. "Of course. Sorry."

"Are you sure?" Frowning, he studied her.

She cleared her throat and smiled to distract him. "So weren't you a little tempted to go to the bar? I admit I considered it for a moment, just for the chance to see Tex ride the bull."

"You've got a point there. But I'm sure one of the others will record it on their phone."

"You're right. I always forget about those high-tech phones. There's no such thing as privacy anymore."

Noah's mouth finally edged toward a smile. "True. I, for one, am damn glad camera phones weren't common when I was in college."

"Oh, God," Elise laughed. "It's a miracle anyone has the guts for a one-night stand anymore. I don't think I'd want to risk that kind of…" Her words slunk away from her throat when she realized what she'd said.

Two minutes at the table with him and she'd already

broached the subject of their illicit coupling. Heat rushed through her so quickly she felt dizzy and sick.

What the hell was she doing here in a deserted restaurant with the one man she shouldn't be alone with?

"Well," he said.

She had to look at him. She couldn't keep staring at the table. But when she finally raised her eyes, Noah didn't meet her gaze. He was slumped against the booth back, concentrating on tearing the label slowly off his bottle.

"We're not going to talk about this, right?" she blurted, unable to handle the awkwardness a moment longer.

His gaze finally lifted, his blue eyes snapping with anger.

Anger?

The heat left her as quickly as it had come, chased away by awful fingers of ice. "Noah, you don't have a girlfriend this time, do you? I figured, after you moved to Denver…"

His bark of laughter made her jump. "No, not this time."

"Oh, thank God. You looked so mad for a second."

"Did I?" His voice got softer when he was angry, and he was obviously angry now. Unfortunately, she loved that tone. It struck her like a cross between a growl and a purr.

"I'm sorry I've been…weird."

"Is that what you're sorry about now?"

She pulled her chin in. "What does that mean?"

A man in a white apron and a hairnet shuffled into

view. "Sorry for the wait," he interrupted. "What can I get for you?"

Elise and Noah stared at each other for a long time. She frowned. He glared.

The cook shifted. "Maybe just another beer?"

"I'll have the turkey sandwich," Elise answered.

"Fish and chips," Noah muttered.

By the time they were alone again, Elise was beginning to register what he'd meant. That she was sorry about sleeping with him. That he didn't like that. But *why?*

The silence of the empty restaurant stretched with impossible tension. A pot banged on the other side of the swinging door. Christmas music floated by as someone drove past in the parking lot.

"We work together," Elise said, her stomach somersaulting like a gymnast.

"Yes."

"So…that shouldn't have happened."

"Because we work together," he said flatly.

"Yes."

His expression offered no hint to what he was thinking. "We're allowed to date."

"You live in Denver. That's not dating, Noah. That's just sex. I don't need my coworkers thinking of me that way. It's easier for you."

"Oh, yeah? How many jokes about flight attendants have you had to put up with this week?"

Right. "Maybe that was a bad idea. I apologize. I panicked."

"I noticed."

Elise remembered the look on Noah's face just

before he'd left her room. *You want me to sneak out the window?* He hadn't been laughing.

What a mess. "It wasn't a good idea, Noah. Surely you can see that."

He raised his hands like he was going to say something important, but he stopped just as his lips parted. He took a deep breath, then placed both hands on the table very slowly. She couldn't help but look at them, at the fingers spread wide, at the hard knuckles punctuated by the occasional scar. His nails were squared off well below the tips of each finger.

"You're right," he finally said. "We shouldn't talk about this."

She was lost. Reeling. Why did he sound so flat and resigned? What was going on here?

Her hands felt too light as she nervously shifted her bottle around on the table. If this were work, she'd just demand to know. She wouldn't tolerate this silence. Maybe...

"Pardon me," he murmured, sliding out of the booth.

Still caught in her uncertainty, Elise watched him stalk toward the bathroom. By the time he returned, their food had arrived and the moment was gone.

Her sandwich was a dry mess in her mouth, despite the gobs of mayonnaise slathered on it. Noah glared at his fried fish like it was the number-one suspect in his accounting investigation.

"We should meet tomorrow," she blurted. "I want to know exactly what you've found so far."

"Sure."

"How about nine o'clock?"

He tossed her a hard glance. "Your room or mine?"

"The conference room," she snapped.

"You got it, boss."

Stomach aching, she watched Noah toss his napkin on top of his half-eaten food. He reached for his wallet.

She shook her head. "I'll get it."

"Happy New Year," he said as he walked away, his tone implying the New Year was a curse instead of a possibility. Elise understood perfectly. The year stretched out before her like three hundred and sixty-five opportunities to screw up her interactions with Noah. And the worst thing was, now she didn't even know what she was doing wrong.

Everything, probably.

Elise finished the last drops of her beer, then leaned back in the seat, listening to the faint sounds of dish-washing leaking through the kitchen door. A phone rang behind the bar. Nobody answered it. Cars roared by on the street, their horns honking in a bright staccato celebration.

Elise waited a long time for the bill. When it finally came, the cook shot a meaningful glance at the empty seat across from her. "You know, there's a singles' party at the VFW hall tonight."

"Pardon?"

"For people who don't have a date on New Year's."

She stared at the curls of white chest hair that had escaped above the grimy collar of his T-shirt. He had to be close to sixty. "Are you asking me out?" she whispered, unable to make the words louder in her tight throat.

"Ha!" he barked. "Lady, I have a date tonight. But you should go. Have a good time. Live a little."

Unbelievable. Brain spinning in horror, Elise paid the bill, added a twenty-percent tip just to prove she didn't resent his suggestion, then tossed down twenty bucks in cash for the three beers she was about to grab from the fridge.

The first day of possibility for the New Year was going to lean heavily toward bleary-eyed hangover, and Elise didn't feel the tiniest bit of regret about that. She planned to do a good job of earning it.

CHAPTER SEVEN

AFTER PACING HIS ROOM for thirty minutes, Noah gave up on his plans for getting a good night's sleep. Instead, he headed for the tiny hotel gym. He didn't come across a single soul. Even the registration desk seemed deserted. Maybe the blonde receptionist was in back primping for a New Year's date. Noah hoped so. Nobody else should have to be stuck in this ghostly building tonight.

He ran on the treadmill for an hour, and every beat of his pounding heart was like a hammer driving Elise's name deep into his brain.

She'd said it was a mistake. A mistake. Because they worked together. Because he lived in Denver. Because it could only be one night.

Not because she didn't want him.

Was she lying because she didn't want to hurt his feelings? Or was she telling the truth about not wanting to hurt her own?

Noah hit the stop button on the treadmill. He slowed to a walk, then laid his arms against the front panel to rest his forehead on his hands. His lungs strained for air. Sweat dripped slowly from his hairline. His heart beat so hard he could feel it shuddering in his chest.

Did she want him or not?

He lived in Denver now. It didn't matter. It shouldn't matter.

But rationality had never had anything to do with his feelings for Elise. He'd left his girlfriend on the basis of a brief kiss. He'd been emotionally unavailable to every woman he'd dated afterward. He'd moved halfway across the country to try to leave her behind.

But now he couldn't get the taste of her out of his mouth. The feel of her hands off his body. He couldn't shake the impossible pleasure of being deep inside her.

Oh, hell. His heart was already long gone. Noah had nothing to lose at this point. He may as well take a chance.

"GAH!" Elise sat up quickly, alarmed by the loud trilling in her ear. Her head was jerked to a halt with a brutal snap. For a moment, she thought she was under attack. Then she realized that she'd trapped her hair under her own arm. "Good grief," she groaned, collapsing back to her pillow.

The phone stopped ringing. Elise shifted around until she freed her hair from its trap, then sat up and rubbed her eyes. Had she drunk too much and passed out?

She looked at the clock. It was just after ten-thirty, and the clock sat framed by two unopened beers. The other bottle was open next to it, only a few sips missing.

No, she hadn't partied too hard and passed out. She'd just fallen asleep at eight o'clock on New Year's Eve. Well, at least the New Year hadn't started yet. She was still well within her rights to be pitiful.

Elise pushed her hair out of her face and took a deep breath that was cut off by the renewed ringing of her phone. She fished it out of the pillows and scowled. *Noah.* What kind of havoc did he want to wreak now?

"Hello?" she asked warily.

"Hi, Elise. Are you busy?"

A glance around showed her open laptop, her abandoned beers and the TV silently playing out fireworks that had exploded behind the Eiffel Tower hours before. "Kind of."

"Listen. I thought maybe… Would you like to go for a walk?"

"A *walk?*"

"Yes."

"What? It's cold. And dark." And you're *you.*

"I think…" He took a deep breath. "I think maybe we should talk about this, after all. And it's a beautiful night."

"It's cold," she said again, her pulse tripping with questions.

"Yeah."

He left it at that. He didn't say another word. Noah just waited. And Elise waited, too. Waited to be brave enough to say yes. Yes to a walk. Yes to talking. Yes to the question hiding in his voice.

"Yes," she whispered.

She had the fleeting thought he'd hung up, but he finally answered. "I'll stop by your room in five minutes."

The phone clicked dead, and Elise wasted a good thirty seconds just staring at it. A walk. With Noah.

In the middle of a dark night. Then she realized what he'd said. Five minutes.

"Oh, crap!" She was half-naked and sleep-squashed. Vaulting out of bed, she raced for the bathroom and found even worse news there. She'd fallen asleep on her hand and left three clear finger imprints in her cheek. "Crap!" she screeched.

It took her a full two minutes to pull back her hair and scrub at her face until the finger marks disappeared. She brushed her teeth. Then she had another minute to tug on her jeans and pull a sweater over the tank top she wore. A touch of make up, a few brushes of her hair—

A knock rang through the room. "Just a second!" Elise tugged on her socks and her boots and lunged for the door.

"Hey," Noah said as the smell of fresh soap drifted to her nose. The edges of his hair curled damply against his neck. Her mouth watered.

"Are you okay?" he asked. "Your cheeks are really pink."

She touched her face in embarrassment. "I was rushing. Sorry. Let me just grab my coat."

As she whirled away, she had the fleeting impression that Noah had been reaching toward her, and her whole body stuttered at the thought. Had he been reaching to touch her cheek? Had he meant to pull her toward him for a kiss? Surely not. No. Elise shoved the thought away.

"So…" His low voice rumbled over her as she pulled on her coat. "Looks like I interrupted quite an evening."

Elise glared at the remnants of her pity party before

she rushed through the door, slamming it behind her.
"Shut up."

"Did you steal those beers from the bar?"

"No!"

Noah grinned and fell into step behind her. They
were down the side stairs and out into the night before
Elise's cheeks finally cooled. She tugged on her winter
hat, squared her shoulders, and took a deep breath. She
was ready for battle.

NOAH DIDN'T FEEL THE COLD. He didn't feel anything
past the numbness that had slipped over him when Elise
had stepped into the pale circle of the security light.
Her skin looked white, her cheeks and mouth pink as
roses. And with her blue knit hat pulled down over
her forehead, she looked about eighteen years old and
impossibly sweet. Like an angel.

That patently ridiculous thought shook him from his
reverie, and Noah gestured toward the sidewalk. They
walked in silence for a long while, but the quiet wasn't
content. It was a pulsing, straining quiet, squeezing
them with unspoken thoughts.

Or maybe that was all in Noah's head.

Without a word, they headed down a sloping trail
that led away from the streets of downtown where bars
spilled drunks out onto the streets. The farther they
walked, the quieter it grew, until the only sound was
the occasional music of the black river ahead.

"Noah," Elise snapped, making him jump. She
cleared her throat and shook her head. "Thank you.
It's nice here. Pretty." The last word was hesitant, as if
she weren't used to using delicate language.

They left the safety of the trail lights, and now only

the moon brightened their way. It glinted and flashed off the river, but it was still dark. Dark enough for what Noah needed to do, anyway.

"Two years ago, you kissed me," he said.

Her shoes scraped roughly against the trail, but she caught herself before she stumbled. "I know. I'm sorry."

His jaw tightened. "That's not what I want you to be sorry for."

"I don't get it. Haven't I been sorry enough? Haven't I apologized and… It was just a kiss. Why do things have to be so difficult between us?"

"Because I've had a thing for you for two years, Elise."

She stopped so quickly that pebbles skittered off the trail and rustled into the bushes. *"What?"*

"That's why it's always been so…tense. At least on my side."

"Noah. That doesn't make any sense. You never said anything. You never said *anything!*"

"You were in a relationship. A long one."

"I…no…you had a girlfriend!"

Noah shoved his hands in his pockets and looked up at the sky to give himself a moment. The sky stared coldly back. "I left her. For you. You kissed me and…"

"What?" she whispered, every inch of the word tight with disbelief.

Yeah, he had trouble believing it himself. "I had a thing for you, but I ignored it until the night you kissed me. I called my girlfriend that night and ended it. I knew it was over. And then…" He flashed her a pained smile. "I found out you were already involved with someone."

"No," she breathed.

"Yeah. Pretty pitiful, huh?"

She didn't acknowledge his huff of laughter. "You pushed me away!"

The pain in her voice surprised him into a frown. "When you kissed me?"

"Yes, you pushed me away. I invited you to my *room,* Noah. And you said no. You didn't want me. I don't understand…"

"I didn't want it to start that way. Not with you."

"Oh, God." She covered her mouth with both hands.

Noah shook his head in confusion. Why the hell did she look like she'd seen a ghost? "Look, that's in the past. Obviously, if I was that into you, things were never going to work out with the woman I was seeing. And your relationship was, um, stronger than it seemed, I guess."

She pressed her fingers harder to her mouth. Even in the dark, he could see her knuckles turn white.

"Elise."

The moon glinted off the river behind her, then caught in the moisture in her eyes.

"Hey," he said, shocked by the sight of tears.

"I didn't have a boyfriend," she whispered.

The words must have been warped by the pressure of her hands. He froze in the act of reaching for her. "What?"

"I didn't have a boyfriend." She lowered her hands, her eyes watched him with wide horror. "I was embarrassed. Horrified. I'd thrown myself at you, and…we were going to be working together for a long time. I didn't want that awkwardness between us. Me liking you, and you feeling sorry for me."

"What?" he repeated, disbelief buzzing behind his eardrums.

"I didn't start dating Evan until two months later."

"You're kidding me, right? That's a joke?"

"Noah, I'm so sorry. If I'd known... If I'd known..."

He just watched her, stunned and sorry for what they'd wasted.

"If I'd known," she whispered, "I'd never have let you go."

His sorrow swept away at those words. Those words that let him know she'd spent the past two years with want and need and yearning. Just as he had. "God."

"I'm sorry," she said again, but Noah no longer wanted regret from her. They'd both been stupid. Idiotic. Foolish.

They deserved each other.

He stepped closer. Tears glistened on her pale cheeks, so he framed her face and wiped them away with his thumbs. "Don't cry."

"I'm sorry," she said on a broken whisper. "I lied."

"And I've been lying to you for two years. But not anymore."

Her lips were cool and tasted of salty tears when he kissed her, but it took only a few heartbeats before the kiss turned hot and eager. Not quite desperate. Something sweeter than that, because it was the first honest kiss they'd ever shared.

By the time the kiss ended, their arms were wrapped tight around each other, their breath coming too fast.

Elise buried her face in his neck, and he felt the tremors running up her back. She was skittish and afraid, but she still held tight to him. Thank God.

"How could we have screwed up so badly?" she breathed against him.

He kissed her hair. "We're hard-headed."

"Stubborn."

"Arrogant."

Elise sighed. "And now it's too late."

No, he wasn't going to let that be true. He'd show her it couldn't be true.

"You smell so good," she murmured.

Noah shivered when her teeth scraped his neck. "Elise…"

"You're cold. We should get back to the hotel."

"I'm not—" he started, than snapped his mouth shut. "Yeah, let's get back to the hotel. It's freezing."

Elise giggled—*giggled*—and took his hand to tug him back the way they'd come. They walked faster, rushing toward the streets of downtown, but the hotel was nearly a mile away. When they reached the first little stone tunnel that ducked beneath a narrow road, Noah pulled her to a halt.

She swung toward him with a laugh, but the laughter died in her throat when he eased her against the stone wall and kissed her again. Her breath tangled with his, rushing over both their lips. Firecrackers popped and sizzled in the distance. Fingers of light from passing cars snuck into the tunnel, but didn't reach their bodies.

"Noah," she sighed, with the exact amount of yearning he wanted to hear. She snuck both her hands into his hair and pulled his mouth to hers again, answering any questions about what she might want.

Noah was determined that the next time they had sex it would be on a horizontal surface, he truly was. But her coat was open, and her hips curved so nicely in his hands, as if they wanted to be held tight. She whimpered, tugging him closer, then groaned when he pressed against her.

There was something unique to her. Something that drew him close and took him over. And to think that he could transform someone so strong and unreachable into a whimpering bundle of nerves... Her need humbled him and swelled him with impossible power at the same time.

"Noah," she whispered. "I can't get enough of you."

"Good." He edged his thumbs under her sweater and found another layer of fabric beneath, this one hot from being pressed to her skin. His hands soaked up the warmth and wanted more. He slid his whole hand beneath the shirt and relief filled him up. Her stomach jumped at the touch, and then she arched into him with a gasp.

Suddenly, all sweetness was gone. Their kisses turned frantic. Their hands greedy. He needed her. *Now.*

He unbuttoned her jeans and tugged them open. Finally, he found true heat—his fingers cupped her. Her breath twisted in white wisps on the icy air, but Noah felt sweat limn his body.

"Please," she sighed.

He'd slide into her right now if he could. He already recognized the hitch that broke apart every breath she took. She was so close already. Her nails dug vicious crescents into his back. Her hips rocked into his hand. Just a few more seconds…

She cried out as her body shook apart against him. In case there was anyone nearby, he covered her cries with his mouth and drank them down.

She was still trembling when she fisted her hands in his jacket and pushed him an inch away.

"Think you can manage the trip back to the hotel?" he asked.

"Yes. I feel much better." The white gleam of her smile glowed in the moonlight.

"Me, too."

ONCE THEY WERE ALL REARRANGED and decent, Noah took her hand and they strolled slowly through the tunnel and out into the moonlight.

"That was…" Elise shook her head.

He couldn't help but grin. "Yeah."

"I'm beginning to wonder if you can even perform in a horizontal position."

"We'll have to see."

"Someday I might even get you to take off your shoes. Or pants."

"If you're lucky."

She giggled again, which only made him grin harder. Jeez, they were like a couple of teenagers together instead of thirtysomething adults. A snowflake touched her nose. He felt the sting of one on his cheek. And suddenly the sky was filled with swirling glitter.

"Wow," Elise breathed. She whispered "wow" again when the first fireworks exploded over the buildings of downtown. A flash of red, then a blue flower. Car horns everywhere blared and honked. Elise and Noah raised their faces to the snow to watch the fireworks explode.

"Well, Noah James," she said to the sky. "You're pretty damn good."

"I have the power of the federal government behind me. I pulled a few strings."

"Very impressive."

He pulled her into her arms and pressed a careful kiss to her red lips. "Happy New Year, Elise."

"Happy New Year, Noah."

CHAPTER EIGHT

THEY MANAGED TO MAKE their nine-o'clock meet-ing, but only because the meeting was moved to a less formal location: Elise's bed.

She sat cross-legged in her underwear, winding the hem of her T-shirt around a finger. "It's 280 thousand dollars, Noah. It doesn't matter. Why can't you just let it go?"

He shrugged his broad, naked shoulders and went back to typing on his laptop. Whatever her frustration with him, the man was a gorgeous specimen of male flesh. Neither bulging with muscles nor wiry and lean. He was just…solid. And every small movement showed a shadow or curve of strength in his chest or arm or thigh. Her mouth rose in a half smile at the small peek of crisp hair and tan skin revealed between the top of the rumpled sheet and the leg of his white boxer briefs.

She wanted to toss that laptop away and throw herself into his arms. But Noah was frowning at the computer screen, his dark eyebrows drawn together in a crumpled line. He was grumpy when he was working.

Elise sighed and flipped onto her back to stare at the ceiling. "Tell me again."

"There's money trickling out *somewhere*. There are discrepancies in the bank's internal accounts. Small adjustments made here and there…the tiniest percentages. But I can't find how the money is getting out. Even Tex can't detect the outflow. Where is it going?"

"Over what time period?" she pressed.

Noah grunted. "Years. A dozen years."

"Two-hundred eighty thousand over a dozen years? You're kidding me, right? That's twenty thousand a year."

"Twenty-three thousand."

"That wouldn't even allow John Castle to support a mistress. Or not a very high-end one, at any rate."

"You gave me until Monday."

"And we're here, aren't we?"

He glanced at her over the top of his laptop, his eyes crinkling in a brief smile. "We definitely are." Then he went back to his numbers.

Her gut burned faintly with anxiety and she pressed her hand to it to try to rub it away. "I just…"

Ten seconds passed. He didn't seem to notice that she'd spoken, and Elise was relieved. But her relief snapped away when she glanced over to find him watching her again.

"What?" he asked.

She rubbed her face. "I don't know. I just…I don't want them to be bad people."

"The Castles?"

"Yes."

"You like the old lady that much?"

"I don't know." She rubbed her eyes too hard and saw stars. "This job has been so straightforward. It's working out. I feel like we did something good."

"We're never the bad guys, Elise."

"I know that! But, God, I get tired of feeling like

we are. The Castles made mistakes. They screwed up. They lost their life's work. They almost lost people's jobs and savings. But I don't think they're criminals, because I just don't want them to be." She shook her head. "I'm sorry. It's been a hard year. I'm glad it's over."

His hand touched her knee and squeezed. "I heard about your dad. I'm so sorry."

Her throat tightened, but she swallowed the tears. The year had been bad, and her dad's death had been a big part of that. Still, even though she missed him every single day, she would be okay. She reached for Noah's hand and took the comfort he offered. "Thank you."

"And maybe you're right," he said softly. "There's no proof they're criminals. If I can just find the damn money, maybe we'll discover a happier truth. Now where the hell did the money go?"

"Maybe it never left," she said flippantly. "Did you check all the desks?"

"I'll make Tex do that tomorrow morning." His hand tightened around hers. "I'll wrap it up as quickly as I can, and I'll try for a happy ending, but no promises."

No promises. Did he mean...? "I understand," she said. "Sure. It's no big deal."

"Elise." He shoved the laptop to the side and leaned toward her. "I wasn't talking about us."

"Maybe not, but how else are we supposed to leave this? We live two thousand miles apart. We've been on, what? One date?"

"Seriously? One date? We've had sex four times in a week."

"Well, most of that was in the past twelve hours."

"You're damn right. That alone is a good reason not to let you throw this away."

She sat up. "I'm not trying to throw it away!"

"You'd damn well better not be!"

Fear and love and panic suddenly welled from her chest like a wound. "How are we supposed to date?" she said softly, worried that her heart was breaking right in that moment. *"How?"*

"Elise." His hands, those hands she'd wanted for so long, they closed over her arms and pulled her closer until she straddled his legs. When she looked away, he touched her cheek to bring her eyes to his. "I don't know about you, but I've wasted two years. Two long years."

She had, too. Elise nodded, afraid to speak. She was so bad at this. How could he admit so much without being afraid? She would've walked away before confessing how lonely she'd been. For him. Even when she was supposed to have been in love with Evan, she'd been lonely.

"We'll manage it. I'll fly to D.C. You'll fly to Denver. Vacations. Email. The phone."

"Noah…"

"Listen to me, damn it. This is good. I am not leaving this to chance. And Jesus, I moved to Denver to get away from you, I can damn well move back to get close again."

Her trembling heart stopped beating. Her knees tightened against his hips. "You did what?"

Noah grimaced and collapsed against the pillows. "Nothing. Forget that."

"Forget it? Noah…why would you—"

"You were in love with someone else, and I wanted this thing between us to be over. That's all. I just wanted it to stop."

Her heart was a ball of pain in her chest. "But it didn't," she whispered. "It never stopped."

"No."

Why did he like her so much? She was too hard, too tough, too afraid to bend. But she bent now. She leaned into him and pressed her mouth to his bare chest, breathing out her pain into his skin.

She thought of the countless hours they'd spent together. She'd watched the way he moved, admired his decisiveness, eavesdropped on his conversations with others, noticed the small kindnesses he didn't want others to see.

"Noah." She kissed her way up to his chest, pressed her mouth to his thumping heart. "I love you."

His heart jumped beneath his ribs.

"Don't say anything back. Please. I just wanted to tell you." The weight left her as suddenly as it had come. She'd done it. Something brave and right.

She felt his hands slide gently into her hair. He eased her up and sat up himself so their faces were only inches apart. "Don't tell me what to do, Elise."

"I didn't say it so you'd say it back."

"Too bad." He kissed her so softly that tears sprang to her eyes. "I love you," he murmured. "I've loved you for so damn long."

She couldn't say a word. The fear was back, but it was soaring on wings inside her, gliding in big looping swoops that left her breathless. So Elise kissed him hard and pushed him down so she could press into him. She swept off her shirt and shoved his shorts down, desperate to fill herself up with something more than this awful hope. He was ready for her, but he stopped her hand when she reached for him.

"Shh. Slow down."

But she couldn't. She was going to break if she didn't have him now. She was going to break and sob and confess everything she felt, and that scared the hell out of her.

She met his eyes. "Please," she rasped.

He held her gaze for a long moment before his face softened. Then he reached blindly for the box of condoms next to the bed.

Thank God.

THE WORRY IN HER EYES was killing him. She needed something from him, and Noah was determined to give it to her. Her body rose above him, her waist curving into flared hips. Her breasts firm and proud and peaked by surprisingly dark nipples.

He wanted to turn her over and worship her body, lavish long hours of attention on every bit of flesh. But he did nothing more than hold her hips as she rose above him. Then he was sliding inside her, the tightness enough to make Noah's vision fade to a brief moment of black.

When his brain began processing images again, they were images of Elise. Elise rising above him, her lips parted, eyes closed. He should've been spent by this point. He'd come once this morning and twice last night, but there was something in her skin that soaked into him like a drug. Every time he touched her he was starving. Now her breasts rose on every frantic breath she drew. She arched to pull him deeper. He rocked his hips and watched her gasp.

That little high-pitched break invaded her every breath, and primal satisfaction filled each hollow space inside him. He owned this secret of hers now. This tiny clue to the puzzle of her body.

She put her hand to his chest, her muscles trembling as her body curved forward. "Oh, Noah."

"Yes," he ground out past his clenched teeth.

And then she was crying out, a ragged, desperate sound, and Noah gave up with a groan.

He was still shuddering when she collapsed onto his chest, her hair sweeping the scent of her across his cheek. Their skin slipped with sweat. Their chests rose and fell in warring rhythm.

Noah was finally spent. He was sure of it. He couldn't move. Couldn't even draw a deep enough breath.

Heaven.

He was just starting to doze off when his brain shifted. Something clicked into place. An idea fell free.

Noah's eyes popped open. "Maybe the money never left," he said.

"Mmm," Elise murmured, her body still dead weight on top of him.

He slid her off as gently as he could, but she protested with an outraged cry when she landed on her face. "Sorry," he said as he reached for his computer.

"Are you going right back to *work?*"

"I just thought of something."

"You're thinking right now? What are you, Superman?"

"Man of steel," he said as he paged through his

notes. *Maybe the money never left.* Maybe. His eyes slid over the numbers, looking for an answer. "Hit the showers, sidekick," he said to a limp Elise. She didn't move so he gave her a friendly smack, thoroughly enjoying the way her body shot half a foot off the bed in response.

"Hey!"

"Get in the shower. We're going to the bank."

"You're insane."

Maybe he was, because the sight of Elise rubbing her pink ass as she walked toward the bathroom made him grin like a madman. Maybe he wasn't spent after all.

ELISE CROSSED HER FINGERS behind her back as Noah looked up from his computer, triumph gleaming in his eyes.

Please don't let it be Mrs. Castle. Please don't let it be Mrs. Castle.

"Well," he said, letting that one word hang between them.

"What?" She crossed her fingers so hard that the tips went numb.

"I'm sorry to say it was old lady Castle after all."

"No," she whispered. She didn't know why she was so damn invested in this woman. It wasn't like she was going to be the kindly old grandmother Elise had never had.

Elise set her strangled fingers free and crossed her arms instead. "I can't believe it. You were right."

"I'm sorry," Noah said, leaning forward with a look of patently false worry on his face. "Could you speak up? I don't think I heard you correctly."

She glared at him, then tossed a look over her shoulder to be sure none of the other team members stood in the doorway. "I said you were right."

"Wow. That feels... That feels really good."

"You're being mean."

"Aw." His smug look brightened into a real smile. "Would it make you feel better if I told you she wasn't stealing the money?"

Her breath left her lungs in a rush. "She wasn't?" Elise squeaked, ridiculously relieved at his words.

"Come here."

She edged around his desk, fighting the urge to sit down on his lap and look over the numbers with him.

"You remember my interview with John Castle? He said he'd started taking over some of his mother's responsibilities back in 1998. She'd started 'making a few mistakes,' as he put it."

"I remember. He was the one who steered the bank toward higher-risk loans." She rested a hand on Noah's shoulder, then leaned her hip lightly into his arm. Her body tingled every place it touched his.

"It was so long ago, that I didn't bother pressing him on what his mother's mistakes were. I figured he'd cleaned up behind her."

"He hadn't?"

"I think he missed some errors. The same ones I missed."

Elise fought the urge to punch his shoulder. *"What?"* she demanded.

"During the nineties, Platte Regional Bank offered two options for sweep accounts."

"Okay." Business checking accounts were prohibited from earning interest, but a sweep account allowed businesses to sweep their money into an interest-bearing account each night.

Noah tapped the computer screen. "The first account options swept the funds into an international money market. But the second option…" He glanced up at her. "The second option was an internal sweep that moved the funds into one of the banks high-yield interest accounts."

She still didn't get it. "And?"

"Every internal sweep account she set up during the first six months of 1998 was paying FDIC insurance to the wrong place."

"You're kidding."

"Nope."

"So the money these people were supposedly embezzling…it was actually money set aside for FDIC premiums?"

"Yes."

Oh, this was too good to be true. "And…it's all still there?"

He shot her a grudging look that was as adorable as it was irritating. "Yes. She recorded the correct administrative account, but when she set up the electronic transfer, she input the wrong account number. An unused slush fund. It's all still there. That's how I found it. When you mentioned that the money might still be in the bank, I pulled up accounts with balances that might work."

"Ha!"

"But I was still right," he countered. "The money was definitely missing."

Elise slapped his shoulder, then stifled a squeal when

he wrapped his arm around her waist and turned her toward him. "They weren't bad guys!"

"Does that make you happy?" he growled.

"Yes."

"How happy?" His other hand slid up her knee.

"Ho-ly crap," a voice said from behind them. A voice with a heavy Texas drawl.

"Oh, no," Elise breathed, too horrified to turn around.

"You and *Noah?*"

She finally got the sense to pull away from Noah. His grip went loose with shock. "Tex, listen," she said, holding up both hands in a plea. "It isn't what you think."

"Really? 'Cause I'm thinking Noah James is a stone-cold *stud*."

Her face flamed and she heard Noah's muttered "Damn it," past a haze of static in her ears. But this was her fault. She'd spread the tale of Noah's tryst with the flight attendants.

"Okay," she whispered. "You're right. He is. He's a total stud, and I don't want anyone to know I succumbed to that, all right? So just keep it quiet."

"Hoo boy," Tex breathed. "This is some crazy shit."

"Elise," Noah hissed, but she shook her head.

"Wow. All right," Tex finally said. "I won't mention this, but don't expect me to keep my admiration a secret, man. And Elise…watch yourself around this dog."

"Yes. Of course."

"Wow," he said again, shaking his head as he retreated from the doorway.

Elise rushed to shut the door behind him and turned to find Noah standing with his arms crossed.

"I can't believe it. You threw me under the bus."

"It's only temporary! I don't want to run the risk that we won't be assigned to the same case. It's just for a little while, I swear."

"Oh?" He scowled at her, unmoved. "And then what?"

She cleared her throat. She'd had a lot of time to think while Noah had assembled his team and pored over mind-numbing numbers for hours. "I've been thinking I'm not cut out for this job."

"What are you talking about? You're damn good at it."

"I am good at it. I'm great at it. But I don't love it. And lately I've been eyeing Fraud and Counterfeiting."

He dropped his arms to his sides. "The Secret Service?"

"Yes. There's a big office in Denver. They're short-staffed and I'm qualified. If I like the investigative side of it, I can apply to become a full-fledged agent next year."

"You're serious?"

"It would be a relief. There are bad guys and good guys. There's nothing touchy-feely—"

"Hey, you're pretty good at touchy-feely."

"No, I'm not. And…my mom was from Kansas. I never knew her family. I don't even remember *her*. But I thought… I thought now that my dad is gone, maybe I should get to know her story, her family. I've been in touch with my aunt…" She shrugged. "I've wanted a change. I love my uncles, but spending every weekend with them… I'm too young to live like that. And now…"

"Now," he repeated.

"Yeah. Now." She didn't know what else to say. Her mind was doing that grasping, anxious dance. What was he thinking? What does he want me to say? She took a deep breath. She had good instincts. Look how this case had turned out.

She decided to take the plunge. "I checked out apartments last year. It wouldn't take too long to arrange, assuming I can get the job. Maybe a couple of months. If, you know, we're still…"

Daring a glance in his direction, she found him looking serious. Too serious. Crap. "Or—"

"We will be."

"I'm shy," she blurted out. "I never know what to say at parties."

His eyebrows rose. "What?"

"And I'm not very girly."

"Oh." He nodded, and his mouth softened to something even sweeter than a smile. "We're even, then. I'm a guy and I don't like sports."

"Really?"

"When have you ever heard me join in a discussion about March Madness?"

"Good point. Are you saying I could kick your ass at basketball?"

"Almost definitely."

She thought of knocking into him on the court, their sweaty bodies tangling as they fought over the ball. "Maybe you just need more practice?"

He shrugged as if he didn't care, and she decided she'd have to convince him. A rough hour on the court with Noah would be right up her foreplay alley. So much better than flowers and dancing. And she had the unshakable feeling that Noah James wouldn't think there was anything wrong with that.

"But I have been thinking about trying bull riding," he drawled.

That snapped her from her fantasies. "What?"

"The mechanical kind. Wanna go out tonight and try your hand? We've got a closed case to celebrate…and there are rumors going around that you're an amazing rider, Elise Watson."

He dodged the fist she threw at his shoulder and snuck his arms around her for a kiss. A mechanical bull on their second date? Yep, he knew her pretty damn well.

CHAPTER NINE

"IS THIS WEIRD?" Elise asked anxiously. "It's weird, isn't it?"

"It's not so bad," Noah answered. "I checked the view from your kitchen window and you can only see one corner of my bedroom from there. Not too creepy at all."

"Oh, no," she groaned, hiding her face behind her hands. Noah put down the box he was carrying and pulled her into his arms.

"You're cute when you're mortified."

"I didn't know I'd be able to see into your bedroom! I should've taken the place across town."

"No, I like it. I feel safe knowing a Secret Service agent is watching over me. Literally."

"Shut up. I'm not a full agent yet."

"I still like having you watch over me. And that other place didn't have a basketball court," he reminded her. He kissed her blushing cheek, then worked his way down to her mouth. Embarrassed or not, Elise let him. In the three months since Omaha, they'd only seen each other four times. She'd been busy jumping through hoops to get the Denver Secret Service position. And despite their caution about keeping the relationship secret, she could've sworn that the FDIC had conspired to keep them apart. They hadn't been thrown together on one job since.

But the hours on the phone every week had been wonderful. And the three stolen weekends. And the flowers he sent even though she told him she didn't need them. He made her feel like a girl. A girl who worked for the Secret Service and kicked his ass on the basketball court.

"Anyway," Noah continued as if they hadn't been making out for a full minute. "Spying on me in my bedroom will be a good transition to living together."

"It's too soon," she groaned, more than familiar with this argument.

"But you did get the shortest lease?"

Elise smiled. And then she laughed. "Three months. Short enough for you?"

"Never."

"I just want to be sure."

He kissed her neck, his breath soft against her as he spoke. "You're not sure?"

The words melted through her skin, warming her body and tying her stomach into a tight knot. She couldn't lie to him, not anymore. "I am sure," she whispered, afraid to admit it too loudly. "But I want to give you the chance to be sure."

"Elise—"

"You might change your mind."

"You're so damn stubborn." His voice was somewhere between a whisper and growl. He placed his hands carefully on either side of her face and stared into her eyes. She wanted to squirm or look away, but he deserved more than that, so she looked into his blue eyes and took a deep breath.

"I love you, Elise. I've waited a long time for you, and I'll wait a little longer if that's what you need. But you don't have to keep warning me off. You don't have to tell me you're different. I know you are. I knew it two years ago, and I know it now, and damn it, I love you so much it hurts. So take your three months, get settled in at your new job and then put me out of my misery and let's make it more permanent. Please?"

She took another deep breath, trying to steady her trembling nerves. She'd spent her whole life thinking of herself as awkward and tom-boyish. Could she accept that Noah James truly saw her as sexy and strong?

Clearing her throat, she tried to buy some time. "You've still got issues with authority."

"And you've still got issues with control," he countered. "Working those issues out could be a whole lot of fun."

When she didn't respond right away, he narrowed his eyes in challenge. She thought of their last weekend together, and the way he'd worshipped her body with his mouth.

Anticipation rushed through her like a drug. "Okay, Noah James. You've got three months to nail me down. You'd better put your heart into it."

He smiled, the grin slowly widening into arrogance. "Oh, I'll put more than my heart into it, boss. Way more."

"I'll take it all."

"You bet your ass you will."

The teasing stopped then, and an hour later, Elise was more than convinced of his sincerity. But she decided to keep that to herself for a few more weeks. A little hard work never hurt anyone, after all, and Noah James had proved himself a dedicated worker…and well worth the wait.

* * * * *

HARLEQUIN® A *Romance* FOR EVERY MOOD™

CLASSICS

Quintessential, modern love stories
that are romance at its finest.

Harlequin Presents®

Glamorous international settings…
unforgettable men…passionate
romances—Harlequin Presents
promises you the world!

Harlequin Presents® Extra

Meet more of your favorite Presents
heroes and travel to glamorous
international locations in our regular
monthly themed collections.

Harlequin® Romance

The anticipation, the thrill of the chase
and the sheer rush of falling in love!

Silhouette® *Desire*

USA TODAY bestselling authors

MAUREEN CHILD

and

SANDRA HYATT

UNDER THE MILLIONAIRE'S MISTLETOE

Just when these leading men thought they had it all figured out, they quickly learn their hearts have made other plans. Two passionate stories about love, longing and the infinite possibilities of kissing under the mistletoe.

Available December wherever you buy books.

Always Powerful, Passionate and Provocative.

SD73069

REQUEST YOUR FREE BOOKS!
2 FREE NOVELS PLUS 2
FREE GIFTS!

HARLEQUIN® *Romance*

From the Heart, For the Heart

YES! Please send me 2 FREE Harlequin® Romance novels and my 2 FREE gifts (gifts are worth about $10). After receiving them, if I don't wish to receive any more books, I can return the shipping statement marked "cancel". If I don't cancel, I will receive 6 brand-new novels every month and be billed just $3.84 per book in the U.S. or $4.24 per book in Canada. That's a savings of 15% off the cover price! It's quite a bargain! Shipping and handling is just 50¢ per book.* I understand that accepting the 2 free books and gifts places me under no obligation to buy anything. I can always return a shipment and cancel at any time. Even if I never buy another book from Harlequin, the two free books and gifts are mine to keep forever.

116/316 HDN E7T2

Name _____ (PLEASE PRINT) _____

Address _____ Apt. # _____

City _____ State/Prov. _____ Zip/Postal Code _____

Signature (if under 18, a parent or guardian must sign)

Mail to the Harlequin Reader Service:
IN U.S.A.: P.O. Box 1867, Buffalo, NY 14240-1867
IN CANADA: P.O. Box 609, Fort Erie, Ontario L2A 5X3

Not valid for current subscribers to Harlequin Romance books.

**Are you a subscriber to Harlequin Romance books
and want to receive the larger-print edition?
Call 1-800-873-8635 or visit www.ReaderService.com.**

* Terms and prices subject to change without notice. Prices do not include applicable taxes. Sales tax applicable in N.Y. Canadian residents will be charged applicable provincial taxes and GST. Offer not valid in Quebec. This offer is limited to one order per household. All orders subject to approval. Credit or debit balances in a customer's account(s) may be offset by any other outstanding balance owed by or to the customer. Please allow 4 to 6 weeks for delivery. Offer available while quantities last.

Your Privacy: Harlequin Books is committed to protecting your privacy. Our Privacy Policy is available online at www.ReaderService.com or upon request from the Reader Service. From time to time we make our lists of customers available to reputable third parties who may have a product or service of interest to you. If you would prefer we not share your name and address, please check here. ☐

Help us get it right—We strive for accurate, respectful and relevant communications. To clarify or modify your communication preferences, visit us at www.ReaderService.com/consumerschoice.

HR10R2

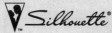

ROMANTIC
SUSPENSE

Sparked by Danger, Fueled by Passion.

RACHEL LEE
A Soldier's Redemption

When the Witness Protection Program fails at
keeping Cory Farland out of harm's way, ex-
marine Wade Kendrick steps in. As Cory's new
bodyguard, Wade has a plan for protecting her—
however falling in love was not part of his plan.

*Available in December
wherever books are sold.*

SPECIAL EDITION

USA TODAY BESTSELLING AUTHOR

MARIE FERRARELLA

BRINGS YOU ANOTHER
HEARTWARMING STORY FROM

When Lilli McCall disappeared on him
after he proposed, Kullen Manetti swore
never to fall in love again. Eight years later
Lilli is back in his life, threatening to break
down all the walls he's put up to
safeguard his heart.

UNWRAPPING
THE PLAYBOY

*Available December
wherever books are sold.*